AMONG

THE

INNOCENT

AMONG THE INNOCENT

MARY ALFORD

Revell

a division of Baker Publishing Group
Grand Rapids, Michigan

Published by Revell
a division of Baker Publishing Group
PO Box 6287, Grand Rapids, MI 49516-6287
www.revellbooks.com

Printed in the United States of America

Library of Congress Cataloging-in-Publication Data
Names: Alford, Mary (Romance fiction writer), author.
Title: Among the innocent / Mary Alford.
Description: Grand Rapids, MI : Revell, a division of Baker Publishing Group, [2022]
Identifiers: LCCN 2021042940 | ISBN 9780800740269 (paperback) | ISBN 9780800741594 (casebound) | ISBN 9781493436361 (ebook)
Subjects: LCGFT: Novels.
Classification: LCC PS3601.L3627 A815 2022 | DDC 813/.6—dc23
LC record available at https://lccn.loc.gov/2021042940

This book is a work of fiction. Names, characters, places, and incidents are the product of the author's imagination or are used fictitiously. Any resemblance to actual events, locales, or persons, living or dead, is coincidental.

Published in association with Books & Such Literary Management, www.booksandsuch.com.

Baker Publishing Group publications use paper produced from sustainable forestry practices and post-consumer waste whenever possible.

22 23 24 25 26 27 28   7 6 5 4 3 2 1

I love how God puts the right people
in your life at just the right time.
That's what happened with *Among the Innocent*.
This book is dedicated to my agent, Rachel Kent,
who has been on my side on this journey from the beginning,
and to my editor, Rachel McRae, because without her faith
in me, this book would not be possible.
Thank you both so much!

Prologue

He drove by the house again. The second time today. All because of her.

The sight of his car rolling down the dirt road in front of her isolated farm filled Beth Zook with thoughts not proper for an Amish girl. A cloud of dust followed the car, instantly covering the freshly washed sheet she'd hung out to dry minutes earlier. Despite the sweltering July heat, he'd put down the window. Was it because he wanted her to see him as he eased by?

He waved when he saw her looking, and she reacted like a moth drawn to a flame. Beth had never met anyone so unpredictable before. One minute he teased, the next his eyes smoldered with such intensity that it frightened her.

Looking at his handsome face sent the butterflies in her stomach scattering. A flash of a smile revealed white teeth, perfect like everything else about him.

Beth waved back, then glanced over her shoulder. What would *Mamm* and her sister say if they noticed? She covered her mouth to suppress the giggle. She'd been giggling a lot lately.

Too soon . . .

Her head warned it was too soon for these emotions, yet

her heart threatened to explode from her chest each time they were together.

Heat flooded her cheeks as she recalled his kisses from the night before. She'd been so afraid her parents would wake and hear her slipping out of her bedroom window. A sense of fear and adventure had followed her each step of the way as she'd crossed the yard in the pitch-black dark of night to the old Miller barn where he'd waited for her.

At first, she'd been afraid to go there after what had happened all those years ago. Four members of the Miller family had been found dead inside that barn. Leah Miller, the oldest daughter, was the only survivor. Whispers around the community about the unspeakable evil that had transpired that night could still be heard.

When Beth told her suitor about the murders, his eyes gleamed with excitement. While he seemed to enjoy envisioning what had happened back then, the barn gave Beth the creeps. But she kept that to herself because he made her feel special. Beautiful. *Important.* For the first time in her life, she longed for things not found among the Plain people of St. Ignatius. A life of pretty things. Like he promised.

Last night when they'd met, he'd asked her to run away with him. Her heart had overflowed with eagerness until reality tamped down her happiness, and Beth realized she wasn't ready to leave her home. Her family. While she remained torn between staying Amish forever and leaving with him, he'd told her he would drive by her house every day until she said yes. Part of her was thrilled—intrigued at the consuming way he watched her. The other part was scared. Beth did not understand his almost feral wildness.

She took the dust-covered sheet down and reached for the

next one, pinning it to the clothesline with unsteady hands. When Mamm wasn't watching, she'd sneak inside and rewash the soiled one. That way there wouldn't be questions to answer.

Out of the corner of her eye, she noticed the car slowing. Brake lights flashed. She picked up the next sheet and hung it.

When he honked, she whirled toward the sound while praying the family wouldn't come to investigate. He slid out and leaned against the rotting fence post near the Miller property. Many times, Beth wished she could be as daring. He did not live by the same rules as the Amish. In his world, anything was possible.

She still couldn't imagine why he wanted her. A man so handsome could have his choice of any girl, *Englisch* or Plain. Why her?

When he realized he had her attention, he motioned her over. Beth felt obliged to shake her head, though she'd thought about him throughout the day. Was eager to see him again. She anticipated his kisses with every beat of her heart.

She touched her hands to her burning cheeks. Such thoughts were not *gut*, but she couldn't help how she felt. With him, Beth felt truly alive. The hardest part was she had no one with whom to share how she felt. Her friend Eva listened, but Beth sensed she might be jealous.

She'd almost told her older sister Colette about him last Saturday night before the biweekly church service, but she'd lost her nerve. Married and ten years older, Colette had three *kinner* of her own.

Besides, her sister was always so serious. She would not understand this reckless feeling.

Until her sixteenth birthday, Beth hadn't either. She'd loved everything about the Amish way of life. Then, she'd started her *rumspringa* and had gotten a taste of the freedom of the

Englischer world. She liked it. Before *him*, she'd planned to join the church and eventually marry Caleb Wagler, but not before enjoying every minute of her running around. Now, Beth was not sure she wanted to spend the rest of her life in St. Ignatius, living on a farm like her sister with a house full of kinner pulling on her apron. *He* offered her excitement. Adventure. Love. How could she not accept those gifts?

She hung the last of the sheets and picked her way across the patches of grass in the bare yard to where he stood. The glint in his eyes as he watched her wasn't anything like the way Caleb looked at her.

Beth stopped a few feet away. With the fence separating them, she snuck a peek over her shoulder. "You should not be here." She tried to sound stern but failed miserably.

Without warning, he jumped the fence. Beth giggled as he grabbed her hands and tugged her closer. "Yes, I should. You belong to me, Beth Zook."

Her heart skipped a beat at his proclamation, and she couldn't help imagining what their life together would be like.

Foolishness, Beth. You waste the day with all your imprudent thoughts, she could almost hear Colette saying.

"Mamm will notice I'm gone soon. You must leave now." She tried to tug her wrists free, but he tightened his grip to the point of pain, and a flash of anger glittered in those deep dark eyes. "You are hurting me," she murmured, tears forming. This was a side of him she hadn't seen before. A cruel side she didn't much like.

He let her go. Smiled. Everything became right again with the curve of his lips. "I'm sorry. I didn't mean to hurt you, Beth." The gentleness in his tone soothed her worries away. "You're just so pretty."

"You are such a flatterer." She playfully swatted at his arm but secretly loved the way he spoke.

He leaned close and planted a kiss on her lips right there in broad daylight. Her legs turned to gelatin. A sigh escaped as warmth coursed through her limbs. After another stolen kiss, he released her.

"It's true. Don't be coy. You know you're pretty." His gaze skirted past her to the house. "And you deserve more than this life. Come away with me now."

More than anything she wanted to, but when she thought about her mamm's pained reaction to her middle daughter forsaking their faith, she couldn't do it. "I told you, I cannot run away with you. And I have to go back to my chores." She turned. Then, emboldened by his claims, she swung around, framed his face with her hands, and kissed him earnestly.

He chuckled at her brazenness. He snatched her hand once more. Though she secretly relished his desire to be with her so badly, she pretended differently. "Please, you must let me go. Mamm will see."

"I don't care." A second passed before he finally relented. "Only if you promise to meet me tonight at our place."

The eagerness in his eyes sent a shiver through her body. It made her hesitate. This was the man she adored. Surely, there was nothing to fear.

"I have something special planned for you," he added with a cajoling smile when she wavered. "Something you'll like."

"If I can," she whispered and pulled her hand free. They both knew she'd be there. As she ran across the scorching earth, Beth peered over her shoulder. He still stood next to the fence, grinning when he noticed her looking. She stumbled over the uneven ground. Heard him laughing.

As she stepped up on the porch, the front door opened and Mamm stood in the doorway, hands on hips. Her wrinkled brow furrowed at her daughter's labored breathing.

"*Komm*, help your sister prepare supper." Her mother studied Beth with narrowed eyes. Took in her flushed face. Her nervous hands. Had Mamm ever felt this way about *Daed?*

"Who is that out on the road?"

Beth struggled to keep her face blank. "Someone passing by, I suppose." With one final glance his way and a secret smile, she hurried to go inside.

Her mother cast another disapproving stare at the car as Beth entered the house.

"I have something special planned for you."

It was hard to keep the excitement to herself. She couldn't wait to see the mysterious surprise he had in store.

one

Heat rose in waves off the blacktop where Leah Miller had parked her police cruiser. Recent statistics showed that the crime rate in St. Ignatius, Montana, was at an all-time low. Today, Leah shot radar at the occasional passing vehicle to occupy her shift until something more challenging came along.

Leah looped her raven hair into a bun at the nape of her neck, seeking relief from the record-breaking hot spell the county was suffering through this July. Her uniform clung uncomfortably to her skin while her thoughts wandered to the things she planned to do when her shift ended. She'd need to check in on Kitty before heading over to have dinner with Marge.

A few years back, Leah had bought her tiny house on Pope Lane. It had taken all her savings, but it was worth it because it represented a huge milestone: putting down roots for the first time since that horrific night. She'd even brought home the stray tabby cat that hung out behind the police station. They were still adjusting to each other, since Kitty had been on her own for a while. In the six months Kitty had lived at Leah's house, Kitty mostly stayed in the laundry room except at night, when she preferred the foot of Leah's bed.

Since Chief Ellis Petri's death, Leah had been spending as much time as she could with her adoptive mother, Marge. Losing Ellis had been hard on both of them, but Marge had been struggling with health issues as well.

Marge and Ellis Petri had been Leah's rock since that night ten years ago when her world changed forever. Several years earlier, Marge and Leah's mother had struck up an unlikely friendship, and Marge had become a frequent visitor at Leah's home. Sometimes Ellis came along. After what happened, Leah had left the Amish community, despite her neighbors offering to take her in. To survive, she'd had to let that part of her life go.

Ellis and Marge had taken her in. They'd become her world.

And now Ellis was gone.

Let it go. The past is written and done, but you're not.

In the distance, dark clouds gathered over the Mission Mountains. A storm was on its way. Despite the sweltering heat, a cold shiver sped down Leah's spine. Something bad was approaching. She could feel it moving in.

It's just the time of year, she told herself. The anniversary of what happened always churned up stuff.

She'd seen plenty of terrible things in her four years on the force. Yet, at sixteen, Leah had become personally acquainted with the devastating effects tragedy had on the living. Her grief had wrapped its spindly limbs around her and took up residence in her soul. That night in the barn—the things she'd witnessed—had imprinted itself in her DNA.

The woman staring back in the rearview mirror was an older version of that frightened Amish girl whose life had changed forever with a flick of a knife. The scar on her neck was a constant reminder of how close to death she'd come and of those who hadn't been so lucky.

Leah dragged in a deep breath and dropped her eyes from the mirror. Better to keep that door closed. Too many bad things hid behind it. For Marge's sake, she needed to stay strong.

Leah shoved her dark aviator sunglasses into place like a defensive shield against the world. She focused on the upcoming car cresting the hilltop.

"Leah? Are you there?" Dispatcher Sugar Wallace's voice came through the police radio, immediately drawing Leah's attention from the approaching vehicle.

"Yes, Sugar, I'm here. What's up?" The car spotted Leah and crawled past. Its speed registered twenty on the radar's screen.

"Henry needs your help on a call out in the Amish community."

Leah's stomach knotted.

"Josiah Zook called from the Mission General Store. He said his daughter Beth is missing."

At the mention of her former neighbor, Josiah Zook, Leah was immediately transported back to that barn again. Watching as a psychopath slaughtered her entire family.

Their deaths came at the hands of a masked stranger who had entered their house, tied everyone up, and forced Mamm and Daed, her sister Ruth, and brother Elijah into the barn. Then, he'd systematically slit each of their throats in front of Leah, saving her for last. She remembered him standing over her. His hot breath whispering against her ear, "You'll always belong to me." Even now, the words had the power to reduce her to that terrified young girl, so certain she'd die along with her family.

"Leah? Did you hear me?" Sugar repeated.

With her heart racing, Leah struggled for calm and failed. "Sorry, yes. I know the family." She'd been friends with Josiah's older daughter, Colette. "I'll head over and assist."

15

"Thanks, Leah. Let's hope the girl shows up soon. I don't want to think about something bad happening to one of those innocent people."

Sugar's words fell like knives in her heart. The Amish were peaceful, God-fearing folks. Violence in the community was a rare thing, yet not unheard of. Leah was living proof. Former police chief Ellis Petri had worked hard to help her achieve closure, yet the suspected killer's end had been just as messed up as his heinous massacre of her family. Even to this day, Leah wondered if the wrong man had died in that fire.

She whipped the cruiser out onto the road and headed toward the Amish community.

The only time she went back there was on a call, and on those occasions, she did her best to avoid her family's homestead. Yet there would be no avoiding it today. The Zook home was a stone's throw from where she'd grown up.

Leah couldn't imagine what her life would have been like without Ellis and Marge. They'd become her entire world. Marge would hold her and assure her everything was going to be okay when Leah woke up in the middle of the night screaming after reliving the nightmare. Yet despite Marge's tender loving care, it was Ellis whom Leah chose to be like. She'd joined the St. Ignatius Police Department after college because she wanted to do good for people, like Ellis.

The sparse community spread out before her. A horse and buggy passed her on the road heading to town. The Amish man waved. Leah returned his greeting. Rolling hayfields spread out toward the stunning vistas of the Mission Mountains. Overwhelming memories came pouring from her heart. Most of them good. All contaminated by that day.

Leah slowed her speed out of respect for the buggy and others that might be traveling the road. A familiar darkness pressed in. Her breaths came quick. Straight ahead, her former house appeared through the haze of summer.

Leah couldn't take her eyes off the old place. She'd lived there until a few months after her sixteenth birthday. In her head the house was as she'd left it that night. Yet the harsh reality was it had sat vacant all those years. Its white paint had faded to gray and was peeling from too many brutal Montana winters. The barn, some distance from the house, hovered over the place like some ancient gargoyle and just as frightening.

A lump formed in her throat that she couldn't swallow. Tears scalded her eyes. Leah's grip tightened on the steering wheel until her knuckles turned white. She wouldn't cry. Hadn't since the funeral. She'd built a wall of stone around her heart no person, including Ellis and Marge, had been able to fully penetrate. It was best that way. Her past had taught her stones could break apart and thrash her heart to pieces at a second's notice.

She shifted her attention to the Zook farm and let the past return to its tenuous resting place.

Officer Henry Landry's patrol vehicle was parked in front of the house beside a second cruiser. As soon as Leah turned onto the drive, another vehicle captured her attention. A familiar one. Ellis's old police SUV. A glaring reminder of more change coming.

A new chief was scheduled to take over the helm of the St. Ignatius Police Department, though no one expected him so soon. Why was Chief Cooper on this call? She leaned forward and peered through the dusty windshield at the vehicles while resisting the desire to call Sugar for answers.

The small police department was still reeling from the intentional shooting of one of their own. Chief Ellis Petri had died

17

on a deserted stretch of mountain road almost a year earlier to the date from a point-blank gunshot wound. With no leads, Ellis's case was dangerously close to turning cold.

Now, someone else would sit at his desk. Drive his SUV. Take his place. Leah did her best to quell her resentment. It was bad enough they'd lost Ellis in such a violent way. That he could be replaced so easily was like twisting the knife in the wound.

Henry had obviously been watching for her. He stepped out onto the porch as Leah pulled up alongside his patrol car. By the time she got out, Henry was standing by her door with a flustered expression on his face. Leah often wondered if a good strong wind might blow the Barney Fife–thin officer away.

"Boy, am I glad to see you. They've been asking for you." Henry pointed to the house and lowered his voice. "*He's* in there too." He wiped sweat from his forehead and cast a nervous glance back to the Zook home.

"Why's he here anyway? I thought Cooper wasn't coming in until later in the week." Leah didn't even bother to hide her disapproval.

Henry shrugged. "He was at the station when I arrived. He heard the call come in."

"What's he like?" The question was out before she could stop it. Gossiping about the new chief was not her finest moment.

"Kind of intense," Henry said with the same amount of anxiety that had consumed Leah since the announcement came through from the mayor. "Sam sure was mad when he didn't get the job, though you're the one who's practically run the force since Ellis passed. I'd hoped you'd take over as chief."

Henry had been on the job only a few years and had made his fair share of rookie mistakes, but Leah had liked him from the beginning and had done her best to help him whenever possible. For that, Henry seemed determined to put her on a pedestal.

"I appreciate the compliment, but I'm just an officer like you. We'll leave the big decisions to someone with a higher pay grade than us."

"Yeah, right," Henry confirmed with a nod. "We'd better get inside. I can't explain it, Leah, but I have a bad feeling about this."

Did he mean the case or the new chief? With those uneasy words hanging between them, Leah followed Henry into the simple Amish home that belonged to people she'd once loved like a second family.

As Leah stepped foot inside the living room, it was like going back to her youth. The simple furnishings hadn't changed much. Same threadbare sofa. Same two functional rockers near the woodstove. A chest in the corner held the quilts Miriam and her daughters had crafted. Hooks adorned the walls near the door for coats and lanterns. A scenic calendar on one wall was turned to the current month. Behind the sofa, a framed picture of the Ten Commandments had been there for as long as Leah could remember.

Back then, she and Colette Zook had done everything together. They talked about what their lives might be like in the future. A husband. A houseful of kids. Their enduring friendship foremost in every part of their lives.

Regret seeped into Leah's heart. She'd left the community and Colette and never looked back, even though her dear friend had tried to reach out to her many times. It wasn't right, the way she'd cut Colette out of her life. In her defense, at the time it seemed like the only way to keep from losing her mind.

"Leah, oh Leah!" Miriam Zook spotted her and immediately

pushed to her feet. "I am so glad you came." Miriam sobbed inconsolably. "Our Beth is missing. Josiah checked the entire property, but there's no sign of her. We're afraid something has happened." The show of emotion was out of character for the woman, who rarely expressed her feelings.

Leah patted Miriam's arm. "We're going to do everything we can to find your daughter and bring her home to you." She did her best to comfort Miriam while praying her words wouldn't come back to haunt her.

Miriam seemed to latch on to what Leah had said as if it were a lifeline. Her dark, red-rimmed eyes searched Leah's face. She sniffed twice and squared her shoulders.

Leah guided the woman back to the sofa, where she sank beside her husband and a young girl who appeared to be around eight. The Zooks had another child. She hadn't realized the family had expanded. Her last contact with the family had been at the funeral.

"This is our daughter Katie." Josiah made the introductions. Katie was a younger version of Colette. Same silver-blond hair and deep blue eyes.

Josiah placed his arm around his weeping wife. He'd aged in the ten years since Leah had last seen him. The Amish way of life was not an easy one. His hair, now almost entirely white, matched his neatly trimmed beard. The worry on his face drove home the reason they were all here. Josiah was an honest, trusting man who kept his faith in *Gott* and his attention on hard work. Worry wasn't part of his subsistence. Until now.

Another man who had been seated in a rocker near the woodstove had risen when Leah entered the room. Leah's attention latched on to the new man in charge as he came her way. Tall and fit, he was probably former military if the way he carried himself was any indication. He wore his dark hair cut short. Brown eyes captured hers as he closed the space between them. Henry's description of the man came to mind. "Intense" seemed fitting.

He extended his hand. "I'm Dalton Cooper, the new chief. Sorry to have to make the introductions this way." He kept his voice low enough for only her to hear. "Sam and Ethan are searching the property and surrounding area."

Leah shook his hand and forced words out. "It's nice to meet you, Chief Cooper."

"Dalton," he said with a brief smile. He glanced past her to where Henry stood in the doorway still. "Why don't you run through what we have for Leah?"

Henry snapped to attention and opened his notepad. "The call came in around 7:15 a.m. Mr. Zook phoned from the Mission General Store to say his daughter was missing from her room. She'd gone to bed at the same time as the rest of the family the night before, but when she didn't come down for breakfast, Mr. and Mrs. Zook checked in on her and discovered her bed was empty. That was at 6:00 a.m."

Around the time when the morning household chores were ending. Leah looked around the familiar room, mulling over Henry's statement.

The stale aroma of that morning's breakfast, probably still uneaten, wafted out from the kitchen. She remembered the many times she'd spent the night here growing up. At daybreak, the family gathered around the table. A flicker of a smile touched her lips as she recalled Miriam bustling about to make sure everyone was fed and ready for the day.

"Beth is around sixteen, correct?" Leah asked Josiah. No doubt going through her rumspringa, a period when Amish youth enjoyed more freedom to go out into the world and experience what it felt like to not be Plain. Most returned to join the faith. Some did not.

Images of Leah's own rumspringa came to mind. She and Colette had committed only small acts of defiance. Colette did her best to keep Leah on the right path, but she didn't know about *him*. He'd turned Leah's head away from the path chosen for her and she'd regretted it ever since. Calling himself John, he'd induced her to do things she wouldn't normally have done, like slipping away in the middle of the night to meet him in her family's barn . . .

"*Jah*, that is correct." Josiah's firm response intruded into Leah's regrets. He adjusted his glasses on his nose, brows slanted together in a familiar frown. Josiah had always been a solemn man.

Leah cleared her throat and posed the question she knew would not be well received. "Is it possible Beth may have gone out after everyone fell asleep? Maybe to a friend's? Perhaps she spent the night there?"

Miriam's head shot up. Anger ignited in her eyes. "Nay. It is not possible. Beth is a *gut* girl. She would not go sneaking out of the house. She is happy with the Plain life and is going to be baptized soon. She and Caleb Wagler will marry one day. Beth would *not* do such a thing." Miriam collapsed against her husband, deep sobs racking her body.

Most Amish parents did not question their children about what they did during rumspringa. It stood to reason the Zooks wouldn't know everything going on in Beth's life, yet Leah had obviously touched a nerve. She let the matter drop.

"Would you mind if I checked Beth's room?" She addressed Josiah again as Miriam continued to weep. The man stared at her blankly. Josiah's simple world had been sent into a tailspin and he was clearly struggling to understand.

Leah focused on the little girl seated beside her mother. "Do you share a room with your sister?"

Katie nodded slightly while keeping her attention on her clasped hands.

"Would you mind showing me around your room?"

Katie twisted her skirt in her hands and snuck a peek at her father. Leah suspected she had information about her sister's disappearance she might not wish to share in front of her parents.

Josiah gave an approving nod. Katie rose and headed for the stairs without a word. With a glance at the new chief, Leah followed.

The little girl clutched the railing as she slowly climbed the stairs and headed down the hallway to the same room that Colette once shared with Beth.

A wealth of memories waited inside the room. She and Colette had been like sisters back then. Once more, guilt pierced Leah deep. She should have reached out to Colette. Kept in touch. If she were being honest, she'd missed her friend through the years, missed their girlish conversations. Colette had stood at her side, clutching her hand, at the cemetery. And afterward, her friend had reached out to her through visits and letters. Leah had been the one to shut her out. Because remembering the life she'd left behind was just too hard.

She focused on the child. "Do you enjoy sharing a room with your sister?"

Katie's huge eyes found hers. The little girl's bottom lip trembled. Was Katie's reaction due to worry for her sister or guilt over harboring Beth's secrets?

"*Jah*, she is a *gut* big sister. She brings me sweets from the store where she works."

The news surprised Leah. She had had no idea Beth had worked outside of the farm. Leah made a mental note to check with the owners of the store if Beth wasn't found soon. She glanced around the small, tidy space. "Which is your sister's bed?"

Katie pointed to the one near where Leah stood while her eyes darted to the open window, where the morning breeze whipped the curtains around.

Leah searched inside the drawer of the nightstand. Nothing but an extra prayer *kapp*. Where would Beth keep things she didn't want her parents to see? Leah's had been under the mattress. A search there produced nothing. Whatever deep, dark secrets Beth might have been keeping, she'd hidden them well.

"Was Beth excited to be going through her rumspringa?" Leah did her best to make Katie feel at ease.

"I guess so." Katie's words were vague, offering little, while her gaze kept returning to the window. Leah swung toward it. Did the girls open the window to cool the room against the oppressive heat, or had Beth left it that way when she slipped out the night before?

"Katie, did Beth sneak out to meet someone last night?" Leah's direct question struck a reaction in the little girl. Tears glistened in her eyes.

Leah moved to Katie's side. "You're not in trouble," she said gently. "I'm just trying to find your sister."

Katie hiccupped several sobs. "*Jah*, sh-she snuck out last night. Beth thought I was sleeping, but I wasn't. I told her Mamm and Daed would be mad when they found out. She begged me not to tell . . . and I didn't." Katie scrubbed at the tears that were streaming down her cheeks. "I did not tell anyone but you."

Leah squeezed her arm. "It's okay. You're doing the right thing. Beth needs our help, and this will hopefully let us bring her home safely. Do you have any idea who she was meeting?"

Katie vigorously shook her head. "Nay. She did not tell me, but I'm positive it was a boy. An Englischer." The last word came in a whisper. "I saw her with him once before when she didn't know. He drove a car and he smiled a lot. Beth did too. She had a funny look on her face when she came back inside."

Beth had let an Englischer into her life. What kind of ideas had he put in her head? Leah thought about her own forbidden romance with John, and her concern for Beth intensified.

"Can you tell me what he looked like, Katie?"

"I did not see him very clearly." Katie gulped back fresh tears. "They talked over at the Millers' barn, and I only saw him for a moment before he pulled her into the barn. He was taller than Beth and he had dark hair. That's all I remember."

Beth had met the stranger in *her* old barn. Too much of a coincidence to dismiss.

She grabbed her phone and called Sam. "Where are you?" she asked the second he answered.

"The pasture behind the Zook house. So far, there's no sign of the girl."

"Check the barn next door." Trembles ran through Leah's frame, and her bad feeling doubled. Was it just the memories of what happened to her family bleeding into this case because of the approaching anniversary? Or something far more deadly?

Sam's silence confirmed he understood the significance. He'd been on the force back when it happened. "We'll head there now," he said quietly.

Leah punched End and stuffed the phone into her pocket. The little girl beside her watched her with huge, worried eyes.

25

More than anything, she wished to reassure Katie everything would be okay, but her gut wouldn't allow it. The mention of the barn amped up her concerns to a whole new level.

"Katie, do you remember anything about the car the Englischer drove?"

The little girl stared at her for the longest time. "I-I think it may have been black. But it was dark, so I cannot be sure."

"You're certain it was a car and not a pickup truck?" Leah pressed. They needed answers. *Now*. Every passing minute reduced Beth's chances at survival.

"*Jah*, I am positive it was a car."

"Good, that's very helpful," she assured the girl. "Thank you, Katie."

The room's window faced Leah's old homestead. As she peered out at the barn, goose bumps sped up her arms despite the oppressive heat. The rickety door stood wide open. While she tried to process the few details they had so far, Sam and Ethan entered her line of sight. Both men paused in front of the open door, staring at something she couldn't see before they went inside.

Leah's pulse ticked off every second they were out of her sight. Twenty beats passed before the men rushed from the building, their stricken faces chilling Leah's blood.

"Stay here," Leah told the little girl and crossed the room. Descending the steps as fast as possible, Leah was certain they'd found Beth Zook. And she wasn't alive.

Two of his uniformed officers ran past the Zooks' front windows. Seeing the terror on their faces catapulted Dalton to his feet.

"Henry, stay with the family," he said as he hurried to head the men off before they came inside. The small four-officer St. Ignatius police force hadn't dealt with many serious crimes in the past. He sensed that was about to change.

Before he reached the screen door, Leah Miller pounded down the stairs. Their eyes connected briefly. The same wave of emotion swept over him that had hit him when he'd first introduced himself to her. Fear lived in the depths of those green eyes. A deep red scar on her throat flared despite her attempts to hide it with makeup. No doubt a constant reminder of what she'd been through.

He and Leah were kindred spirits. Though she'd lost so much more than he could ever imagine, they had both been affected by the same crime. Only she had no idea of their connection.

Leah broke eye contact, yanked the door open, and headed outside. Dalton caught it before it slammed in his face. She'd seen her fellow officers' reactions as he had.

"You found her." Leah addressed the senior officer, Sam Coeburn. It wasn't a question.

Sam was silent for a moment. "I didn't think I'd ever see something like that again," he muttered, his face ashen.

"Let's take this conversation away from the porch," Dalton told his officers. He didn't want the Zooks to hear the fate of their daughter like this. Once the group moved away from the open windows, he asked, "What did you find?"

Sam dragged in several breaths and struggled to get the words out. "The girl, Chief. She's dead. Her throat's been cut and there's blood everywhere . . ."

"Where is she?" The thought foremost in his mind was how devastated the family would be when he had to deliver the news of their daughter's death.

"In the old Miller barn." Sam looked anywhere but at Leah. The similarity to what happened all those years ago clearly was not lost on him.

In an instant, Dalton's worst nightmare materialized before his eyes. When he'd agreed to assist with the missing persons call earlier, not in his wildest dreams did he imagine they'd be facing a homicide with ties to the past. His past.

"We do this by the book," he told them. The town of St. Ignatius was unique in that it resided on the Flathead Indian Reservation, as did this Amish community. The Flathead police would need to be brought into the investigation along with the sheriff's office. Since the original call was to the St. Ignatius police, they would take the lead.

Dalton hit the radio on his uniform. "Dispatch, have the coroner come out to the old Miller place right away and contact the tribal police and the sheriff's department in Polson. Have them send the crime scene investigations unit here as well."

"Yes, sir." The tremor in Sugar Wallace's tone confirmed she understood what had happened.

He'd met Sugar earlier. The fifty-something woman had dyed-red hair piled high on her head. Sugar wore too much makeup and called him "hon," and he was pretty sure she'd checked him out. But he believed behind that in-your-face abrasive exterior beat a heart of gold. Still, her personality would take some getting used to.

Dalton ended the transmission and faced his waiting officers. "We secure the crime scene right away. Everyone glove up but try not to touch anything unless you have to. When CSI arrives, they can take over and we'll assist."

Henry stepped out on the porch, his gaze ping-ponging between the four. "What's going on?"

Dalton sensed the young officer might still be green. He'd read all his people's files. Henry had served under Petri's watch for a short time before the chief had died from a gunshot wound while out on a call. "Close the door," Dalton told him. Until they had more to go on, he wasn't ready to break the news to the family.

Henry glanced back inside before he shut the door and came down the steps.

"Sam and Ethan found the girl." Getting the next part out proved harder. "She's dead. I need you to stay with the family and keep them inside and away from the windows until we've had time to investigate."

Henry's mouth flopped open. He repeatedly shook his head. "I can't. They'll see the truth on my face."

"Yes, you can," Dalton insisted. "Do your job, Officer. This will be hard enough for the family as it is. Be strong."

Henry's hesitation confirmed his lack of confidence. He slowly nodded, hitched his thumbs in his belt, and adjusted his pants, then swung toward the door. Dalton watched him disappear inside the home before turning to Leah. "Did you get anything useful from the girl?"

Her attention fixed on him, and Dalton tried not to get sucked into the storm going on inside those tumultuous green eyes. Some of her raven hair had escaped from its restraint, and she tucked it behind her ears. "I did. Katie told me Beth snuck out last night. She said she'd seen her sister with an Englischer over near the barn once before."

The past slapped him in the face. Had the real killer returned to take up his old games? The time of year was not lost on Dalton. Stuffing down the resentment flowing through his veins proved hard because it was always there whenever he thought about Harrison's death. Dalton had known Harrison since he was just a child. Knew he wasn't a killer. "Can she identify this man?"

Leah shook her head. "She thought he had dark hair, and he drove a dark-colored car, but that's it." She shrugged. Like him, Leah had to be comparing the details of this murder to the ones that had taken place in that same barn ten years earlier.

A vague description of the perpetrator was all they had to go on. It could fit any of a dozen men around the area. And it fell on his shoulders as the chief of police of little more than a few hours to solve Beth Zook's murder. His stomach churned. Dalton didn't believe for a moment the killer would stop with her. He had a bloodlust and he'd just begun his deadly games again. More bodies would follow unless they apprehended him soon.

Dalton stared across the short distance to the barn. Rising heat appeared like a vapor between the two properties. Though it was not even midday, the temperature had already reached the sweltering point. What appeared to be a bloody handprint on the barn door grabbed his attention. He hadn't noticed it before because the door was open. Now, the crimson blood appeared a stark contrast to the weathered gray exterior of the barn. It served as a warning that the horror of the day had just begun. He remembered reading about a handprint found on the same barn during the Millers' murder investigation. It was determined to be left by Leah as she fled to the Zooks' to get help for her family.

When Dalton first heard about Ellis Petri's murder and the subsequent vacant chief of police position, he'd immediately contacted the hiring committee even though it meant leaving behind a promising detective position in Denver. Not to mention the suggestion from his commander that he was making a mistake by chasing ghosts. When he'd received the call to set up an interview, he tried not to get his hopes up. But Dalton soon learned he was the only outside candidate to apply for the position. The committee had offered him the job the same day.

In Dalton's opinion, the offer came by God's own hand. After ten years, he had the chance to find out the truth beyond the story Ellis Petri had given. He would stop at nothing to know what happened to the Miller family . . . and to Harrison.

"Let's take two patrols over and park on the road near the barn. It stands to reason Beth and possibly the killer may have crossed the same path as Sam and Ethan to the barn. There might be evidence left behind we can't afford to disturb." Dalton turned to Leah. "You'll ride with me." As the only surviving witness to the original murders, she might remember something useful to the case now. And he wanted her close.

Adrenaline shot through his veins. He'd expected it to take months if not years of going over the murder files—chasing down leads missed by Ellis—to have answers. If this was the work of the Miller family's killer, was the timing an accident or deliberate in anticipation of the tenth anniversary of that crime?

Leah clutched her arms tight around her body. Her troubled eyes seemed to confirm her mind had traveled down the same dark road as Dalton's.

A tragedy such as hers changed a person. It had certainly changed him. He'd grown up with Harrison. As kids they'd played together. Toward the end of his mother's life, he spent more time with Harrison's family than at his own home. Though Dalton was Englisch, neither Harrison nor his family treated him differently.

In the years since Harrison's death, the mystery of what really happened chased him through his tour of duty in Afghanistan and into his college years as well as his marriage.

"Are you ready?" Leah's voice intruded into his pain. Dalton's attention went to her face. She shoved her dark sunglasses in place and climbed into the passenger seat of his SUV without waiting for his answer. Though he'd only met her a short time earlier, he had the feeling she did her best to keep people at a distance. Something they had in common. Since Harrison's death and the devastation that followed, he'd done the same.

Let it go . . . Give it to me. That small voice whispered in his head.

"Sam, you and Ethan follow me." Dalton rounded the front of the SUV and climbed behind the wheel. In the passenger seat, Leah stared straight ahead.

Dalton fired the engine, reversed, and then headed down the dusty dirt road. His curiosity about the woman beside him grew. Ellis Petri and his wife had adopted her shortly after the grisly tragedy that had befallen her family. She'd excelled in school and had worked on the force for several years now.

He pulled off the road near the Miller place. He and Leah got out. "Go slow," he told his people as they headed for the barn. "Keep your eyes open and disturb nothing."

Leah's full attention remained on the barn. This investigation would no doubt reopen old wounds. From Sam's account, Beth Zook's injuries matched those of Leah and her family. Dalton's instincts wouldn't let him accept they had a copycat. Which left one other option. The killer had returned.

He glanced past the structure to the crumbling house while a quick prayer ran through his head. *Please be with Beth's family, Lord. Give them your strength.*

After today, the Zooks would never be the same again.

The Miller house and barn sat some distance off the road. According to what he could ascertain, the property had remained vacant since the night of the murders. But he was familiar with every inch of it. He'd come here many times after Harrison's death without anyone knowing. Desperate to understand why Ellis Petri would go after someone as innocent as Harrison for such a heinous act. Especially without iron-clad proof.

"Tire tracks." Leah stopped and pointed to the dusty earth nearby.

Dalton knelt and studied them. "Sam, get photos of these. We'll have CSI make molds. Maybe they can match them to a particular make of vehicle." He rose and glanced at the woman at his side. Her tension was almost palpable.

As they neared the barn, he saw two sets of footprints that came from around the side of the building. One much larger than the other.

"Which way did you and Sam enter the property?" he asked Ethan.

The former marine picked up on what he was asking right away. "Those aren't ours."

"The smaller set probably belongs to Beth. It's possible the second is the killer's," Leah said, her voice scratchy.

Without words, they moved to the barn's entrance, which faced the Zook farm. Up close, the blood-red handprint acted as an omen of what they'd find inside.

Dalton eased open the door and went in first while Leah trailed behind him. Shadows clung to everything despite the time of day. The scent struck him head-on. Metallic and overpowering. Even in the dim light, there was no mistaking the brutality that had taken place within these dilapidated walls.

Beth lay in the middle of the barn on the dirt floor, dressed in a simple white nightgown, blood covering the front of it.

Someone gasped. Dalton's attention shifted to Leah, her face as pale as the white gown.

"Do you need to step outside?" he asked gently. The reminder of that night long ago had to be crippling. He'd certainly understand if she needed to take a moment.

Leah swallowed repeatedly and visibly collected herself. "No, I'm fine," she mumbled and moved to the dead girl's side. Dalton pulled in a ragged breath before joining her.

They faced each other across Beth's body. Her sightless eyes stared into space. Beth's throat had been slashed.

Upon taking the police chief position, Dalton had read the report of the Miller murders. He'd seen the crime scene photos. They matched what he witnessed here almost perfectly. However, for reasons only the killer could explain, he hadn't shown the same vengeance toward Leah as he had the rest of his victims. It appeared the perpetrator had some type of connection to her, whether real or made up in his twisted mind.

A noise broke his concentration. Dalton realized Leah was struggling to keep from being sick.

"Go outside, Officer. That's an order."

Without answering, she rushed from the barn.

Dalton stared down at the lifeless young woman. Terror and excruciating pain had undoubtedly filled Beth's final minutes on this earth. "I'm sorry this happened to you," he whispered. Beth Zook had had her whole life ahead of her. She didn't deserve this.

Blood spatter spread out around the body like a halo. The attack had been a violent one. Most of Beth's nails were broken. She'd fought her attacker. It was possible they'd recover some trace DNA from underneath her fingernails.

Someone entered. Dalton turned his head as Ethan came his way.

"This is a terrible thing, Chief. A terrible thing."

Dalton didn't respond as he concentrated on Beth's body. He saw that she clutched an item in her left hand. He freed the paper from the girl's lifeless hand.

"What is that?" Ethan asked.

Leah had quietly returned to the barn. She and Ethan peered over Dalton's shoulder at the note.

As carefully as possible, Dalton unfolded the paper.

"What's it say?" Ethan asked.

Dalton glanced at Leah. Her haunted expression solidified his own suspicions. The nightmare that had taken place in this barn ten years earlier had come calling again.

Bright red words jumped out at him from the page. There was no doubt in his mind the killer used Beth's blood to pen the note. The message written here was intended for one person alone.

"Tell Leah I'm back."

two

Awounded sound tore from that place inside Leah where the pain festered. She dropped to her knees, covering her mouth with hands that shook. Words written on a paper held by a dead woman confirmed the truth. Harrison Troyer had died an innocent man. And the true killer was coming after her again.

When she'd learned Harrison had set an abandoned home on fire to commit suicide, the very idea seemed inconceivable. The sweet boy she'd met at the biweekly services was not a killer, much less capable of ending his life in such a violent way. But Ellis had assured her Harrison had been the one who killed her family. He'd told her the fire had burned so hot it destroyed everything inside, including Harrison's body.

Now, she had proof Ellis had been wrong and the real killer wanted to play his morbid games again. Did she have the strength to survive another round?

Someone lifted her to her feet and urged her outside. A blast of heat slapped her in the face, plastering damp tears on her cheeks.

Leah stared into Dalton's eyes. Anger. Frustration. Pity. All there. All for her.

She couldn't let him pull her from the case, no matter what. The answers she'd desperately needed all these years would finally be revealed, and she wanted to be there to bring the true killer down. Leah owed it to her family. To Harrison.

"I'm okay." Leah backed away, and he let her go. She needed to put distance between them for her own peace of mind.

"You're not," he said quietly. "Take a beat. Collect yourself. You shouldn't even be working the case, and you wouldn't if we didn't need all the manpower we have on staff." His words struck like blows. He'd heard about her past. He was clearly a man who'd done his research before taking this job.

With a final searching gaze her way, Dalton returned to the barn.

As she watched him disappear, Leah wondered how she could possibly not let what happened to her family enter into this investigation when the killer himself had thrown it in her face. Desperate to free herself from the clutches of despair, she started walking and didn't stop until she'd reached the old pine tree next to her former home. The room above once belonged to Leah and Ruth. Memories of her sister's laughter, her smiling face, brought more tears.

"Why? Why did you let this happen? Why take them? Beth?" Leah clenched her fists until her nails dug into her palms, but the pain wouldn't be denied. "I love you, sis." Ruth's smile faded. Replaced by that night. The whimpering sound her sister made as she died was branded on Leah's heart. "Leave me alone. Go back to your hiding place. Leave me alone." Yet the memories wouldn't.

Like Beth, Leah had been on the cusp of adulthood back then and excited to grow up. When Harrison Troyer showed up in the community at the beginning of the summer months to help his cousins on the farm, they'd become instant friends. She'd thought there might be more until John came into her life.

Had Beth felt this same way? She'd obviously kept secrets from her family, like Leah had. Met up with an Englischer who didn't understand the Amish ways.

Like John.

Incredibly handsome and worldly, John had stolen her heart, or so her sixteen-year-old self had thought. Leah had slipped out many a night to meet him in the same barn where Beth died. They'd kissed. He'd begged her to run away with him, but she hadn't wanted to leave her family. That's when she'd seen the ugly side of John. Leah had thought he would hit her, but he'd stormed from the barn instead. Gotten into the car he'd parked down from her house and sped away. Her heart broke at the prospect of never seeing him again.

And then . . . a few hours later a masked man had broken into her home, forced her family inside the barn, and killed everyone but her.

"You'll always belong to me." He'd whispered those words while slashing her throat. Leah had known it was John.

When Ellis told her Harrison had committed the murders, Leah didn't want to believe it. Yet the chief had been so certain, and the killer had worn a ski mask. Perhaps after the trauma of the attack, she'd been mistaken about the voice. Now, with the killer back and all but confirming his connection to her, Leah was certain John had returned.

Something caught her attention above. Movement near the cracked window of her old room. Tattered gingham curtains waved. Just the wind? Leah shielded her eyes against the sun's glare. A figure. Barely visible past the curtains. Someone was in the house.

Without thinking of her own safety, Leah raced to the entrance. Ramming her shoulder against the warped door, she forced it open and charged inside. Ten years of dust covered everything, yet time had been encapsulated in this compact space. The sight of her mamm's knitting next to her favorite rocker sucked the breath from Leah's body.

Pushing aside those heartbreaking memories, Leah drew her weapon and eased toward the stairs while recollections of the many times she and Ruth had slid down the banister crowded in. She stuffed them down deep as she reached the landing. Braced for the confrontation to come.

The first door on the right belonged to her parents. As quietly as possible, she opened it and peeked inside, fighting the haunts waiting there.

The room was vacant of anything resembling human life. Next, she checked her brother's room. Nothing.

One more room. With the weapon shaking in her hand, Leah stood before her old door. She drew in a breath and opened it. Breached the threshold. Barely cleared the entrance when something hard slammed against her head, dropping her to her knees. The world around her blurred. Someone grabbed her arms and hauled Leah up on the filthy bed that had once been hers.

A hand snaked around her neck. She stared up into the past. Same angry eyes. Same ski mask. Same killer.

"I told you, you would always belong to me. Now you realize I meant it." As he continued to choke the life from her, Leah thrust her weapon between them. Her attacker's eyes widened when he spotted it. He jumped from the bed. She managed to fire a shot at the fleeing figure. The bullet lodged in the doorframe, and a moment later, the killer disappeared from view.

Leah staggered to her feet. Putting one foot in front of the other, she gave pursuit. After ten years of waiting to be sure, she couldn't give up now.

As she reached the landing, Leah struggled to focus on the space below. Nothing moved. She leaned heavily against the banister as she descended the stairs. The front door stood open. Before she had the chance to give chase, Dalton and Ethan rushed into the house.

Leah doubled over and blew out a relieved breath before lowering the gun. "Did you see him?" Her voice came out raspy.

"Who?" Dalton skimmed over her face, seeing the terror she couldn't hide.

"The killer. He was just here. He tried to strangle me." She massaged her tender throat. "Didn't you see him?"

"Stay with her," Dalton ordered Ethan, then bolted from the house.

With her heart pounding in her ears, Leah sank down to the bottom step and tried to capture the shreds of her composure.

"You all right, Leah?" Ethan asked with obvious concern.

She nodded because it hurt to speak.

Ethan combed a hand through his wavy black hair. A native of the Salish tribe, Ethan was in his early thirties, former military, and had twin daughters to raise alone after his wife passed away. "What brought you over here anyway?" He looked around at the simple reminders of the life she'd once lived.

She swallowed painfully. "I stepped away to clear my head. Then I noticed movement in a room upstairs."

Before she'd finished her recounting, Dalton returned. "There's no sign of him."

Leah repeated what she'd said to Ethan. "He must have been waiting for me behind the door." She drew several needed breaths before continuing. "He struck me here." She pointed to her head. "Then threw me on the bed and started choking me." Her voice shook as she relayed the menacing words the killer had uttered. "I don't think he wanted to kill me."

"More likely he wanted you to know he was back and could get to you anytime he wanted." Dalton's jaw tightened. He shifted toward Ethan. "Get some crime scene techs over here now."

Ethan followed the command immediately while Leah tried to stop the trembles. She'd given so much already. Now another innocent life had to be sacrificed to satisfy a madman's lust for murder.

After several minutes passed, Dalton came from upstairs carrying something in an evidence bag. She hadn't even been aware of him leaving, yet the moment she got a good look at the bag, Leah knew the killer had left another note.

"We should wait outside until the techs can examine the house thoroughly." Why wouldn't he tell her what it said?

A pressing alarm closed in as she followed him outside. "Tell me what it says," she asked when he wasn't forthcoming.

Dalton's brows slanted together. "Are you sure you want to hear?"

Did she? What choice was there? "Yes, I want to know." She *had* to know.

Dalton put on new gloves and took the paper out of the evidence bag. He slowly unfolded the note and read it aloud. *"I've waited ten years for you. You thought he'd protect you, but I proved he was no match for me."*

The meaning behind those chilling words threatened to take her legs out from under her. "He's admitting to killing Ellis." She couldn't believe it. John, or whatever his real name was, had killed Ellis.

41

"It appears so," he said quietly. Dalton's gaze swept over her. "Are you okay? We should have someone look at that." He pointed to her head.

She dismissed his request with a wave of her hand. "It's nothing. I'll be fine."

Dalton took a deep breath. "All right. It seems that for whatever reason, the killer is obsessed with you, which means you're in danger. From this minute on, you are going into protective custody. We can't afford to take any unnecessary risks."

Leah barely heard what he said. "Marge could be in danger too." The thought of her sweet, adoptive mother who suffered from dementia being subjected to the killer's brutality was terrifying. "I need to see her." Leah didn't think she could bear it if something happened to Marge.

"I'll send Sam to her house right away. He'll bring her to the station and we can explain what's happening there. I want you with me."

Dalton's intense gaze held hers. For a moment, it was hard to think clearly.

"Marge doesn't do well outside her home. She's having problems with her memory." Leah did her best to explain Marge's condition. "She knows Sam. If you have him tell her I asked him to stay with her for a while, it'll be better."

Other than attending church services, Marge rarely left the house anymore. Sometimes Leah was able to coax her out for a walk and the occasional visit to the grocery store. She couldn't imagine how Marge would react to having to leave the security of her home and go to the police station.

Dalton hit the mic on his radio and spoke to Sam. Once he ended the transmission, he shifted his full attention to Leah. "We need to speak with Beth's family right away. With all the additional police presence, they're bound to wonder what's happening."

Leah pulled her thoughts together. There would be no hiding the truth for long. "You're right. They should know what happened to their daughter."

"They trust you, and your relationship with the family will help." Dalton scanned the activity taking place around them. "We have to set up a command post. With three separate law enforcement agencies working the case, we need a central location to compare notes." His focus returned to her. "Once we've spoken to the family, let's head back to the station and start analyzing what we have so far."

Several techs from the crime scene unit arrived with Ethan. Dalton handed them the note and explained where he'd found it. "Ethan, can you assist here?"

"Sure thing." Ethan pressed Leah's arm briefly and gave her a reassuring smile. "The medical examiner just arrived. Hopefully, he'll give us some idea of the time of death soon."

"Thanks, Ethan. Leah and I are going to speak with the family now." Dalton turned toward her with a solemn expression on his face. "Ready?"

She wasn't. Any more than she was ready to play the killer's games again. But the choice had been taken from her. She'd play because she had to know the truth if she was ever going to lay those ghosts to rest.

Dalton stared up at the Zooks' house. The midmorning sun cast a glare on everything around. "I hate having to deliver news like this. Especially to these good folks. They don't deserve it," he murmured and shifted toward Leah. "You didn't either."

Despite what happened to Harrison and the secrets that drove Ellis Petri to come after him so aggressively, Leah was another innocent victim like the rest of her family.

Climbing the porch steps felt like summiting a mountain, each one laden with dread. He opened the door and stepped inside the house, his heart as heavy as his footsteps.

The family remained where he'd left them. No one stirred as he and Leah entered the living room. If he didn't know differently, he'd swear these were wax figures made in their likenesses.

Leah sat beside Miriam Zook. The woman turned. Saw something in Leah's expression and collapsed against her in a fit of sobbing.

The inevitable couldn't be postponed. Dalton pulled the rocker over near Josiah while Henry watched from the corner, the dark news to come keeping him glued to the spot.

"I'm sorry to have to tell you this, but we found Beth at the Millers' barn." He took a breath before delivering the worst news of their lives. "I'm afraid she's dead."

A wail ripped from the depths of Miriam Zook's soul. It tore through Dalton's mind and burrowed in his heart.

Josiah seemed incapable of blinking, much less forcing out a coherent sentence. Out of the corner of his eye, Dalton noticed the little girl coming down the stairs. She stood in front of her mother, watching as she grieved. Katie didn't comprehend what was happening. She would in time.

"Henry, why don't you take Katie into the kitchen to get her mother some water," Dalton suggested.

Henry steered the child away from the devastating adult conversation taking place.

Josiah swallowed several times and fought against the tears in his eyes. "What happened to my daughter, Chief Cooper?"

Leah still held the weeping woman. Something akin to compassion shone in her eyes as they met his. She understood the Zook family had now become part of a dark and ugly club. One no one wished to join.

"Your daughter's death is being ruled a homicide," Dalton said quietly.

"No!" Another heart-wrenching cry tore from Miriam's lips. She pulled away from Leah, her eyes red rimmed and swimming with tears. "Who would do this to my child? Who?" she demanded.

Dalton couldn't tell her that he believed Beth's death had come at the hands of a serial killer obsessed with one victim. "We don't know yet, ma'am," he said. They didn't have the killer's identity yet, but he was determined they would in time. "We'll find the person who's responsible and see justice served. I promise we will."

"My poor Beth. My poor little girl." Miriam sobbed uncontrollably.

Josiah's keen eyes latched on to Leah. "Chief Petri was certain young Harrison Troyer killed your family back then. Once Harrison died there were no more deaths. Was he wrong?"

Dalton's expression froze in place. Every time he heard Harrison's name mentioned in connection to Leah's family's case, he wanted to scream. The sweet young kid he remembered was not capable of such violence.

"It's still very early in the investigation," Leah said quietly.

Tears fell unchecked from Miriam's eyes. The sight of them forced Dalton back to the moment. He had an investigation to run. A grief-stricken family in need of answers.

"I want to see my child." Miriam's chin wobbled as she struggled to hold on to some control.

"I'm afraid that won't be possible until we've finished with the investigation," Dalton told her. "But as soon as we are able, we'll release Beth's body to you."

Miriam buried her face in her hands, her body quaking.

"Who would do such a thing to our Beth? We are simple people. We live simple lives." Josiah's voice broke.

Everything Josiah said was true. The Amish were pacifists who didn't believe in harming anyone. Yet someone had brought violence into this community.

"Was Beth having trouble with anyone?" As much as Dalton hated putting the family through the rigors of answering questions, they'd lost valuable time, and the first hours of any investigation were critical.

"Nay." Josiah's answer came quick. His stern voice filled with rebuke. "Everyone in the community loved Beth. There was no trouble."

Katie came back into the room with the glass of water in her hand. She held it out to her mother without response.

"We'll just put it over here for later." Leah set the glass on the table next to the sofa. "Katie, we have to tell your parents what happened last night."

Miriam jerked toward her daughter. "What is she talking about?"

Katie's bottom lip trembled, her eyes full of trouble.

"You didn't do anything wrong," Leah assured the child gently before facing the parents. "Katie told me she saw Beth climb out of the window last night. She noticed her sister meeting with an Englischer once before, near the barn."

Anger flashed in Josiah's eyes. "Why are you telling such lies?" he spat out to his youngest child before addressing Leah. "Beth would not sneak out of the house. My daughter is mistaken."

Beth's parents probably didn't have a clue what was going on in their daughter's life.

Miriam dragged in a deep breath and sat up straight while wiping her eyes. "This is Eva's fault. She has led our Beth astray," she said in Pennsylvania Dutch, unaware that Dalton understood the language.

"Hush," Josiah warned his wife.

"What about Eva?" Leah asked. The couple had forgotten she'd once been one of them.

The man clamped his mouth shut, refusing to talk.

"Josiah, we need your help," Dalton urged. "If you have information that will assist us in finding out what happened to Beth, you must tell us."

Miriam ignored her husband's stony reaction. "Eva Hostetler. She and Beth are of the same age and going through their rumspringa together. Eva is . . . a spirited young woman. She is always encouraging Beth to do things she should not do."

"What type of things?" Leah pressed.

"Things like smoking," Miriam hissed. "She and Beth both work at the Mission General Store. The owner is a *gut* friend. She told us they caught Eva and Beth smoking out back." Miriam shook her head in disgust. "And Eva wants to leave the faith. Beth said as much."

Dalton's gaze connected to Leah's. They'd need to speak with Eva right away.

"My daughter Colette." Miriam clutched Leah's arm. "How are we going to tell Colette about her sister?"

Leah patted her hand. "Colette and I were once close. Let me speak to her. Maybe she can help us figure out who's responsible for hurting Beth."

Miriam wiped her eyes. "*Denki*, Leah. That is most kind of you."

Dalton nodded toward the door. It was time to leave the family to their mourning and start on the investigation. Leah rose along with Dalton.

"If you remember anything that might be useful, please reach out to us," he told the family. "As soon as we have anything, we'll be in touch. Again, I'm so sorry for your loss." He clasped Josiah's hand.

No one from the Zook family responded.

Dalton headed outside with Leah and Henry. Once they were out of earshot, he said, "I want to speak to Colette right away and then Eva Hostetler. Beth shared her secrets with either her sister or her friend. One of them knows something." He shifted to Henry. "Why don't you give the officers a hand canvassing the Miller house and barn for evidence? We can't afford to dismiss anything, no matter how insignificant it might seem."

The young officer stared from Leah to Dalton before nodding. With another troubled look toward the house, he started for his cruiser.

After he'd gone, Dalton watched the activity taking place near the barn. Since Harrison's death, he'd become desperate for the truth behind what happened that night. The fire that Ellis Petri had claimed was started by Harrison had been investigated by an arson expert, who concluded that an accelerant had been used. Ellis said Harrison had been carrying what appeared to be a fuel can in his hand when he entered the abandoned house. The former chief believed Harrison had chosen death over being accused of murder. Now the real killer had returned. And the clock was ticking.

three

He crept past the house, trying to be as inconspicuous as possible. He'd hidden the car at the place where he was staying. Too risky to drive it for a while. They'd be looking for it. Instead, he'd taken a truck no one would be missing yet. This was his game, and he wanted to be part of every twist and turn.

She was there. Each time he saw Leah, memories of that night and the euphoric sensation of holding her life in his hands made him want to experience it again. And again. Just like he had earlier. She'd been at his mercy in the house. He'd chosen to let her live. For now. But when the time was right, he'd finish her off. A smile crept across his face.

Beth had proven no challenge at all. From the beginning, she disappointed him. Falling for him without him even trying. Though she bore a faint resemblance to Leah, she was much weaker. Leah would now prove his greatest challenge. But he would break her.

He kept the truck's speed nice and slow. By now, all the local police and tribal officers were assembled, along with the people from the sheriff's office. Their cars encircled the Zook farm. All because of him. The family had heard about their daughter's fate. He would have given anything to be able to witness their pain.

As he peered over at the activity, he noticed someone he didn't recognize. Who was this man? He slowed even more. Watched as he spoke to Leah. Inches separated them. Something in the way the man looked at her filled him with rage. He pounded on the steering wheel as he drove.

He'd waited for years for the right moment to claim her as his, and the right moment was now. The game had started. No one would stand in his way. No one.

As much as he wanted to stay and watch from a distance, he had something important to do. He continued driving before turning onto the dirt lane where his next conquest lived. She wouldn't know about Beth yet. But soon. He enjoyed taunting her with hints of his relationship with Beth.

He rolled to a stop past her house and climbed out. The noonday heat slammed into him. This godforsaken stretch of land was useless for anything but dying.

As expected, she was there waiting on him. Not timid like Beth. She enjoyed flirting.

She made her way across the bare ground, a smile spreading on her face. The girl thought it exciting to meet like this. Her parents would not approve, which made it more appealing. The rules of the Amish were impossible to keep. Especially for someone like her.

"There you are," she said as she reached him. She gave the truck a curious once-over. "Why are you driving a pickup? Where's your car?"

He smiled the way he always did, but his thoughts were still back with Leah and the new chief. If the man got in the way, he'd have to take him out.

"It needed some repairs, and I wanted to see you."

This pleased her. "I thought you might not come," she said, perfecting her pout.

"I'm sorry I'm late. Something came up."

"That's *oke*. You are here now." She clasped his hand. "You were not with someone else, were you?" Though she smiled, he saw behind it. She was fishing for reassurances he cared for her more than Beth.

He suppressed a laugh and assured her she was the one for him. She imagined he loved her, but his heart belonged to only one. Not that it mattered. Eva would be dead in a matter of days. Her usefulness fulfilled, he'd grow tired of her like he had Beth. She was but a means to draw out the one he wanted. The one who belonged to him. *His* Leah.

"I'll let you take the lead with Colette since you two are friends."

Leah rousted herself from troubled reflections. She turned and found Dalton watching her with a curious look on his ruggedly handsome face. Dalton Cooper was one of those men who would grow more attractive with passing time.

Their eyes held. A flicker of something she couldn't name made it hard to breathe normally. Leah forced her attention away. Her tears were just below the surface, and the last thing she wanted was to fall apart in front of the new chief.

"Leah?" Dalton's husky tone reached out to her. A shiver passed through her frame.

"Yes, I'm sorry. That's fine." Leah stared up at Colette's simple home.

"Are you sure you're up to this? If it's too much, you can wait in the patrol."

She'd been pitied, felt sorry for, tiptoed around for years. She didn't want it from Dalton.

"I'm fine. It's just . . ." She didn't finish. "Do you think he really killed Ellis?" She blurted the words out. *"You thought he'd protect you, but I proved he was no match for me."*

Dalton rubbed his throat. "It's possible, or maybe he's simply playing with you. If he's been following your activities, he'd realize Ellis and Marge cared for you. Probably figures his claiming responsibility would cause pain." He pinched the bridge of his nose. "There are more questions than answers at this point. We'll have to look closer into the call Ellis responded to on the night he died."

The interior of the SUV became claustrophobic. Leah needed air. She stumbled from the vehicle. A few beats later, Dalton exited the car as well.

Leah stepped up on the porch and knocked a couple of times. Beside her, Dalton shoved his hands in his pockets and rocked on his heels.

Somewhere inside the house, a baby cried. Colette had married David Stoltzfus the year after Leah left the faith. Though she hadn't spoken to the other woman since the funeral, Colette had still invited her to attend the wedding. Leah hadn't gone. It was just too painful to see the people she'd once been close to.

Footsteps headed toward the door. A second passed before it opened and a somewhat older and more frazzled Colette stood there, a baby on her hip.

Colette's mouth fell open when she spotted Leah.

"Hello, Colette."

"Leah." Her smile froze when she noticed the man in uniform

beside her. Colette gasped and lifted her chin. "Something has happened."

Leah remembered Colette had been with her at the hospital when Ellis confirmed her family had all succumbed to their injuries. Now, she must do the same. "I'm afraid so. May we come inside?"

"*Jah*," she said eventually, and yet she didn't move. Leah gently pulled the screen free and stepped inside with Dalton.

Colette blinked several times before fixing her attention on the sleeping child in her arms. "Let me put Sadie down first." She headed down the hallway without waiting for an answer. Two children, a boy around six and a girl who could be three or four, peeked their heads out from the kitchen, watching as Leah and Dalton moved to the living room to wait.

Colette said something to the two kids. They disappeared into the kitchen. Soon, Colette returned, her worried eyes skipping from Leah to Dalton.

"Colette, this is Dalton Cooper. He's the new chief of police."

Colette didn't acknowledge Dalton. "What has happened, Leah? Please, tell me."

"I'm afraid it's bad news. You should sit."

"Tell me," Colette insisted.

"It's Beth, Colette. I'm so sorry. She's gone."

A wealth of emotions chased across her friend's face. Shock, followed quickly on its heels by heartbreak. Tears filled Colette's eyes. She dropped to the sofa, covering her face while her shoulders quaked with sobs.

Leah sat beside her. "I'm so sorry."

Colette struggled to collect herself. "Gone? How? What happened to my sister? Was it an accident? Sometimes the cars in town go much too fast around the buggies."

Leah briefly looked to Dalton. "I'm afraid not. We found her in my old barn." Getting the next part out was hard. "She was murdered."

The connection wasn't lost on Colette. "The barn? The same place where . . . ?" She didn't finish. Didn't need to. The horror on Colette's face would be forever branded in Leah's memory. "Who would do such a thing? I just saw her. She spent the night here a few days ago. We attended service together." Her voice broke in a sob. "I cannot believe she is gone." She searched Leah's face as a new horror dawned. "Have my mamm and daed heard?"

"They have. Your father called us to report Beth missing. Colette, Katie told us Beth snuck out last night to meet a boy. Do you have any idea who she might've been seeing?"

Colette struggled to speak. "No, not really. Beth never spoke of another man other than Caleb, but he is a *gut* boy. He wouldn't hurt her, and he certainly wouldn't ask her to do anything against our parents' wishes." Colette appeared to struggle to make sense of what happened. "Beth was going through a rebellious time. She stayed out later than usual and I suspected she smoked, although she denied it . . ." Her voice cut out as she realized something.

"What is it?" Leah prompted, watching Colette's face closely.

"Something strange did happen when Beth spent the night. She kept looking out the window as if she was expecting someone. When I asked what was going on, she told me nothing."

"But you didn't believe her," Dalton inserted, and Colette shifted her attention to him.

"No, I did not. Later that night, the baby woke up. While I tended to her, I heard a car drive by. And I am almost positive the front door opened. I asked Beth about it the following day, but she said she did not know anything." Colette shook her head. "I think she lied to me. Beth must have slipped out to meet someone."

"But you have no idea who?" Dalton asked.

Colette rubbed the side of her face. "I do not. But she was keeping secrets from Mamm and Daed and me. And she talked once about leaving the St. Ignatius community."

"Was she serious?" Leah couldn't get over how similar Beth's story was to her own.

Colette shrugged. "I'm not sure. She laughed and told me she was only teasing, but I don't believe she was."

If Beth was planning to leave the faith, she would have needed help. She'd be on her own, without her family's support. There was little doubt in Leah's mind that the Englischer who had talked Beth into doing things she wouldn't normally do was the same person who killed her.

"There's something else," Colette said tentatively. "I found it hidden in the room where Beth stayed on occasion. I'll get it." Colette rose and left the room.

When she returned, she carried something in her hand. Colette held it out to Leah. A necklace with a small heart-shaped locket. The sight of it sent Leah back in time, and she fought to grab enough air into her lungs. She recognized the locket because *he'd* given her one just like it. As much as she hadn't wanted to believe it, the locket confirmed the truth. He was back. John was back.

***

Dalton waited until they were in the SUV. "You recognized the locket. You've seen it before."

Leah slowly nodded. "I had one just like it. He—John—gave it to me."

"John? This is the Englisch man you were seeing?"

She whipped his way in surprise. "You read my case file?" She almost sounded hurt.

"I did. There was no mention of a necklace in the file."

Leah's brows knitted into a frown. "I don't understand. I told Ellis about it."

Ellis seemed to have skipped over lots of evidence. "What happened to the necklace?"

She stared at the locket in the evidence bag. "I don't know. The last time I saw it was the morning before the murders. I kept it under my mattress."

"It's not there." In the past, he'd searched the entire house looking for something to make sense of what happened.

Leah's eyes narrowed. "How do you know?"

Dalton realized he'd slipped up and said, "I searched the room earlier, remember? When I found the note."

After a second, she nodded. "This one appears similar to the one John gave me, but I'm not sure."

"Still, it's an awfully big coincidence. We'll send it to the lab after we've spoken to Eva. Maybe she knows how Beth ended up with something forbidden by the Amish faith."

Dalton started the SUV and left Colette's farm. Beside him, Leah had the sunglasses firmly in place once more along with her wall. He skimmed over her profile. She had the type of looks that couldn't be classified as breathtaking as much as mysterious. He wondered what she would be like had tragedy not overshadowed her life.

"Before we speak with Eva, there's something we need to talk about."

Instantly she sat up straighter. "What is it?"

His heart went out to her. In so many ways, they were both stuck in the same grief cycle. "I realize Ellis Petri believed the Amish boy who died in that fire killed your family, but considering what happened to Beth and the connection the killer claims to your family's murders, we'll have to reopen your case." Speaking of Harrison in such an impersonal way felt wrong. Yet for the time being, he wasn't ready to reveal his connection to Harrison.

"It's been ten years. Why would he wait so long to return?" she said as if trying to convince herself this wasn't the same monster who had destroyed her world.

Dalton didn't have a good answer. "Maybe he's been in jail or another part of the country." He shrugged. "Whatever the reason, the likelihood we're dealing with a copycat is slim." He shifted his gaze to the mountains in the distance and saw God's presence in them. A sense of comfort settled inside him. God hadn't been part of his life growing up in a house full of anger and abuse.

"Ellis seemed convinced Harrison Troyer killed my family, but—" She shook her head.

"But what?" he asked curiously. The report he'd read showed Leah had originally said she didn't recognize the killer's voice. She'd later changed her story and said it belonged to an Englischer she'd been seeing. Yet the former chief had become fixated on Harrison to the point of not investigating any other leads.

"Harrison was sweet and only here for the summer to help his family. He didn't seem the type to do such a terrible thing."

Dalton listened as Leah confirmed what he'd always known in his heart.

"The report mentioned someone following you before the attacks."

Her frown deepened. "Yes. I noticed it several times before that night." She stopped abruptly, leaving something unsaid.

"Tell me about this Englischer you were seeing."

Leah's body language turned rigid. She didn't like being questioned. "He called himself John, but I don't believe that's his real name." She looked Dalton's way briefly. "Anyway, I met him while walking home one day. He just walked up behind me and started talking. John told me he'd been hiking around the country. I'd never met anyone as charming as him before. He filled my head with stories of his adventures around the country. For an Amish girl who had been nowhere, it was exciting." She chanced a look his way.

"Go on," he prompted when she remained silent.

"There's nothing else to say."

Dalton was almost certain there were things she'd left out. "Did he ask you to run off with him?"

Her head jerked back to him, confirming the truth. "How did you know?"

"Beth's sister said she considered leaving the faith. I'm guessing this Englischer tried to convince her to run away with him like John did you."

"And he killed her when she didn't agree?"

Dalton witnessed all her doubts as they crossed her face. On the surface, the theory didn't make sense. But the correlation between what had happened to Beth today and Leah's family ten years ago was strengthening.

"I realize it's weak, but it is something to tie the two cases together. Did you consider leaving with him?"

A far-off look entered her eyes. "I was flattered when he asked me," she said so softly he almost didn't hear her. "But I loved the Plain life. The thought of living any other way seemed impossible to comprehend at the time. And so I told him no." She shuddered at the recollection. "John got so angry with me. He stormed out of the barn and drove away." A whisper of a sigh escaped her lips.

"Did he come back that night and decide if he couldn't have you, no one would?"

"I wasn't sure until now," she admitted. "Maybe I didn't want to think the man I'd brought into my life had killed my family." Their eyes met. "But this is John—no doubt about it. He's back and he's killing again."

Dalton touched her arm. "We'll get him, Leah. This time we'll get him." And they would. Because he'd do whatever necessary to bring the killer into custody. End Leah's nightmare and his once and for all.

four

"The turnoff to the Hostetler farm is coming up soon."

On occasion, Leah and some of the other officers would be called to a disturbance out in this part of the community. Mostly it involved teenagers drinking and getting rowdy. They'd come to Amish country because it offered isolation. There were only a few farms spread out this way.

"There it is." She pointed up ahead to where a battered mailbox stood beside a dirt drive.

Staying focused on the case proved all but impossible. The moment she'd entered the barn again, all Leah could see was her family instead of Beth's lifeless body. Little Ruth crying against Mamm's side. Elijah too terrified to speak. Her daed doing his best to reason with the man who was beyond rational thinking.

"How well do you know Eva Hostetler?" Dalton asked, dragging her attention back to the present. Since their brief conversation earlier, he'd been quiet.

As she stared at the remoteness surrounding the Hostetler place, tension coiled her stomach into knots. She could almost feel *his* presence. Was he watching? Leah struggled to keep it together.

She cleared her throat. "Not very. Eva would have been a

child when I left the faith. Still, she and Beth were good friends, and I'd see her at the biweekly services and occasionally at the Zook home."

Dalton slowed the SUV's speed to make the turn. Dust billowed past them. Even in the air-conditioned interior, the heat from outside beat through the windows.

The narrow drive contained dozens of potholes. Like many of the men around the community, Eva's father farmed for a living. Her mother kept the house along with Eva. Gertrude probably sewed quilts and wall hangings to sell in town for extra income, much like Leah's mother had.

The small farmhouse came into view backdropped by a larger red barn. The weathered and peeling white paint of the house was a stark contrast to the red of the structure.

Dalton stopped out front. He touched her arm as she started getting out of the vehicle. "Hold up a second."

Leah resisted the urge to jerk away from the personal contact. Instead, she squared her shoulders and faced Dalton. Once more, she wondered why someone who could probably have his choice of positions would come here when he had no connection with the area.

He frowned at her reaction. "Do you remember the names of Eva's parents?"

Leah pulled in a breath and answered in a less-than-steady voice, "Noah and Gertrude."

When he continued to watch her without responding, Leah got out and tried to collect herself. After what had happened to Beth, her emotions were all over the board.

Leah remembered Gertrude as a stern woman who had a handful of boys. Eva was the last child and the only girl.

Dalton followed her up the steps. They stood side by side

in silence and waited for someone to answer the door. The midday meal would be finished by now—the men returned to the field. Gertrude and Eva would be cleaning or doing other household chores.

The door opened. It took Leah a moment to realize the young woman standing before them was Eva. Her dark brown eyes held curiosity. "May I help you?" Eva's attention lingered on Dalton, a little smile playing on her lips. Even this Amish girl wasn't immune to his good looks.

"Eva?" Leah's use of her name brought the younger woman's attention back to Leah. Recognition widened her eyes. Leah doubted if Eva remembered her from when she was Amish, but the story of what happened to her family had been talked about in the Amish community for many years.

"You are Leah Miller. The one—" Eva stopped. She didn't need to finish for Leah to understand what she meant.

"That's right." Keeping the resentment out of her tone was hard. It wasn't Eva's fault. If the nightmare had happened to anyone else but Leah, she, too, would have been curious.

"Is your mother here?" Leah asked

Eva looked from Leah to Dalton. "Mamm is in the kitchen. My daed and brothers are in the field."

"Can you get her please?"

Eva turned on her heel without answering. The screen door slammed behind her.

"I sure hope she knows something about this man Beth was seeing," Dalton whispered. Had Beth and Eva been close enough to share such secrets? She and Colette sure hadn't.

Two sets of footsteps came their way. A much older-looking Gertrude appeared in the open door while Eva hovered in the background, her expression anxious.

"What is this about?" If Gertrude recognized Leah, she didn't acknowledge it.

"May we come inside, Mrs. Hostetler?" Dalton asked quietly.

Like many Amish, Gertrude appeared wary of police presence. She stepped back without giving a verbal consent.

Dalton opened the screen door and waited for Leah to go ahead of him. Gertrude led them into a small family room similar to that in the Zook home. A place to gather after a hard day's work.

Gertrude stood stock-still, waiting.

"We're here to speak with Eva actually," Leah told her. The young girl fidgeted nervously beside her mother.

"Eva?" Gertrude's tone held shock. "Why?"

"It's about Beth Zook." Leah kept her attention on Eva as she delivered the news. "I'm afraid I have some bad news. Beth was killed sometime last night."

Gertrude gasped. Her wild eyes gave away her struggle to comprehend words that were not familiar to her or her people. "Killed?" She dropped down to the sofa, her chin trembling.

Tears hovered in Eva's eyes. The news came as a surprise.

"She was murdered," Leah added quietly. "You and Beth are friends, aren't you, Eva?"

Eva pressed a hand over her mouth, yet a sob escaped as she settled beside her mother. Gertrude put her arm around the girl.

"Eva and Beth have been *gut* friends for many years. How could this happen to Beth? She is the sweetest thing."

Like Ruth and Elijah.

The questions she was asking reminded her of the ones Ellis had asked her once she'd been released from the hospital.

Leah pulled herself together. "We're hoping Eva might shed some light on Beth's movements over the past few days. Maybe tell us if she was having problems with anyone?" She glanced at Dalton, who watched both women's reactions carefully.

"Eva has not seen Beth since the service," Gertrude answered for her daughter. "The girls no longer work together."

This news came as a surprise. Beth's mother had told a different story. "I thought you and Beth worked at the Mission General Store?"

Eva shook her head slightly, her eyes on the floor.

"Eva has decided to give up her rumspringa and return to the Amish life. She will be baptized soon and become a member of the church," Gertrude said proudly.

"What did you and Beth talk about the last time you were together?" Leah believed the only way they were going to get answers was to get Eva away from her mother.

Gertrude's stern attention turned to her daughter.

"Nothing." Eva's face colored. "We did not speak of anything."

"Mrs. Hostetler, may I trouble you for a glass of water?" Dalton asked, and Gertrude's hawk-like gaze jerked his way.

She slowly nodded. Gertrude rose and looked to Leah.

"Nothing for me, thank you."

Gertrude tossed Dalton a troubled look when he followed her to the kitchen. Being alone with a strange man was not something an Amish woman would find acceptable, yet she held her tongue.

There wouldn't be much time. Leah claimed the seat Gertrude had left. "Please, if you know something that will help us find out who hurt Beth, you have to tell us."

Eva's startled eyes flew to the doorway as if expecting her mother to reappear. "I do not know anything. Beth didn't tell me everything."

"That's not true, is it? She told you about the Englischer she was seeing." Eva jerked back as if Leah had struck her. "You're not in trouble," Leah assured her. "But we believe this man killed your friend and possibly others." The words were hard to say. The idea that the person responsible for her family's deaths had been waiting for just the right moment to return was unimaginable.

"Please, Eva. Help us. Tell me what you know. Even if it doesn't seem important, let me decide."

Tears glistened in Eva's eyes. "I don't know who he is, but I am certain he would not harm Beth. He's a *gut* man—according to Beth," she added almost as an afterthought.

"Okay," Leah forced herself to say. Was it possible Eva was seeing this man? Was it John? Her heart raced. "What did Beth say about him? How did they meet?"

"He stopped into the store one day."

"Were you there?"

Eva shook her head. "Nay." Her answer came out a little too sharp. Eva twisted her hands in her lap. Her anxious behavior seemed to confirm she wasn't telling the truth.

Leah realized she was getting nowhere. "How long has Beth been seeing this man? Did she ever mention his name?"

Eva grew increasingly nervous. "Nay, and she hadn't been seeing him long. I believe they may have been having trouble." There was a hint of something in Eva's tone bordering on satisfaction. It had Leah wondering if Eva might have been jealous of Beth's relationship with the Englischer.

"Why do you say that?" Leah pushed harder when she heard Dalton talking to Gertrude.

"Beth told me she was worried he might be growing tired of her."

Eva knew more about this man than what she'd told them. "Your mother said the last time you spoke to Beth was at the church service. Is that true?"

Eva's worried gaze shot to the door as if she was expecting her mother. "It is true. We didn't speak of anything unusual, just the things young girls talk about."

On a hunch, Leah pulled out the evidence bag holding the necklace she'd tucked inside her pocket. She showed it to Eva. "Do you recognize this? Did Beth tell you who gave it to her?"

Eva's eyes flashed surprise. "I had no idea she had a necklace."

"Did he give you one too?"

Eva shook her head in denial. "I don't know what you are talking about. The Amish do not wear jewelry."

The conversation down the hall grew closer. Almost out of time. "What about Caleb? Was Beth having problems with him? Did he know about this Englischer?"

Eva rose and backed away. "There were no problems, and I cannot say what Caleb knew."

Leah stood and pulled out a card with the police station's number along with her cell phone number. She dropped it into Eva's apron pocket. "Call me if you want to talk more. Eva, if you know this man, he's dangerous, and I don't want anything to happen to you."

A second later, Gertrude entered the room with Dalton. His attention went to Leah, who shook her head slightly.

Dalton faced Gertrude. "Mrs. Hostetler, if you or your daughter remember anything, please get in touch." Gertrude's only answer was a displeased sniff.

He and Leah stepped outside into the growing afternoon clouds. Leah waited until they were inside the SUV before she answered the questions on Dalton's face.

"She knows something, but she's not talking, at least not yet. And I believe she and Beth may have been seeing the same man. Eva recognized the necklace. I think he gave her one as well. He may be playing the two against each other."

Dalton shifted toward her. "That had to put a strain on their friendship."

"I doubt Beth knew about it." Leah's mind worked through the tangled details so far. "At some point, we'll have to speak with Caleb Wagler."

"Agreed." Dalton started the engine and headed back down the drive.

"I don't believe Eva will speak to us further, and it has nothing to do with Beth. She's protecting this man."

Dalton's hands tightened on the wheel. "If he's the killer, she's in danger. We have to find a way to reach her. I'd hoped she'd open up to you without her mom present."

"Me too. I'll take another run at her. Maybe I can catch her without her mother again. Somehow, I'll find a way to convince Eva to trust me." The only question was how.

Dalton looked her way. "How are you holding up?"

She shook her head. "I still can't believe this is happening again." The words came out on an unsteady breath.

"I'm sorry it is, but we'll figure it out, I promise." The determined look on his face made her believe he would do everything in his power to make it happen. More than anything, she wished she could stay here in the safety of this vehicle with Dalton. Let someone else play John's ugly games. But she couldn't, because she was the one he ultimately wanted, and she'd waited ten years to make him pay for destroying her life.

Dalton parked outside the station. He'd caught glimpses into the real Leah Miller's personality throughout their time together. He believed there was so much she hadn't told him about that night, and he wanted to beg her to trust him. Yet how could he ask for trust when he had his own secrets?

"Leah, wait." He stopped her when she would have gotten out. She slowly faced him with her hand still on the door. For a second, he thought about telling her everything. He wanted to, but they weren't there yet. "I'm sorry you're having to go through this again," he said instead. Those soulful eyes holding so much pain got to him. "It's going to be okay." And it would, because he'd make sure of it. Yet to get to okay, they'd have to go through a whole lot of bad.

For a moment, the killer stalking her was the last thing on his mind. This woman had gone through more than anyone should have to experience, and it wasn't anywhere close to being finished.

"I hope you're right," she murmured and brushed a hand over her eyes and got out. She headed inside the station without him.

Dalton blew out an unsteady breath. He understood why he felt a strong connection to Leah, but was it simply the past they shared? In many ways she reminded him of his wife. He hadn't been able to save Allison from the cancer that claimed her life. Would he be able to save Leah?

The station was alive with activity when he entered. Beth's death was the biggest case the force had seen since Ellis's death.

Dalton stopped in front of the dispatch station, where the flamboyant Sugar Wallace manned the controls. "Anything new on the case?" he asked the woman with piled-high red hair and nails to match.

Sugar abruptly put a caller on hold. "No, but you got a call while you were out." She handed him a slip of pink paper. The message was from Mark Sorenson.

His former Denver police lieutenant was worried about him, with good cause. Mark knew the real reason Dalton had come to St. Ignatius, and he'd cautioned him about getting his hopes up. Mark would be checking in to see how things were going. When Dalton had a better idea of what was happening, he'd reach out to Mark.

Sugar eyed him with raised brows as if waiting for an explanation he wasn't prepared to give her.

"Thanks, Sugar." He tapped the pink slip against her desk.

"Uh-huh," she murmured, her disappointment clear. "Team's all set up in the conference room. Coffee's hot. Sounds like you're gonna need it."

Dalton headed down the corridor to where his people and officers from other branches gathered.

Henry and Ethan came up to him as he entered the room.

"How's the family holding up?" he asked his youngest officer.

"Not so good. Their bishop and several deacons arrived as we were leaving." Henry glanced around the room at the impressive amount of police force. "I've never seen anything like this."

Dalton patted his back. "You're doing a good job, Henry. I want you to go over to the Mission General Store and speak to the owners. See if they remember seeing Beth talking to a man. Leah said Eva Hostetler told her that's where Beth met the Englischer."

"You got it, Chief," Henry readily agreed. "So, we think he's the one who killed her? How does it connect to what happened to Leah's family?"

"That we can't say for certain yet. Once you've spoken to the owners, maybe they can give you some insight."

Henry hitched up his belt over his skinny frame and headed out.

Dalton stepped away to a quiet corner and called Sam. He'd been told about Sam putting his name in the hat for the chief's position. The man had worked under Ellis Petri for almost fifteen years. He'd investigated the Miller murders. But according to the mayor's committee, while being a great officer, Sam lacked leadership skills. He hadn't even been in the running. When Dalton had introduced himself earlier, there'd been a hint of resentment in the officer. He sure hoped they could work together without having a problem. "How are things going?"

"It's been quiet, Chief. Marge didn't much like it at first when I mentioned I'd be parked outside. I told her there'd been some burglaries in the area."

"Good thinking. If anything seems suspicious, call me right away." Dalton ended the call and shoved the phone into his pocket. He approached the conference room table, where Leah had been speaking with a female member of the tribal police. Her arms were wrapped around her body in a defensive gesture.

Their eyes met. Things he hadn't felt since he'd lost his wife took life inside, but he dismissed them. Too soon, his heart warned. Allison had only been gone a few years.

The woman said something, and Leah turned away. The moment passed. Had she felt it as well?

He moved to the front of the room and kept the briefing short. The lead CSI tech believed they'd lifted a viable fingerprint from the bloody one on the door. Imprints from the tire tracks were taken along with the shoe prints outside the barn. Beth had DNA beneath her fingernails that would be analyzed.

The young Amish girl's death had occurred while the community slept, which meant they wouldn't have any witnesses. Dalton tried not to show disappointment. This was the beginning stage of the investigation. It promised to be long and grueling.

Dalton hesitated before delivering the news he was certain would be controversial. "From the note left on Beth's person as well as the one found at the adjoining house, we have to assume this killer is the same one who murdered the Miller family ten years earlier."

Sheriff Ingalls interrupted immediately. "Hold on there, Chief Cooper. Those murders are closed. I assisted Ellis with the case. Harrison Troyer killed himself rather than go to jail." His glance slipped to Leah.

Dalton flinched at the man's description of what had happened to Harrison. "That was the belief, but we can't afford to overlook anything at this point. And Beth Zook's killer referenced those murders."

"So, you're reopening the case?" Ingalls clearly didn't approve.

"Yes, I'll be looking at it again in light of Beth's death."

Sheriff Ingalls kept his opinion of this to himself. "What can my staff do to help?"

Dalton had no idea at this point, but he had a feeling they would need every single one of the people seated around the table and then some.

"We're looking into the man Beth had been seeing before her death, but we can't discount the boy she was going to eventually marry, Caleb Wagler, as a suspect. If he knew about the other man in Beth's life, he might have become jealous." Dalton didn't know the Amish man, but in his gut he didn't believe Caleb was responsible for Beth's death.

"We can speak with him and his family." Sheriff Ingalls rose and motioned to his deputy.

"Thank you, Sheriff. I appreciate the assist. Let's meet here later today. Hopefully, we'll have some answers by then."

Dalton waited as the room cleared. All he wanted to do was go back to Ellis Petri's old office and dive into the file from the Miller case again. Something had to have been missed.

Sugar stepped into the room, and he turned. "What is it?"

She tossed a pointed look at Leah. "You have a visitor. Said her name is Eva Hostetler."

Leah rose quickly. "Is she alone?"

Sugar confirmed with a nod.

If Eva had shown up without her mother, she obviously had more to say than what she'd felt comfortable mentioning in front of Gertrude Hostetler.

"I'll be right out." Leah waited until they were alone. "I'll use Ellis's—*your* office, if I may."

Dalton's heart went out to her. No matter his personal opinion of Ellis, the man had taken Leah in and treated her like his child. He could certainly understand Leah's loyalty.

"Of course. I'd like to sit in on the interview, unless you think Eva will shut down."

Leah's face gave nothing away. "Why don't we take our lead from Eva? I'll bring her down. I just hope she has information, because we sure need to know John's true identity before he has the chance to hurt someone else."

five

Adrenaline coursed through Leah's body as she reached Sugar's station, where Eva waited, her hands clasped in front of her. Her curious gaze skimmed the men working there.

"I'm glad you came." Leah stopped beside Eva, who clearly wasn't as sure.

The girl's dark hair peeked out from beneath her prayer kapp. The light-blue dress created a pretty contrast to the white apron pinned to the garment.

This could have been Leah. Same dark hair. Same headstrong outlook on life.

"I am not sure why I came." Eva glanced nervously to Sugar. "Beth is my friend and I love her. I want to help you find out what happened."

Leah kept her tone even. "I understand. Why don't you come with me? We can talk someplace more private."

Eva hesitated, her attention on the front of the building. "Mamm will miss me if I'm away for long. I told her I was going to the store."

"This won't take long, I promise." Leah clasped her elbow

and led her toward Dalton's office. As she stepped into the room, the ghosts from the past were there waiting. Ellis had brought her here for the first time after she'd been released from the hospital. He'd been a gentle but firm man who changed her life for the better. She could almost picture him sitting behind the desk, his reading glasses resting at the edge of his nose, his thinning gray hair combed over to the side to cover obvious bald spots.

Eva stopped midstride when she spotted Dalton. "Maybe this isn't a *gut* idea."

Dalton rose. "It's okay. I can wait outside while you and Leah talk." He stepped from the room and closed the door.

Leah pointed to one of the chairs in front of the desk. "Please, Eva, we need your help."

Eva reluctantly took a seat.

Leah slipped into the chair beside her and reached for the girl's hand. "I know it's hard, but Beth would want you to help. Do you know something you couldn't say in front of your mother?" she asked as gently as possible.

Eva emphatically shook her head. "That's not why I'm here. I mean, I am not sure why I'm here."

"Did you ever see Beth with this Englischer?"

The truth became apparent in the flash of surprise on Eva's face. "I told you I don't know who he is."

"But you do know something."

"Maybe," Eva whispered without looking at Leah. "Beth told me her boyfriend wanted her to leave the faith and run away with him."

Colette had mentioned the same thing. "Was she considering it?"

Eva nodded. "*Jah*, though she was afraid she might miss

her family if she did." Her troubled eyes found Leah's. "Beth enjoyed the freedoms she found during our rumspringa. She wanted more. And he gave her little gifts. It made Beth feel special." A tiny smile touched Eva's lips. Leah wondered if she might be talking about herself instead of her friend.

"Like the necklace?"

The smile disappeared. "I told you I don't know anything about that."

Leah couldn't get over the impression that Eva might be involved with the same man that Beth was seeing. "Eva, this man is dangerous. If you know who he is, you must tell us."

"No, you are wrong," she insisted. "He's nice—Beth said so." She became increasingly agitated. "He treated her as if she were special."

Leah held Eva's gaze. "Eva, are you seeing this man too?"

The girl jumped to her feet. "You don't know what you're talking about. I have to go." She started for the door.

"Eva, wait." Leah grabbed her arm. "You're in danger if you see him again."

Eva jerked her arm free. "Please leave me alone!" she shouted and ran from the office. Leah followed in time to see the girl race past Dalton and exit the station. She crossed the street, barely escaping an oncoming car. The driver honked. Eva dashed from the road and down the street.

Leah's heart sank. The interview couldn't have gone worse. She'd wanted answers for herself and pushed Eva too far when she wasn't ready to talk.

Dalton stopped beside her. "What happened?"

"I blew it," she said without looking at him. "I pushed too hard." A rookie mistake she knew better than to make.

"Don't count her out yet."

Leah wasn't so sure. She turned to Dalton. "I want to stake out her place. If she won't talk, maybe we can safeguard Eva from herself by keeping watch. The family won't agree to us being on their property. We'll have to find a way to set up where we can see the house without alerting Eva or her family to our presence."

"We can do that." He smiled at her. "I'll take the first shift."

Leah looked away. Dalton Cooper was a handsome distraction she couldn't afford. She cleared her throat. "I'm coming with you. This is my fight too," she said when he tried to protest. "I'll even bring my special coffee."

His smile disappeared. "Leah, that's not a good idea. He wants you."

"And I want to stop him. This is my job, Dalton. I'm a police officer. I don't want to be treated like a victim," she said with conviction. She'd lived in the shadow of that night for years, giving the killer far too much power over her life. She wouldn't live in fear any longer.

Dalton didn't respond.

"If Eva's slipping out to meet this man, she won't be able to do so until after the family has gone to sleep."

"Like Beth." His voice was soft.

"And me. I want to be there for her. Like I couldn't do for my family." She almost didn't get the last part out.

"Okay," he finally agreed. "But I'm not letting you out of my sight for a second. And that's an order."

Her heart kicked out an unsteady beat at his protectiveness. Something about him made her wish for a second that she could be normal. "Copy that," she whispered.

His infectious smile returned, and she bit her bottom lip and tried not to react. He sure had a nice smile.

Leah gave herself a mental shake. She was thinking way too much about the new police chief.

She and Dalton returned to his office, where Leah reclaimed her former seat, feeling a little unsteady.

Dalton leaned back in his chair and pinned her with that piercing gaze. "I need you to tell me what happened on the night Ellis went out on that call." The unexpected question took her by surprise and sent her back into a vortex of emotion. "I've read the report," he said, anticipating her response. "But there has to be more than the bare details included in the report. Help me understand why Ellis went there alone. The caller indicated shots were fired in the woods near the Amish community."

She remembered every detail of that evening as if it had happened yesterday. She told Dalton about having dinner with him and Marge when the call came in. Leah had volunteered to go, but Ellis said he'd handle it. She'd always suspected that Ellis's death was somehow connected to her dark past. Now, the killer had all but confirmed the truth, and she wished more than ever she'd insisted on going.

Dalton was justified in wanting answers, no matter how difficult they might be.

"I later learned the property owner had reported the same thing happening before. Ellis had answered that call as well."

Dalton's frown confirmed that he considered Ellis's behavior strange. "He never documented the earlier one." He paused for a moment. "The report said you were the one to find him," he added softly.

Leah would never forget that either. It felt as if her life would forever be grounded in death. "His SUV was parked along the side of the road. Ellis was slumped over the steering wheel.

He'd been shot in the head at point-blank range. He'd been dead for a couple of hours when I found him." And once more her world had been turned upside down.

"Any suspects?"

She shook her head. "None. There were tire tracks left behind by a pickup, according to the crime scene unit, but in this state, pickups are everywhere. It's been a year, and we're no closer to finding out what happened than we were that night."

Dalton's brown eyes bored through to her soul. "That's different from Katie's identification that the killer drove a car."

"I think Ellis may have known the person who shot him." She admitted what she hadn't told another living soul before. She looked at Dalton and wondered about his past. He'd treated her with respect and concern, yet she sensed there was something more to his story than what she knew. "It must be hard taking over a new police force and having to deal with a murder case right off the bat. What made you want to come to St. Ignatius? We're mostly a quiet town. What happened today and to my family are unusual."

Dalton gave her a measured look before he responded. "I've seen plenty of action in my time. On the force in Denver and as a marine. I wanted a change of pace." A hint of a smile touched his full lips. It didn't reach his eyes. "I'm guessing I'll have to wait on that."

Chief Dalton Cooper had secrets of his own, and she planned to find out what they were. Leah rose. "I should check on Marge. I'm worried about her with everything that's happened."

"Mind if I ride over with you? I'd like to meet her." The question stopped her midstride.

She guessed his real reason. "She doesn't know anything, Dalton. Marge has been struggling since Ellis's death." And

Leah felt as if she were losing Marge bit by bit as the memories of their time together slipped from Marge's grasp.

"I'd still like to meet her. I can imagine losing Ellis has been hard for her and you."

It had been an emotional day, and she wasn't sure how much more she could handle. Leah cleared her throat. "Where are you staying?"

He grimaced. "At the Mission Valley Cabins. Until I can find someplace permanent."

She'd been to the cabins on multiple calls. It wasn't a place for the chief of police to be staying. "You can stay at my house. I'd be happy to move in with Marge until you find your own place. I'm there all the time anyway. It'll be better than the cabins, I promise."

His eyes widened. "Really? That's very generous. To be honest, I wasn't looking forward to being at the cabins, however short a period of time."

Leah laughed. "For good reason. They're a dump." She dug into her pocket and handed him the house key. "I'll need to collect my cat and bring her with me, otherwise she'll want to sleep with you."

He chuckled. The sound of it washed over her like a gentle shower. "Well, as much as I love animals, I've been told I snore, and your cat might not take too kindly to the noise."

"Probably not. Kitty was homeless for a while. She's still pretty skittish and picky about who she bonds with." It had taken Leah six months just to be able to get Kitty to tolerate the occasional petting. "I'm not even sure she likes me."

He laughed again. They walked toward the station entrance.

"If you think my being there will be too much for Marge, I can wait in the vehicle. When you're finished, I'd like to stop by the ME's office and speak with him. Hopefully, by then the crime scene unit will have something useful."

Leah shook her head. She could almost hear Marge telling her they didn't turn anyone away. All were welcome in the Petri home. "No, you should come in. She'll want to meet you." Leah waited while Dalton checked in with Sugar. The brassy dispatcher blurted out something snappy to which Dalton appeared to struggle to keep from reacting. Leah grinned to herself. Sugar took some getting used to.

The midafternoon streets were quiet. Only a few vehicles passed in front of the station. Mainly pickups, the most common form of transportation in the area. Not unusual.

While they drove to Marge's, Leah leaned back against the seat and watched the shops pass by without seeing them. The eyes of the man who had attacked her all those years ago filled her mind. After ten years, many things about him had faded, except for his rage-filled eyes. They would haunt her forever.

Dalton pulled onto the peaceful street where Ellis and Marge had lived for all their time in St. Ignatius, and Leah straightened in her seat. "How did you know the address?" His face gave nothing away and yet . . .

"It must have been on some paperwork."

She couldn't explain it, but something about Dalton troubled her. Why would a big-time detective from Denver choose to come to a small rural town like this to be the chief of police?

He stopped beside Sam's parked cruiser. Leah rolled her window down.

"Leah. Chief," Sam said. "Everything's quiet here. I told Marge I'd be sitting outside the house for a while." He focused on Leah. "She thought my being here had something to do with Ellis, and I didn't correct her."

Her mother's dementia was getting worse, and it broke Leah's heart to witness the struggle Marge went through sometimes to recall words. Remember things they'd done in the past.

"Thanks, Sam. I'm just going to have a word with her, and then we'll be on our way."

He nodded. "Take your time."

Dalton pulled into the drive and they traversed the distance to the house. Every time Leah saw it, she was reminded of that frightened sixteen-year-old self who had come here for the first time after the worst moments of her life.

"You okay?" Dalton asked. She realized he'd been watching her closely and seeing far too much.

"Just thinking about the first time I came here. I was so scared."

"I can't even imagine," he said softly.

Leah didn't understand what was happening to her. Dalton had a quiet strength about him that made it easy for her to open up to him, and that scared her. Was it a ploy to get information or did he genuinely care?

She took out her key and realized Marge had forgotten to lock the door again.

Dalton saw it too.

"She's becoming more forgetful," she said and opened the door before he asked another question. The house appeared quiet. "Marge," she called out.

"In here."

Leah spared Dalton a glance before she headed to the kitchen.

When she entered the room, she found Marge seated at the table with a cup of coffee in front of her, a smile on her face. Yet Leah once again was taken aback by the years the woman had aged since her husband's death.

Leah leaned down and kissed her cheek. "How are you today?"

Marge smiled up at her. "Better, now that you're here." She noticed the man next to her, and Leah made the introductions.

"This is Dalton Cooper. He's the new chief," she added reluctantly.

"I see," Marge whispered then held out her hand. "Well, it's nice to meet you, Dalton. Is Leah showing you around?"

"Yes, ma'am, she is."

Leah glanced around the room and noticed a second coffee cup on the counter. She moved to it and felt the side. Still warm.

"Did Sam have coffee with you?"

Marge turned her way. "Sam? No, why?"

"There's a second cup." Leah pointed to it.

The older woman's brow knitted. "I must have poured it and forgot. Would you and Dalton like some? I can make another pot."

Leah shook her head and sat down beside Marge. "We can't stay that long. I just wanted to check on you." She did her best to explain what had happened without mentioning the connection to her own past. She didn't want to cast doubt on Ellis's investigation of the case just yet.

Marge clutched her throat. "Oh my word, that's terrible. The poor girl. Are you safe?"

No matter how old Leah was, Marge still remembered that frightened girl Leah had been back then.

"I am. I promise I won't take any unnecessary risks." Leah glanced up at Dalton. Time was quickly passing and they had a killer to catch. She reluctantly rose. "I hate to leave so soon, but we need to go. Sam will be here with you should you need anything." She hugged Marge tight. The thought of losing this sweet woman to an enemy Leah couldn't fight was terrifying. "I'll be back to check on you again soon."

A smile creased Marge's weary face. "Okay, baby girl." Leah wondered if her use of the pet name she'd given Leah when she first came here was deliberate, or had she forgotten her name?

Marge grabbed her arm, a fearful look on her face. "Be careful. I can't lose you too."

Leah placed her arms around her mother's shoulders and hugged her. "I'm not going anywhere, and you aren't losing me." She gave Marge a kiss on the cheek.

Dalton's phone rang and he answered it.

While she listened to the one-sided conversation, Leah noticed a pile of mail on the counter. Since Ellis's passing, she'd taken over managing the finances for Marge. She'd do a quick sort-through to make sure there wasn't anything urgent.

"Thanks for the information, Sheriff," Dalton said before ending the call.

Leah looked his way with an envelope in her hand.

"The sheriff's people spoke to Caleb Wagler and confirmed his alibi. He wasn't involved in what happened."

Leah wasn't really surprised. She remembered the family and Caleb. They were simple, hardworking people who she didn't believe were capable of harming anyone.

She returned to sorting the mail. Something grabbed her attention at the bottom of the pile. A letter. No postage or return address. The envelope had Leah's name scribbled across the front. She dropped it as if it burned her fingers when she noticed the familiar handwriting.

"What's wrong?" Dalton must have seen her reaction and noticed the writing. "If that's from him, he could have left DNA evidence behind." He immediately radioed CSI then pulled out a set of latex gloves and carefully opened the envelope.

A spent shell casing was all that was enclosed.

"A .38. Same as what killed Ellis."

Dalton didn't miss the connection. "Probably taken from the crime scene." The killer wanted to make it clear he had ended Ellis's life.

Leah's attention riveted to Marge quietly sitting in her chair, unaware of the nightmare coming their way. There were times when Leah was almost envious of Marge's fading memories. Many times she wished she could erase hers from her mind and her heart.

He pounded his fist against the dash. Screamed at the top of his lungs. Eva. That foolish girl had gone to the police. Eva knew his secrets about Beth, and she'd gone to speak with Leah and the new man. Had she turned on him? He had to find out. Though he'd told her to meet him tonight, this couldn't wait.

"Stupid," he shouted and whipped the truck onto the road again. He wouldn't let Eva ruin his plans. As he drove past the police station again, he stared at it and almost spat remembering the one who had held the chief's position before. A slow smile spread across his face. He enjoyed taking lives. Especially *his*.

Dust billowed up behind him as he entered the community. He'd have to be careful. The police had someone stationed at the Zook place and they were watching the Miller barn. But he knew a back way into Eva's place in case they were staking it out.

He hated everything about the Amish, including their simple ways. All lies.

He parked on the backside of Eva's property where it intersected with a small gravel road mostly used by Amish buggies. Trees hid the road from the house. No one would spot him here. Late afternoon shadows clung to everything. He got out and waited. Soon, Leah would find the bullet he'd deliberately left for her. She'd fit the pieces together and know the truth. The thought of her pain pleased him, and he couldn't wait to inflict more. He climbed from the truck and leaned against it.

A few minutes later, Eva came through the trees, her smile confirming she had looked forward to seeing him.

He kept his anger in check. There was a problem, but he'd fix it.

She leaned in to give him a hug. He hesitated before gathering her close.

"I wanted to see you," he said when she pulled away.

Eva giggled. "*Gut.* I wanted to see you too. I don't have long. Mamm is working in the living room on her quilt and my *bruders* and daed are in the field. I told her I would take care of the animals before helping her. If I'm gone too long, she will come looking for me."

He grabbed hold of her wrists and squeezed them tight. She deserved the discomfort.

"Ouch! You are hurting me." A wounded look replaced her adoration.

He loosened his hold slightly. "I can't wait to see you tonight."

"I'm not sure I can. Mamm is growing suspicious. She noticed me speaking with you before. Why can't I come to your home?"

His anger churned into an internal storm. Somehow, he kept it under control. "Because I don't really have a home yet. I'm staying with friends."

She accepted his answer without questioning him further. "Where do you want to meet?"

He had her. She was his. The thought of returning to the place where he'd ended Beth's life thrilled him, but the cops were watching. He couldn't do what he wanted to Eva there. "Meet me here. We'll go to the bridge. It's quiet there."

Eva hesitated. "The police asked me about you."

Alarm bells went off. "They did? What did you say?"

"Nothing." She didn't look him in the eye.

"What did they want to know?" He took a threatening step closer.

Her eyes grew fearful. "They asked if Beth was seeing someone other than Caleb. They know about you."

His hands fisted. "Really? What do they know?" His tone remained remarkably calm. He'd gotten good at hiding the monster inside when it served his purpose.

"Only that Beth was sneaking out to meet someone. Her sister saw her. But she wasn't certain what you looked like. They showed me the necklace you gave Beth. Like the one you gave me."

Her hurt tone sickened him.

"That's because Beth found the necklace before I could give it to you. She thought I bought it for her. It would have been rude to tell her differently. Besides, I bought you a far prettier one."

She brought the necklace from her apron pocket and touched it lovingly. "*Jah*, it is so much better than hers."

It amazed him how easily she'd betrayed her friend. "Did you tell them anything about me?" A hard edge entered his tone. Eva would not mess this up for him.

"I would never tell them anything," she fervently assured him.

"Do you think I would hurt Beth or you?"

She hesitated one moment too long. "No, of course not."

He forced another smile. If the police continued to question Eva, she would break. He'd have to eliminate her soon.

"Good, then meet me here at around eleven. I have to go now. Make sure you don't tell anyone about tonight."

She grabbed his arm as he turned toward the truck. "Wait."

He swung back to her. "What is it?"

"Nothing." Her anxious expression cleared, and she slowly smiled. "I—I will see you then."

Because she still had doubts, he tugged her closer and kissed her. "I like you so much better than Beth," he murmured against her ear.

She pulled back and whispered breathlessly, "Really?"

"Really." He let her go. "You should head back. Don't want your mother getting suspicious. Now don't forget about tonight."

She was all his. "I won't, I promise. I cannot wait."

He chuckled as she skipped toward the woods. Once she was out of sight, he drove down to the end of the dead-end road to turn around. In the distance a set of horses pulled a plow. Eva's father and brothers were working the field. Several pointed his way, and he quickly left, his heart racing. If Eva's family noticed the type of truck he drove, they might report him when she was gone. "Foolish!" he shouted to himself. He'd have to be more careful. He couldn't get caught. Not before it was time for him and Leah to meet one final time.

six

"There's no sign of her," Dalton said after checking the time on his phone again. Past 2:00 a.m. They'd set up early. Had watched the upstairs bedrooms go dark and waited in case Eva ignored Leah's warning and slipped out to meet John. They had been sitting here for hours without any sign of movement. "I don't think she plans to meet him tonight. Maybe you got through to her after all."

Dalton checked in with the tribal officer watching the Zooks' place. "Any activity there?"

"No, sir. It's been quiet all night. No activity at the Miller's barn either."

"Copy that," Dalton said and ended the call. He turned his head sideways against the headrest and watched Leah stifle a yawn. It had been an emotional day, starting with the discovery of Beth Zook's body.

She caught him looking and bit her bottom lip. "I think you're right." Her voice held a breathless catch that had him curious. Dalton wondered what her life had been like since her family's deaths. He'd lost Harrison. She'd lost everything.

The spent shell matched the one from Ellis's murder. The killer had wanted them to tie the shell to Ellis.

"Did Ellis own a .38?"

Leah searched his face before his thoughts became clear. "He did. A Ruger LCR. It wasn't his service weapon. You think Ellis was shot with his own gun?"

"It's possible." The Ruger had been one of the weapons their gun expert believed would match the shells.

"Ellis used the Ruger as his backup weapon. He took it out with him on every call. It wasn't found on his person. I've searched the house. It's not there either. I believe the person who shot Ellis took it with him."

His gaze skimmed over her face. "It's late and we're both exhausted. We should go." Still he didn't move. His attention drifted to the scar.

Leah immediately covered the place on her neck. "I hate this. It's a reminder that I lived and those important to me died. There has to be a reason. I just wish I knew why." Tears glistened in her eyes.

He understood guilt completely. It had been a simple act of fate that Harrison ended up in St. Ignatius instead of him. "You're alive because God wants you to be. He has a reason. You'll find it."

"Do you really believe that?" she said almost wistfully. Dalton could see Leah did not. The killer had taken away her ability to trust God. Strange for someone who had once been part of a strong faith-based community. It made Dalton sad that she had to ask.

"I do. We can figure it out together." And maybe he'd finally be able to lay his own demons to rest. The tiny glint of hope he saw in her eyes rocked him to his core. No matter what, he would find a way to fulfill that promise.

"I'm going to have another patrol take over for us. We need

to have Eva's place under surveillance at all times." Dalton called the tribal chief for assistance. Once the patrol arrived, he started the SUV and pulled onto the road. The pressure to find the killer ratcheted up another notch. So far CSI hadn't found anything useful. The tire tracks were identified as a particular brand common around the area because of its low price. It would take weeks if not longer to track down sales, and his team was stretched to the limit as it was. "I'll drop you off at Marge's," he told her as they entered the city limits.

She rolled her shoulders to stretch out the kinks. "Thanks, but Ethan is with her now while Sam gets some sleep. If it's all the same to you, I'd like to return to the station and go over the evidence again. I'm too keyed up to sleep."

He felt the same way. He kept replaying everything that had happened since he'd responded to the call of a missing person and was thrown headfirst into the case he'd come here to solve.

Dalton turned onto the street leading to the station. There was something that had always troubled him. "Did Ellis and Harrison ever have a run-in before the murders? I'm wondering if he may have had it in for Harrison in some way. From what I gathered, the young man was only visiting the area and certainly not prone to causing problems."

Her green eyes filled with surprise. "How do you know so much about Harrison?" she asked point-blank.

Dalton kept his attention on the road ahead. "I've read some of the details of the case. Your family's murder and what occurred afterward were the biggest thing to happen here in a long time."

He could feel her unwavering gaze. Though he hated keeping secrets, Dalton wasn't ready to tell her everything yet.

"There was no run-in," she said at last. "I don't think Ellis knew Harrison until I mentioned him. He asked me to tell him everyone I'd had any contact with before the murders. I mentioned Harrison because we'd talked some after church services." Leah had inadvertently been the one to bring Harrison's name into the investigation. But why had Ellis zeroed in on him alone? Dalton had read Leah's interview. She didn't believe Harrison was the killer. Dalton was convinced Ellis tried to make her believe otherwise.

Leah twisted her raven hair into a knot at the nape of her neck. "Nothing like being baptized by fire your first day."

Her dry sense of humor struck a chord, and he smiled. "Not exactly what I expected."

While her attention was fixed on the passing shops in town, Dalton sent a couple of curious glances her way. He couldn't deny he was attracted to her courage. He thought about his wife, Allison. She'd been the love of his life. Allison had put up with his need for the truth behind Harrison's death even though it had bordered on obsessive at times. And that obsession had put a strain on their marriage. Ultimately it had taken him away from her when she'd needed him the most.

I'm sorry, babe. I let you down.

The blazing lights of the police station captured his attention as he parked.

He and Leah stopped next to the second-shift dispatcher, who was the complete opposite of Sugar. This young woman appeared to be in her twenties, and had her dark hair pulled back into a ponytail. She wore a sweater despite the heat and a dark-colored dress.

Her blue eyes lit up as she introduced herself to Dalton. "It's nice to meet you, Chief Cooper. I'm Justine Raber." The name sounded Amish. Had Justine been Amish at one time?

She didn't wear makeup and her dress was plain. "The medical examiner called for you. He said you can reach him any time."

"Thanks, Justine." He turned to Leah. "I know it's late, or more to the point, early, but I'll see if I can reach the ME. Hopefully, he'll have something for us." He glanced over to where Justine had gone back to work. "Is she—?"

"Not anymore. Justine's family left the faith. Believe it or not, she's actually Sugar's niece."

"You're kidding." The dispatcher glanced their way and smiled before returning to her task. "How often does that happen here?"

She held his gaze. "It happens. Want some coffee?"

"Yes, please."

She smiled at the hint of desperation in his tone. "I'll get us some."

He went into his office, leaving the door open, and returned the medical examiner's call. The ME told him Beth's time of death was somewhere between midnight and four in the morning. Her carotid arteries on both sides of the neck were severed as well as the trachea. She'd died in a matter of minutes, but she'd fought back before he cut her throat.

"We matched the fingerprint on the barn door to Beth," the doctor told him. "She must have tried to escape before he caught her and killed her."

Just like the one left by Leah when she'd fled the barn that night ten years earlier.

"But the main reason I called is to let you know we were able to retrieve a hair sample from the Zook girl's neck. It doesn't match the victim."

Dalton's heart pounded at the revelation. "You think it belongs to the killer?"

"There's a good chance. The victim probably yanked it from the killer without him realizing it. We'll see if we can match the DNA profile."

Dalton glanced up. Leah hovered in the doorway. He waved her in. She set a cup in front of him.

"I appreciate the call, Doctor Melendez."

"My pleasure. I'll be in touch when I have more." The call ended and Dalton filled Leah in.

"That's good news." She sat across from him. "What I don't understand is where he's been for the past ten years. He clearly enjoys the game. Why wait until now to start up again?"

Dalton grabbed his coffee and leaned back in his seat. Darkness lay beyond the lights of the station. It was barely four in the morning. Dawn was still some time away. "Prison maybe. If so, we may be able to get a DNA match."

"And if not?" She pinned him with those troubled green eyes.

"Then we keep looking. He came back here for a reason."

Leah visibly trembled. "I think we both know the reason. This is the same person who killed my family. And the anniversary of that date is only a few days away."

Dalton believed the same. The killer's timing was intentional.

He shifted gears. "Do you mind me asking you some questions?"

Her body language changed before his eyes. She did mind, but Leah wanted to catch the killer more. "Go ahead."

"What do you remember about the vehicle following you around that time?"

She took a sip of coffee. "Not much really. It was a pickup truck like so many others you see around the state. I don't remember the color. And the driver hung back. I'm sure to keep me from seeing his face. I only saw it a couple of times. Still, it gave me the creeps."

"Did Ellis investigate?"

Leah's attention dropped to the cup in her hand. "He said he did. But he told me nothing ever came from it."

The tire tracks near Ellis's body were from a pickup truck. A fluke? After nine years he couldn't imagine it was the same truck. The killer was probably good at stealing transportation.

"I could use some fresh air." He rose and stretched the kinks from his back. "Want to join me?"

"Yes, please." Dalton held the door for her, and they stepped out back of the station. Despite the early morning hour, the heat remained oppressive.

"Is it always like this?" He did his best to peel his shirt from his body. In Denver, the periods of heat usually abated with the night.

She smiled sympathetically at his discomfort. "Not usually. Makes it hard to concentrate, doesn't it?"

"You could say that."

She held up her cup. "This isn't helping."

He laughed. "No, it isn't."

He found himself even more curious about Leah Miller. She wasn't married—he'd read her file. Was there someone special in her life?

Leah took a sip of coffee and lifted her face to the slight breeze. Some of her hair had worked free of the bun. He fought the urge to tuck the strands behind her ear.

What was wrong with him? He'd come to St. Ignatius for answers. Nothing more.

Leah sighed. "I really hate what happened to Beth, and I wish I could bring her back, but I've lived most of my adult life fearing the past. Afraid to make connections. Keeping people at a distance for fear they'd be taken from me." She shook her head. "I'm tired of living like that."

In a way he'd lived the same. So focused on finding out what happened to Harrison that nothing else mattered. He hadn't seen how sick Allison was until it was too late. After his wife's death, he'd thrown himself into the case even more. Not being able to see the future beyond the past. Maybe this was a chance for both of them to find a way to move beyond the nightmare.

"I want this to end. More than anything," she whispered.

He did too. For her. For himself.

A clattering noise grabbed his attention.

Leah jerked toward the sound.

One of the cans had been turned over. Dalton drew his weapon, his shoulders tense. A sense of being watched put him on alert. He grabbed the flashlight and shone it down the alley. Nothing. "Let's go back inside."

Out of the corner of his eye, he saw something move. Dalton whirled back toward it. Something scurried away. A rat. Dalton bent over with relief. And then what sounded like footsteps running in the opposite direction near the shop next door had him wondering if his relief had come too soon.

The scent of cigarette smoke wafted their way. "That's near the coffee shop next door." Leah flashed the light that direction. Nothing moved.

Dalton hit the mic on his shoulder. "Justine, where's Sam?"

"He should be coming on duty at any time."

"Tell him to head around to the alley. We need to search it right away."

"I'll radio him now."

"Stay close to me," Dalton said once the transmission ended.

They didn't have to wait long before Sam's patrol crawled down the alley with his spotlight searching the back side of the shops.

He stopped just past the coffee shop, and Leah and Dalton went over to him. Sam had gotten out and focused his flashlight beam on the ground between the two buildings.

"What do you have?" she asked.

"Cigarette butts." He knelt beside them. "Someone's been here recently smoking. It's thick in the air."

A shiver sped down her spine. "It could be kids. There are several who like to hang out around here and smoke." She prayed it proved to be so innocent.

"This close to the station?" Dalton clearly had doubts. He radioed for CSI, and the three searched the nearby shops. All the doors were still locked. There was no sign of anyone tampering with them.

"Let's get you back inside," Dalton told her. "Sam, do you mind waiting here for them?"

"Not at all. You think this was him?"

Dalton shook his head. "I'm not saying that. But we can't afford to discount anything."

He and Leah went back inside to his office.

"Leah, I'd really feel more comfortable if you were in a safe house until we arrest this guy."

She immediately rejected the idea with a wave of her hand. "I'm not hiding. This is my battle, and I'll see it through to the end."

He let out a long, frustrated-sounding breath. "Leah . . ."

"Don't worry. I can handle myself."

But could she? "Leah, you're his target. You need to stay out of sight."

She shook her head firmly. "This is my fight, Dalton, and I'm not hiding out. He killed my family. I want to be part of bringing him in. So unless you order me off the case, I am part of this."

He ran his fingers through his hair. "All right, but you don't take any unnecessary risks and I want you close."

Sam stepped into the room, his attention darting between her and Dalton as if he'd interrupted something.

"What's up?" Leah prompted.

"CSI finished up. The butts on the ground have been there for a while. They took them in to examine anyway. I doubt if they'll yield anything useful, though. Whoever was smoking out there tonight took their cigarette with them."

"Maybe the smoker was a kid and didn't want to get in trouble?" Still, the excuse sounded flimsy even to Leah.

"Anyway, I'll be at my desk if you need me. I've got some paperwork to fill out," Sam said and stepped from the room.

Leah slipped into the chair across from Dalton. A lock of his dark hair had fallen across his forehead, which made him appear almost vulnerable.

Those intense brown eyes found hers. He moved slightly and grabbed his head. "I have a bugger of a headache."

Leah smiled sympathetically. "Ellis kept some aspirin in his desk."

Dalton rummaged around until he found the bottle and took a couple. "I can't help but feel we're running out of time. Walk me through what happened the night of the murders. You said you met John in the barn earlier that evening."

Leah stared at a spot past Dalton's shoulder. Her breath

became familiarly shallow. Her body tensed. She was back in the barn with John. "Yes, I saw John earlier in the evening. He seemed excited about something." And she'd been such a foolish girl. Attracted like a moth to a flame by John's charm. "He said he had something he wanted to ask me." She stopped as she recalled the look on his face. "When I arrived at the barn, he barely gave me time to come inside before he asked me to run away with him. He said he wanted us to leave right then. That night." Leah focused on Dalton once more. "I couldn't believe it. Though I was infatuated with John, I wasn't ready to leave my family."

"What did he do once you refused to leave with him?" Dalton's deep voice washed over her, somehow reassuring.

"He changed. Immediately. He became enraged." And she'd always known. Despite Ellis's insistence otherwise, she'd known John killed her family. "He stormed from the barn. I returned to the house and eventually fell asleep." Elijah's room was next to hers and Ruth's. Her parents were across the hall.

"I'm not sure what happened. I awoke to find a masked man standing over me. He held a knife to Ruth's throat and forced us all downstairs. We were herded into the barn." She stopped. Fought back tears. "And then he killed each one of them and forced me to watch. When he came to me, he whispered, 'You'll always belong to me.' His voice sounded strange. High-pitched. I think he wanted to disguise it as part of the game." She pulled in a couple of breaths and let the storm abate. "And then he slit my throat, only it wasn't as deep as theirs."

"He wasn't trying to kill you."

Her mouth twisted bitterly. "No, he was saving that for now." She rubbed her fingers over the scar on her throat before continuing. "I somehow managed to get to my feet." Her eyes met his. "I could tell they were in bad shape. I tried to get help."

"You ran from the barn. That's when you left your handprint on the door."

She slowly nodded.

"You're certain this was John?"

"Yes." She hesitated before telling him something she hadn't shared with another living soul. "And I think the person following me in the truck may have been John. Either it was part of his game or he wanted to cast doubt."

Dalton reached across the desk and clasped her hand. "I'm so sorry," he whispered. "You didn't deserve having your family taken from you. But you have no idea how strong you are. Having gone through what you did and surviving."

The tender way he said the words was her undoing. A sob tore from her lips. She'd worked so hard to rise above what happened. Make sure she never became a victim again, and yet tonight, she felt like that sixteen-year-old girl.

"Leah." Dalton said her name softly and released her hand. He came around to gather her in his arms.

She struggled for composure and finally found it. Leah pulled away and scrubbed tears from her face. "I'm sorry. I don't usually lose it like this."

"Don't be sorry. Having to relive what happened again and again must be incredibly hard."

"I just want this to be over. I want him stopped."

"And he will be."

She put space between them. "Do you think he's killed before my family? The pleasure he took in killing them. The way he appeared so organized—that couldn't have been his first time."

Dalton seemed to realize her need to shift the conversation away from herself.

"Let's find out." Dalton returned to his chair. "I'm checking the National Crime Information Center database to see if I can find a similar MO."

Leah's phone buzzed and she pulled it out. Before staking out Eva's house, she'd worked with the county's sketch artist to create a rendering of what John would look like today. "It's the sketch." She brought it up and showed it to Dalton. "As soon as it's light out, I want to get this in front of Katie and Eva."

He returned his attention to the computer screen without responding.

"Did you find something?"

"Maybe," he murmured. She came and looked over his shoulder.

"Twelve years ago, two young women were found dead off a country road. Their bodies were badly decomposed, throats slashed."

Leah leaned closer. "Where did this happen?"

"Wyoming."

"What's his connection to Wyoming?"

"Not sure." Dalton read through the two cases. "I'm going to contact law enforcement and see what I can find out. Maybe they had a suspect."

"Wouldn't that be great?" Leah sighed and returned to her seat.

"You look exhausted. Why don't I take you home so you can get some rest."

She shook her head. "I'm okay."

Truth be told, she hated sleep. Too many bad things waited for her there.

seven

Bright sunshine assaulted Dalton's eyes as he and Leah left the Zook home. Katie hadn't been completely certain, but she believed the man she'd seen with Beth was the same one in the sketch of John.

He shoved his sunglasses over his eyes to subdue the glare of the sun through the windshield of the SUV.

"You're doing everything you can, Dalton," Leah said as if sensing his frustration.

Would it be enough? He wasn't so sure.

Lord, we sure could use your help.

Had his personal connection to Harrison gotten in the way of working the case? So far, every piece of evidence—every lead—had ended in them being no closer to identifying the killer beyond the name he'd given Leah. With the anniversary of her family's death approaching, Dalton believed they were sitting on a ticking time bomb.

Dalton slowed and turned onto Eva's drive, dodging potholes until they reached the house. He spotted the tribal police vehicle set up on the side of the road and waved to the officer inside.

They needed Eva to give a more positive ID. Would she cooperate? He had no idea.

The quiet of the countryside settled around them as they exited the SUV. Somewhere out there a killer waited. If they didn't stop him soon, he'd come after Leah again.

Leah knocked a couple of times and waited while her eyes darted around the farm. She'd been jumping at shadows since the attack, with good cause.

The information he'd received from Wyoming confirmed there were no suspects in the two Jane Doe murders. Leah and Beth were Amish. They had no way of telling if the two victims in Wyoming had been Amish. Was it possible John had been practicing on homeless women or runaways? Perfecting his MO?

The door opened. Gertrude stared back at them with the same distrust as before.

"Gertrude, we'd like to speak to Eva again," Leah told her.

Gertrude Hostetler's eyes darkened. "Why? What is this about?"

Dalton's patience stretched to the breaking point. "Mrs. Hostetler, your daughter may have information to help us find out who killed Beth. May we speak to her?"

Eva materialized behind her mother.

Gertrude spun. "They say you know something about Beth's death?" she said in Pennsylvania Dutch.

The girl recoiled. "It's not true. I know nothing."

Gertrude clutched her daughter's shoulders with her claw-like hands. "Do not lie to me."

"I am not lying, Mamm!" Eva insisted and tried to free herself.

"But you have been doing bad things. I saw you with him," Gertrude spat out in Pennsylvania Dutch.

Color drained from Eva's face.

"What do you mean? Who did you see?" Leah asked.

Gertrude jerked toward Leah. She'd again forgotten Leah had once been Amish. Had no idea Dalton understood the language.

Gertrude released her daughter. "Nothing."

More lies. As much as he wanted to press her, soon she would shut down entirely. "Mrs. Hostetler, Eva is not in trouble. We just want her to look at a sketch and tell us if she recognizes the person."

Without looking at him, Gertrude agreed. "Do as they wish."

Eva's large eyes locked on Leah. "I told you I do not know who Beth was seeing." She tugged at her apron nervously.

"It will only take a second." Leah brought up the photo of the sketch and turned it toward Eva. "If this is the man Beth was seeing, he's dangerous, Eva. He killed Beth and he's killed before. You could be in danger."

Eva looked away, but not before Dalton saw her reaction. She recognized the man.

"I told you I don't know this person and I don't know what happened to Beth. Please, just leave me alone." She turned on her heel and ran from the room.

Another strikeout.

"It is sad what happened to Beth," Gertrude muttered unexpectedly. "She was a *gut* girl but troubled." She lowered her voice. "Wishing to leave the faith and go out into the Englischer world." She clicked her tongue. "Such a shame."

Dalton believed Eva had deliberately disparaged Beth to keep her mother from looking too closely at her own behavior. Still, he didn't understand why the girl would defend the man who had killed her friend.

"Thank you for your time." He touched Leah's elbow, indicating they should leave.

"She recognized him." Leah confirmed his belief when they were in the vehicle.

"Yes, she did." He started the SUV and reversed. "He has her under his spell. She's still shielding him even though she knows he's dangerous." Dalton spared her a glance. "Maybe that's part of the attraction. Whatever the reason, we don't need Eva's identification to start looking for this guy."

Dalton reached the main road and left the Amish community behind. His main objective was to keep Leah out of the crosshairs of a ruthless killer who had proven he would stop at nothing to finish his diabolical game.

He watched them from a safe distance through the trees behind the house. He'd been careful not to alert the officer watching the front.

Before they'd even left the property, Eva texted him using the cell phone he'd given her.

The police were here. They are asking about you.

How soon before Leah realized Eva was protecting him? If she hadn't already.

What did they ask?

Best to keep Eva guessing for now, until she found out the truth for herself.

They showed me a picture of a man who looks like you. Did you kill Beth?

He squeezed the phone tight and fought the urge to throw it hard.

> Why would I harm Beth? She was my friend—nothing more. You are the one I want to be with. Can I see you tonight?

A long moment passed before she finally answered him.

> If I can.

His lips curled into a smile. She would be there. He watched as Leah and the new chief drove at breakneck speed away from the property.

> Can you slip out now?

> Now? Where are you?

> The road behind your house. There is a police officer watching the front of your house. But I want to see you.

Leah had made her doubt him. Eva would need a little romancing if he were going to convince her to meet him tonight, but it was imperative that she do his bidding.

A few minutes later, she slipped out from the cellar door at the back of the house and came his way.

She saw him in the woods and stopped. Always so brave before, now Eva hesitated. Further proof she'd served her purpose.

"Why are you standing over there?" He held out his hand to her.

She swallowed several times before she slowly closed the space between them and clasped his hand.

He tugged her close. "I can't believe you'd think I would hurt poor Beth." He did his best to appear hurt.

"I'm sorry, but the picture looked just like you."

He squeezed her tight. "But it wasn't me. The last time I spoke with Beth, she mentioned a man following her. Perhaps it's him. There are lots of men who look like me around here. I'm pretty common looking."

She laughed and swatted at his shoulder, no longer suspicious. "You are not. You know you're handsome."

He faked modesty. "You flatter me, Eva. You're the real beauty."

She kissed him fervently, then pulled away. "I cannot stay long. Mamm is hovering over me like a hawk."

His mouth thinned. "She smothers you. You'll never be the vivacious woman you were meant to be if you stay here. Come away with me. I'll make all your dreams come true."

Eva blushed and covered it with a giggle. "Did you say these things to Beth?" Though she'd meant it as a joke, he could tell Eva was jealous he'd paid attention to Beth first. She'd gone after him despite her friend telling her how much she loved him.

His grip tightened on her hand. "Why would I say such things to my friend?"

Her brow wrinkled with doubt. "Beth said you did. She said you told her you loved her."

He should have known Beth would brag to her friend. "That never happened. She became jealous of the way I felt about you. She wanted more, but I refused."

This pleased her. "Silly Beth."

"Yes, silly Beth." So easy to fool these young girls. They believed anything he told them.

"I must go. My mamm will want me to help with the midday meal, and we are going to visit the Zooks later today."

"But I will see you later, right?" he pressed her.

"Yes, I will be there. Maybe I'll even run away with you." Eva winked before freeing her hand. She passed quickly through the trees and stopped at the property edge before dashing toward the cellar door. In a few hours, his problem with her would be over.

* * *

The task force meeting ended in more frustration. Everyone on the team had been working overtime to find Beth's killer and yet they were getting nowhere.

"I'm going to take the next shift with Marge," Leah told Dalton after the meeting ended. She worried about Marge's safety as well as her mental state.

Dalton's brown eyes slipped over her face, filled with compassion. "I'll come along."

Having him close made her feel safe. Not only that, she just liked spending time with him.

Leah found her thoughts drifting to things she'd written off as impossible.

Dalton grabbed the case files and unlocked his desk. He retrieved his service weapon and holstered it.

As they passed by Sugar's station, Dalton told her where they'd be should anything break with the case.

"Sure thing, Chief." Sugar winked at Leah. She could almost read Sugar's thoughts. Leah chose to ignore the innuendos.

"She's an interesting character," Dalton said as they drove through the quiet midday streets of St. Ignatius.

Leah braced before facing him. Had he seen Sugar's wink?

"Sugar means well, and she has a good heart, but she's a bit boisterous."

Dalton chuckled. The husky sound of it washed over her.

"That's a nice way of putting it." He looked her way, and a moment of awareness passed through her body. "And yes, I saw the wink."

Leah's cheeks grew hot. "She's been trying to fix me up since I joined the force."

"I'm guessing she hasn't come up with any viable candidates yet?" His tone held amusement.

Normally, Leah avoided personal discussions, but Dalton had a way of putting her at ease. "Not for lack of trying. Sugar goes to my church. Every new man around my age who shows up is evaluated and grilled."

He laughed again, and she found herself smiling.

"So, you're holding out for the perfect man?"

She'd dated some in college but usually ended it when the questions got too personal. How did she explain to a stranger that her entire family had been murdered? "No, I don't think I'm cut out for relationships." Leah peered his way and noticed the humor leave his face. "What about you? It's hard to believe you're still single."

His jaw tightened before he answered. "I was married once. My wife died."

Leah suppressed a gasp. "I'm so sorry, Dalton. I didn't know. That must have been hard."

His hands tightened on the wheel. "Harder than anything I've ever gone through."

"What happened to her?" she asked softly.

Dalton dragged in a breath. Let it go. "Ovarian cancer. Allison fought hard. She was one of the strongest people I've ever known."

Leah squeezed his arm, yet the gesture felt inadequate.

"She's been gone for almost five years now, and I can still

see her smile." He swallowed visibly. "Allison had the type of smile that lit up her face. Made you feel better just seeing it."

"She sounds like a wonderful woman."

He nodded. "The best. She never met a stranger. Always had time for others even when she was sick. And she put up with me and my obsessive behavior."

An odd choice of words, but she didn't push.

They arrived at Marge's house to find Ethan's patrol parked out front.

"I had breakfast with Marge earlier," he told them. "She seems in good spirits."

"Appreciate it, Ethan. We'll take it from here." Leah was happy to find the door locked. She fished out her house key and unlocked it.

"Marge, it's me," she called out as they stepped inside.

"In here, baby girl." Leah followed Marge's voice to the family den. Memories of Ellis were etched into every crevice of this room. He'd used it as an office for as long as Leah could remember.

Marge beamed at her. "I'm glad you're here." She offered her hands to Leah, who kissed her cheek. A frown shadowed Marge's face when she peered at Dalton as if trying to understand how she knew him.

"You remember Chief Cooper from yesterday?"

Marge's expression cleared. "Well, of course I do."

Leah wasn't sure she believed her mother. With the dementia manifesting itself more since Ellis's death, Marge kept the extent of her memory loss from Leah.

"How are you today?" Dalton asked her.

"Oh, I'm doing fine." She patted the photo book in her lap. "I've been going over some old family photos." She squeezed Leah's hands. "Come sit with me, baby girl."

Leah settled beside Marge while Dalton claimed Ellis's favorite recliner.

"At times I still can't believe you're all grown up. I still remember that teenaged girl who changed Ellis's and my lives. You came to us with only that pretty handmade dress and your apron and prayer kapp. I kept them for you, honey. Thought you might want them one day. That light blue dress reminded me of the one I wore when I was your age. Though mine was darker."

Leah studied Marge's smile. Was it another confused memory? "What dress do you mean?" she asked gently.

Marge touched her furrowed brow. "Just one I had as a teenager. My mother made it for me. You remember this picture?" Marge pointed to one taken the summer after Leah graduated from high school. As much as Leah wanted to press Marge further, her mother's emotional and mental states were fragile.

Ellis had managed a few days off and they'd taken a trip to the Florida coast. She'd been so happy that day. Had almost been able to forget the past for once.

Leah leaned her head on her mom's shoulder. "You forgot to use sunscreen and got a terrible burn." She couldn't get Marge's strange comment out of her head.

Marge chuckled. "That's right. It hurt for days."

Leah tucked her arm in Marge's. She'd lost her family to a killer—probably Ellis to the same man. Now she was slowly losing Marge to a different kind of killer.

"I love you," Leah whispered to the woman who meant the world to her. "So much."

Marge turned her faded eyes Leah's way. "I love you, too, baby girl." She cupped Leah's cheek. A reminder of that time when she'd come here for the first time. Leah had been so scared, but Marge had made her feel welcomed and loved.

"Look at me going on about these old photos when we have a guest. I'll whip us up some lunch." Marge hurried away before Leah could protest.

"She's a nice woman," Dalton said once they were alone. "It must be hard for her since Ellis's passing."

Leah swallowed several times, but the lump in her throat wouldn't allow her to speak.

"It's hard watching those we love grow old," Dalton murmured. "Each time I visit my parents, it seems they've aged years." A reminiscent look came over his face.

"Where do they live?" There was much she didn't know about his life. But she wanted to.

"Near Rexford."

Less than three hours away. "I didn't realize you were from Montana." She'd assumed he'd grown up in Denver, since he worked there.

"I grew up near Rexford. Joined the marines at eighteen. Then I went away to college in Denver after I returned. After graduation, I attended the police academy and joined the Denver force."

"Is that why you chose to take the chief position here? To be closer to your family?"

"Something like that." He glanced around the room. "This is a nice room."

Leah understood he wanted to change the subject. She of all people could sympathize. She hated talking about her past. "This was Ellis's office. Every time I come here now, I see him sitting at his desk working on something. Usually nodding off with his glasses slipping down his nose." She smiled at the memory. Leah had lost track of the times she'd woken up in the middle of the night and come downstairs to find her dad fast asleep in his chair.

"He sounds like a good man."

"He was." And she'd wanted to follow in his footsteps more than anything. "He and Marge weren't able to have children of their own. They adopted me and spoiled me rotten."

A trace of a smile creased his face. "From everything I've heard, he was good at his job."

She nodded. "The law was in his blood. Which was why what happened with Harrison never made sense. I worked cases with Ellis. His instincts were spot-on. It's almost as if he'd made up his mind about Harrison's guilt and nothing could change it."

"And now we have another death and the true killer at large."

"Yes. Poor Beth." Because of Ellis's single-mindedness, Beth had lost her life.

Dalton leaned forward in the recliner, and the sincerity in his eyes held her in place. "It isn't your fault, Leah. You were just a kid. What Ellis did was wrong but not your fault."

"Why are you talking about Ellis in such a way?"

Leah jerked toward the door where Marge stood in the entrance, determined to defend Ellis no matter what. Leah had witnessed that fierce loyalty between Marge and Ellis many times.

"We were just discussing a case."

Marge frowned and came into the room, her hands clenched. "Ellis was a good cop. What happened to that boy wasn't his fault."

What happened to that boy? Leah rose and went to her. "What do you know about it?"

Marge stared at her for the longest time, a confused look entering her eyes. "That boy who went missing. Ellis tried to find him in time, but he just couldn't."

It dawned on Leah that Marge meant the young kid who

had died from exposure a couple of years back. For a moment she'd thought . . . "You're right. Ellis did everything possible to find the boy."

Tears filled Marge's eyes. "He was a good cop and a better man. I miss him."

Leah hugged her close. "Me too."

Acting on an instinct she couldn't begin to explain, Leah pulled out her phone and showed Marge the sketch of an older version of John. "Do you recognize this man?"

Leah kept her attention on Marge's face. Something flashed in her mom's eyes. "I'm not sure. Who is he?"

"We believe he's the one who killed Beth Zook."

Marge handed Leah back the phone. "That poor girl. To lose her family like that."

Leah had done her best to explain about the young Amish girl's death, but her mom had confused what happened to Leah with Beth.

"That was me, Marge. Remember? Beth died yesterday."

Her mom eventually nodded, but Leah wondered if she truly understood.

"I have sandwiches for you both." Marge's expression cleared as her coherency returned.

"Thank you." She clasped Marge's hand.

As they entered the hall, Dalton's phone rang. "It's Henry. You two go ahead. I'll only be a moment."

In the kitchen Leah noticed the dishes piled up in the sink, the disorder that she couldn't associate with her sweet mom. "Why don't you have a seat and I'll start cleaning up while we wait on Dalton."

"Nonsense. I can help." Marge grabbed a dishcloth while Leah dumped dishwashing liquid into the sink and began scrubbing the first dish. Her mother insisted on doing the dishes by hand, even though Ellis had installed a dishwasher for her. Marge said she did some of her best thinking while washing dishes.

Nearby, the drawer where Marge and Ellis kept some petty cash stood ajar. When her mom's back was turned, Leah opened it and looked inside the envelope. Empty. Ellis normally had a couple hundred dollars there in case there was an emergency or someone in need.

There were a few kids in the neighborhood who had been arrested for breaking and entering. Marge would make an easy target. She had a habit of inviting anyone who came to her door into her home.

"Has anyone from the neighborhood been here lately?"

Marge waved her hands in front of her. "The only people who stop by for a meal from time to time are your fellow cops. Ellis works such long hours, he's rarely home anymore."

Leah turned away. Fought back tears. Was it time to have someone stay with Marge during the day? Perhaps she should move in permanently.

Dalton came back into the room. Right away, Leah could tell something was wrong. "What is it?"

"Henry received a call about a vehicle parked along the highway heading out of town. It's a black car."

Just like the one Katie remembered. "I'm coming with you."

He stopped her. "Stay. Sam is on his way here to take over for Ethan." He lowered his voice. "She needs you, and you should try and get some rest. You look beat, and this thing is a long way from being over." The warmth in his eyes reached out to a part of her locked away since that night long ago.

"If you're sure . . ."

"I am." He shifted to face Marge. "I'm sorry to have to leave."

"I understand. Ellis was called away from many a meal. At least take some food with you." Marge wrapped up a couple of sandwiches.

"Thank you. That's very kind." He headed for the front of the house.

Leah went with him to the door.

"Keep it locked, and I meant what I said, Leah. Get some rest. I need you sharp." His words left her feeling a little breathless.

He reached for her hand. An unfamiliar sensation sped up her arm. Calmer than her experience with John. It made her wish she had it in her to explore.

"I will," she said in an unsteady voice so unlike hers.

"Good. I'll call you later and let you know what we've found." With another searching look, he stepped outside and closed the door.

Leah slid the lock into place and leaned back against the door. She'd written off the prospect of sharing her life with someone, yet maybe she'd been wrong. Maybe it was time to start living again.

eight

You *acted foolishly.* He could almost hear his stepfather's rebuke.

Stupid, stupid, stupid. He'd forgotten to check the gas gauge, and the car had run out of fuel only a short distance from the cabin where he'd been crashing. Would the car lead them to search the cabins near the lake?

Now, police officers were crawling all over the car. He had to get out of here while he still could.

Another patrol vehicle pulled up alongside the car. From his vantage point in the trees, he saw the same man who had been with Leah before. The new police chief.

The man got out and panned the area, his gaze closing in on his hiding spot. He ducked behind the tree while his breathing quickened. If discovered, he wouldn't go out willingly.

Seconds ticked by. His pulse slowed. With the police distracted, he crept through the trees until he reached the clearing near the quiet vacation community where he'd been crashing. He tossed his belongings into the truck and then donned the wig and a ball cap that helped him disguise his appearance to match his driver's license photo. The only road leaving the community wound past the cops. His hands grew sweaty on the steering wheel as he pulled the truck onto the main road and crawled past the first cruiser. Several officers glanced his way with varying degrees of distrust. A roadblock had been set up where a rail-thin officer motioned him to stop. He moved the gun within reach should he need to take out the threat.

The young officer leaned toward his open window. "License and registration, please."

He'd anticipated this request and had them handy. "What's going on, Officer?"

"We're checking all vehicles in and out of the area. Wait here. I'll be right back." The officer took his identification and went to run it and the vehicle registration. The driver's license was a fake, but a good one. Would the officer question him about the truck not being in his name?

He glanced at his car and watched them tearing it apart.

"Here you go, sir."

His attention jerked toward the cop. "Sorry, Officer." He forced a smile and tried to appear normal.

The young cop's eyes narrowed. "Are you always this jumpy?"

He chuckled. "Not usually. I guess it's being stopped for no reason."

The cop's eyes narrowed. "Why are you in this area? And why are you driving a truck that's registered to a Marissa Pennington?"

He felt the rage rising but kept the smile on his face. "That's my sister. She lets me borrow her truck whenever she and her husband aren't using it. I'm on my way to meet up with her now." He noticed a couple more cars stopping behind his truck and hoped the young cop wouldn't press the matter.

The officer spotted the vehicles and stepped back. "You be safe now, sir."

"Thank you, Officer."

The officer tapped the hood of the truck and waited for him to pull away.

He slowly eased down the road with a knot in his stomach and tried not to call additional attention to himself. As he put some distance between himself and the cop, he looked in the rearview mirror and noticed the officer leaning toward the next vehicle. In the cop's mind he was already forgotten. All was well. At least for now.

Conversation drifted into the room where Leah had fallen asleep. She sat up quickly, rubbing sleep from her eyes. She reached for her phone and discovered over an hour had passed. Several missed messages from Dalton confirmed John's car had been stolen from a man living near Cheyenne, Wyoming. The same location as the two previous unsolved murders. The puzzle pieces tied the killer to Wyoming somehow.

Her mind went back to the conversation she'd had with Dalton earlier and the growing closeness she felt toward him. Dalton had occupied her thoughts a lot.

Another message came through. Dalton was outside. She texted him back to let him know she'd be right out.

Marge's troubled voice could be heard from somewhere within the house. Who was she talking to?

Leah opened the door and stepped out into the hall. In the living room, the TV played softly, but there was no sign of her mom.

"Marge?" Leah called out.

"I'm in the kitchen, baby girl."

Leah stepped into the room where Marge sat alone at the table.

"Were you talking to someone?" She studied the older woman's flushed face.

"There's no one here but me." Marge picked up her coffee cup and went over to the pot.

"I thought I heard you speaking to someone just now."

Marge turned and smiled. "Probably just the TV. You want some coffee?"

Was it, or had she been talking to herself and hadn't realized Leah heard? "No thanks. I'm heading back to the station. Dalton is outside waiting for me. I'll have a word with Sam before I go." She kissed Marge's cheek. "Don't forget—"

"I know—keep the doors locked. Do you really think that person will come after me?"

Leah had to make her mom understand how serious the danger was. "It's possible. I believe he's responsible for Ellis's murder, and we can't afford to take any unnecessary risks."

Tears glistened in Marge's eyes. "I can't believe anyone would want to hurt my Ellis. He always did his best for everyone."

Leah squeezed her shoulder. "I know. We'll find out who did this, I promise. You just don't take any chances. If you need anything, call Sam. He's right outside."

"Don't worry about me. You just take care of yourself."

"I love you."

"Love you too, baby girl."

Leah hated leaving her, but she had unfinished business and a killer to bring to justice.

She waited until Marge locked the door before heading over to where Dalton spoke to Sam. Heat rose in her cheeks under

Dalton's intense gaze. There was something about him that reminded her that she was still a woman, and despite having written romance out of her life after John, she was attracted to him.

"Marge says she's going to call you if she needs anything," she said in a somewhat unsteady voice. "But I would appreciate it if you would check in on her from time to time."

Sam smiled. "It's my pleasure."

She got in next to Dalton and tried not to think about her reaction to him. He was her boss, and she was in a fight for her life to bring in a killer before he claimed another innocent person.

"You look rested," he told her.

Leah shifted in her seat. "And you don't. Seriously, when was the last time you slept?"

Dalton chuckled at her directness. "Too long ago to remember."

She cleared her throat. "Has there been anything new from the investigation?"

"Not really. It appears the killer wiped the car clean, so there were no viable prints. We're reaching out to the car's owner now."

Tension coiled through her body. With the anniversary of her family's deaths approaching, their faces were always close. She'd gone over every single detail of that night. John's handsome face contorted in anger when she'd rejected him sent shivers between her shoulder blades.

He'd tried to hide himself, distort his voice, and yet she'd known. If she'd agreed to go away with him, would her family still be alive? The guilt gnawed at her insides.

Dalton parked out front. They stepped into the station and

were greeted by Sugar's booming voice. "Someone phoned here and wanted to speak to you, Leah."

Leah frowned. "Who was it?"

"She wouldn't give her name, but she said she needed to speak with you right away about Beth Zook."

Her pulse kicked out a frantic beat. "Did she leave a number to call her back?"

"No, but she said she was calling from one of the tourist shops. Told me she'd like to meet you at the mission around four."

An uneasy feeling filtered through Leah.

"She said she would only speak to you." Sugar leveled a narrowed look her way. "You think it's a setup?"

"It could be—unless it's Eva." Leah looked at Dalton. "Maybe something we said got through to her."

"Or it could be the killer trying to lure you out."

"You really think he'd take such a chance in a public place? He'd have to know we'd have officers there. Let me go in alone. You can be parked down the street."

"Leah, it doesn't take long to kill someone."

She flinched. Truth be told, the idea of facing off with John again terrified her. Still . . . "I don't think we can afford to dismiss this."

He blew out a weighty sigh. "You're right, but I'm calling in the tribal police for additional backup, and we'll have people stationed around the area in case something goes wrong."

"Thank you." With almost an hour to kill, her thoughts raced over every possible outcome. Leah needed something to take her mind off the meeting. She claimed the chair across from his after they entered his office. "What do you think the killer's connection is to Wyoming? With the two unsolved cases and now a car stolen from the state, there has to be one."

"You're right, there is. We just haven't found it yet." He settled into his chair and watched her from across his desk.

Something unnamed passed between them that had her rising unsteadily to her feet. "I'm going to grab a cup of coffee. I could use the caffeine." She headed for the door without looking at him. "You want me to get you some, because . . ." Leah stopped talking when she realized she was babbling. She pulled in a breath and turned back to him.

"No, thank you," he said softly, the edge of his mouth quirking into a smile. "I've had way too much already. I'll call the tribal police and get them set up."

Leah didn't answer. She reached the break room and poured coffee with unsteady hands. What had gotten into her? Was her awareness of Dalton simply because of this case dredging up old feelings from the past? She sipped the coffee and felt it burn her anxious stomach. Everything in her life had been stunted by the murders of her family, including her ability to fall in love. She'd give anything to be normal again.

Dalton stuck his head in. "If you're ready I'd like to get everyone in place ahead of the meet."

His gravelly voice washed over her, reminding her of all the things missing in her life. Things she'd never really considered important until now.

Leah forgot about the coffee. "I am." She released a quavering breath, then followed him outside to the SUV.

"Are you sure you're up for this?" Dalton faced her over the top of the vehicle.

"Honestly, I don't know anymore. This case has me so mixed up. I keep thinking about all the things that happened back then. Things I should have done differently." She shifted toward him. "This is all my fault."

His piercing gaze softened. "You didn't ask for any of this. You were just a girl seduced by a killer. He told you what you wanted to hear. It wouldn't have mattered what happened—whether you went with him or not—he's unbalanced."

"I want to believe that." She wanted to trust Dalton completely.

"You can," he whispered as if he'd read her thoughts. "I promise you can trust me."

With his attention on the road ahead, they made the trip to the St. Ignatius Mission in silence while Leah tried to find the calm she'd need to face what lay ahead.

The historical mission came into view. Dalton pulled into a parking space a short distance down from the building. "Let me verify the others are in place before you go inside." He called a number and waited. "Are your people ready?" A second ticked by while he listened. "Good. Thanks." Dalton ended the call and set the phone on the center console. "Everything's set. Keep your guard up. If this isn't the killer, we have no idea what their motive is."

She reached for the door handle. For some reason, Leah turned to him once more. "Thank you, Dalton. For the first time since this happened, I believe we might actually solve this case."

And she did. For ten years she'd waited in limbo for John to return. Always certain he would. Now he was back, but she was different. Leah wasn't the naïve teenager he'd been able to fool, and she wasn't alone. She had Dalton and a team of law enforcement officers determined to catch him.

His smile eased the tension on his face. "Be careful, Leah. Don't take any chances."

"I won't." She slid out and closed the door. She walked toward the redbrick mission made with native clay, its steeple pointing to the clear blue Montana sky. The Mission Mountains in the background created a majestic scene. Leah remembered all the times she'd visited the mission through the years. Many times with her Amish family. A few with Marge. Others on her own.

She ascended the steps and went inside. The sanctuary was empty, the temperature only slightly cooler than the blistering heat outside.

Leah stood in the entrance and surveyed the beauty of the building. It always took her breath away. Built in the late 1800s, the sanctuary was stunning and combined stained glass and fifty-eight Christian murals. She inched down the aisle to the front toward the main altar.

Who was this mystery woman, and why did she wish to meet here alone?

Tension crackled through her veins as the meet time came and went. Something felt off about the whole request. She watched the door and waited, her heartbeat ticking off the passing time.

Leah slipped into one of the wooden pews and turned sideways so she could see the entrance as well as the side door.

The mission was laden with history and so unlike the small church where she had attended with Marge and Ellis. She and her mom still went faithfully each week, though Leah didn't feel the connection with God she'd experienced before her family's massacre. That night, while her family was being led to the slaughter, she'd begged God to protect them. Only he hadn't. And since then, she'd been going through the motions of worship. Her heart was encased in ice.

Someone entered through the front door. Leah rose with her hand on her service weapon. An older couple she didn't recognize came in. At this time of the year, there were plenty of tourists around the city.

"Isn't it beautiful?" the woman said to her husband, who murmured a response.

The time on the phone reflected twenty minutes had now passed. Leah moved up the side aisle toward the front to avoid having a conversation with the couple.

If this was a setup, what was his endgame?

Leah pretended to stare at one of the murals while her nerves stretched tight. She'd give it a few more minutes and then leave. Perhaps it was some kook who had heard about the case and Leah's connection to it and was trying to gain a small amount of notoriety for themselves. Strange, but it sometimes happened.

She was heading for the door when something lying on the floor caught her attention. A single slip of white folded paper. Her breath evaporated from her lungs. Leah leaned over and picked it up. Something fell from inside. A picture taken with one of those instant cameras. She reached for the photo, and her limbs became glued in place. It was her. Taken right here at the mission when she'd sat in the pew. The killer had been watching her this whole time.

She jerked toward the front of the mission. The couple inside the sanctuary. They were gone.

Leah ran from the building and flew down the steps.

Dalton reached her side quickly. "What's wrong?"

Leah handed him the photo. "He was here. I think he had the couple leave it."

She unfolded the crumpled paper and read the words written there.

Are you enjoying my game? I'll be seeing you again real soon, Leah. It's almost our time.

Leah ran back inside while Dalton shadowed her. Both had their weapons drawn.

"The male. There was something strange about him. He must have worn a disguise to make himself appear older." Leah flew out the door and down the steps. The older woman stood near the building.

"Where's your husband?" Leah demanded and grabbed hold of the woman's arm.

The smile on the woman's face disappeared. "He's not my husband. He told me he wanted to play a joke on his girlfriend." The woman glanced past Leah to Dalton, and her eyes shot open wide. "What's going on? Am I in trouble?"

"Where did he go?" Dalton demanded.

"He ran that way." Then she turned back toward Leah, looking contrite. "He said you would get a kick out of it."

Leah released the woman and ran in the direction she'd pointed. The two tribal police officers guarding the back hurried their way. "Did you see anyone leave the church?" she asked the female officer.

"Sure, an older man," Officer Rebecca Trahan responded. "He didn't fit the description of the person we're looking for." She realized her mistake. "Was it him?"

"We think so. Which way did he go?"

Rebecca pointed.

"Stay with the woman. She's a witness," Dalton told Rebecca. "You come with us." He motioned to the second officer.

With Dalton close at her side, they carefully moved away from the church, searching every possible hiding place.

"He's gone," she said in disbelief and did a 360-degree turn-around. How had he managed to slip away?

The tribal officer shook his head. "Nothing. I'll radio my people and have them search the surrounding blocks."

"Thank you." Dalton's attention shifted to Leah. "Let's go speak to the woman again. Maybe she can remember something useful."

Rebecca had moved the woman inside the mission. She sat near the front with Rebecca standing close.

Leah slipped into the pew beside the woman. "How did you meet this man?"

"At the coffee shop. I'm here visiting my sister. She wasn't feeling well today so I thought I'd do a little sightseeing on my own." She appeared embarrassed by what had happened. "He came over to me and seemed so nice. Though I think he was trying to make himself look older than he was."

Leah looked at Dalton in surprise. "Why do you think that?"

The woman smiled. "It was his voice. He sounded much younger. I can't believe I agreed to do this. It's so unlike me, but he came across as harmless." She glanced between Leah and Dalton. "Am I in trouble?"

Dalton shook his head. "No ma'am, but I will need you to give us a description of the man."

She ran her hands down the front of her jeans. "Well, like I said, he appeared to want to look older. He wore a newsboy cap, but his hair was graying where I could see it." She looked to Dalton. "He isn't as tall as you, young man. He had a beard and mustache that were gray, and he wore those reflective sunglasses over his eyes." She pointed to her face. "Other than that, he had on jeans and a dark T-shirt."

Dalton finished writing down the description. "I'll need your contact information and your sister's name and her address."

"Oh my. Well, of course." The woman gave it to him.

"Thank you, ma'am. And in the future, don't go along with any practical jokers."

The woman jerkily rose. "Don't worry, I won't. Once is enough."

"She has no idea she was in the presence of a serial killer," Dalton said once the woman had left. "He could have ducked into one of the stores and disposed of the disguise. We're spread thin as it is. Let's check with some of the closest businesses. Maybe someone remembers this guy."

She wondered how Dalton was functioning on virtually no sleep. "I can call Henry and have him help me with the search. You need some rest."

Dalton shook his head. "As soon as we finish our canvass, I'll go to your place and grab a shower and a few hours of sleep. I'll be fine." He was stubbornly putting her welfare ahead of his own. Dalton had all the attributes of a true hero and a heart of gold. She'd seen it many times already.

"We can get there faster by driving."

"Copy that." Outside the mission, Dalton started the SUV and pulled out into the light late-afternoon traffic. He made the turn and stopped at the first tourist shop.

Several people milled around, browsing for souvenirs to take home.

Leah recognized the woman behind the counter. She'd gone to high school with Gina Cardone.

Gina spotted her and came over. She hugged Leah tight. "I can't believe it's you. How are you? Gosh, it's been years."

Leah froze at the unexpected contact, then forced herself to relax. "It has. I'm good." She pulled away and wondered if there would ever be a time when she didn't have this reaction.

Gina scanned Leah's uniform. "I heard you were a police officer."

Leah still remembered how hard starting school had been after her family's deaths. The looks she'd received from other students. The rumors about the murders were rampant.

In the Amish community, a child's education ended with the eighth grade. She'd struggled to catch up. Gina had been kind, and they'd promised to stay close. Gina was someone else she'd disappointed.

"We're actually here on police business." She introduced Dalton. "Did you notice a man come in here earlier who may have been trying to appear older?" Leah gave her a description.

"No, I'm sorry. The folks you see here now are the only ones who have been in the store. Why? What's this man done?"

"He's wanted for questioning. If you see anyone resembling him, give me a call." Leah handed her a card with her numbers.

"Of course. It's good to see you again, Leah. We should get together for lunch sometime."

Leah forced a smile. "I'd like that." And she would. She was tired of living every second of her life stunted by that July night.

She and Dalton stepped from the shop.

"He could be anywhere." Leah sighed and studied the faces of those passing by. John was good at blending in.

Dalton reached out and squeezed her shoulder. "His behavior is becoming more reckless." He glanced up at the streetlights. "Do those surveillance cameras work? They might have caught something."

"They do. It's worth a try." They started back to the SUV.

Dalton glanced at his watch. "Henry should be coming on duty soon. I'll have him get the camera feed."

Inside the SUV, Leah looked over at Dalton. Thoughts of the case and the noises of the street disappeared, and suddenly it was just her and Dalton. Leah dragged in a breath and faced forward. It was just the case. It had to be the case, because she couldn't accept that she might be coming back to life.

nine

Dalton hadn't felt this way about a woman since Allison, and that worried him. He was losing pieces of their life together. She deserved better. Allison was the love of his life, and she'd sacrificed so much for his quest for answers.

He stopped by the break room for coffee and a chance to clear his head. He needed sleep and a shower, and not necessarily in that order. The burnt taste of the coffee worked its way to his stomach, where it churned up acid. Dalton ran a hand across his bleary eyes and prepared for another grueling task force meeting without answers. The necklace left at Colette's hadn't provided any answers. There had been no records around the area of any like it being sold. John was smart—he'd probably purchased it elsewhere. Still, Dalton had to believe he'd eventually make a mistake. At least he sure hoped so.

Dalton called his former commander because he needed to hear Mark's gruff, no-nonsense way of putting things to make him feel better.

"'Bout time you called."

Dalton smiled. "Sorry, brother. Things have been crazy here." He told Mark everything that had happened.

Mark blew out a long breath. "I sure wasn't expecting this. What can I do to help?"

As a strong Christian, Mark had been an example of the type of man Dalton wanted to be. "Pray. This thing is quickly going ballistic, and we need answers. Ask God to give them to us."

"You got it, my friend. Call me anytime if you want to talk or run something by me. Whatever you need. I'm here for you."

"I know." And he did. "We'll talk soon." Dalton ended the call and swallowed the last of his coffee.

No point in putting off the inevitable. Dalton stepped into the conference room, where members of the different agencies had gathered. A sense of gratitude washed over him. Everyone was trying hard to solve this case. Most knew Beth and her family. It had become personal for them.

Dalton moved to the front of the room. "I know it's been a long couple of days and we're all tired. For those of you who don't know, there was a sighting of the killer at the St. Ignatius Mission." Dalton told them all about the incident. "Unfortunately, there were no fingerprints or DNA left behind. The feed from the surveillance cameras was a bust. He knew where they were and how to avoid them."

Dalton pointed to Ethan. "Were you able to speak to the car's owner?"

Ethan confirmed. "I did. The guy said the car was parked at his farm in the barn. He said he rarely used it and didn't even realize it was missing for a while. The local PD backed up his story."

Another in a series of dead ends.

"Listen, I know we're all working overtime as it is, but we can't afford to let up. I appreciate what you're doing. Get some food. And we've set up extra cots in one of the conference rooms, so grab sleep when you can. Ethan, I'd like for you to relieve Sam. Watch your backs, everyone. This guy is dangerous, and we don't know where he might strike." His eyes surveyed the men and women. Would they be ready for what the killer would throw at them next? His head ached. The world around him swam in his exhaustion.

"You need rest."

He turned to find Leah watching him.

"Come on. It's about time you got settled into my house. Maybe we can grab something to eat, and I'll get Kitty and take her to Marge's."

Dalton's stomach rumbled in answer to her words. "Food does sound good, but I think it's best if I stick with you at Marge's. We'll stop by after we eat and get the cat."

She slowly smiled. "There's a greasy spoon around the corner. They make a mean burger, unless you're a vegetarian."

He laughed. "I'm not, and that sounds pretty awesome."

She held out her hand. "Give me the keys. I'll drive."

Dalton was just tired enough to let her. He slid into the passenger seat. As afternoon faded to evening, Leah pulled out onto the street and drove a short distance before turning the corner. The name of the restaurant was the Rusty Penny, and it looked like it'd seen better days.

He eyed the sign doubtfully.

Beside him, Leah laughed and got out. "Trust me. You'll like it."

He hesitated briefly before exiting the vehicle.

The restaurant appeared to have been a saloon in another life. A long bar ran across one wall with stools. The floors were scuffed wood. The ceilings were high and covered with tin. The walls were adorned with photos from around the area.

A woman who had to be in her eighties waved at Leah from behind the bar. "Take your usual seat. I'll be right over."

"Thanks, Gladys." Leah headed past the handful of patrons to the back of the building and to one of the booths lining the wall.

"You must be a regular." Dalton slid in across from her and admired the view of the mountains from the windows.

"I am. I'm embarrassed to say I'm a terrible cook, and I enjoy food too much to suffer through my own cooking."

He chuckled at her description.

Gladys approached with menus. "Who's your friend?" She pointed to Dalton.

Leah wore an amused look on her face. "This is the new police chief, Dalton Cooper. Dalton, meet Gladys."

"Nice to meet you, Gladys."

The woman grunted. Dalton held out his hand only to have it ignored.

"We'll have two Cokes and two burgers."

Gladys ambled away without a word.

"She's a cheerful one. Does she have a last name?"

Leah laughed. "Probably, but I've been coming here for years and all I've ever heard was Gladys."

Dalton clasped his hands together on the table. "Fair enough."

Leah leaned back in her seat and studied him as if she were watching something strange. "I think Kitty is going to like you, and she is very particular about who she lets get close."

He chuckled. "What about her owner?" He regretted his joke the moment it was out. Before his eyes, the wall he'd seen her use to keep people out returned.

"I've learned I'm better off with animals. For the most part, they don't try to kill you."

What a terrible way to live, and yet he was barely one step

134

ahead of her. He'd had the perfect woman, but he'd been too consumed with Harrison's death to appreciate her fully.

An awkward silence returned. Dalton found himself grateful when Gladys brought over their food. "Thank you," he told her. Gladys waved a hand and walked away.

"I don't think you're going to be able to charm Gladys." Leah took a big bite of the burger, smearing mayonnaise across her mouth. She grabbed her napkin and wiped it off.

"I'm not usually the charming type. I think it's best to be straightforward."

Something akin to admiration showed in her eyes. "I prefer straightforward."

He wondered why she'd chosen to stay in St. Ignatius. Couldn't be much to do around here for someone her age. "Did you ever want to venture out into the world and leave your small-town roots behind?"

She wiped her hands on her napkin and took her time answering. He had the impression Leah didn't much like giving pieces of herself away.

She shrugged. "I guess I find something comforting about living in a small community."

As someone who had survived such a horrendous tragedy, she probably took comfort in knowing those around her. Having things rarely change. "You never wanted to get married?" he added softly.

She cleared her throat. "At one time. The Amish are all about family. Growing up, Colette and I used to talk about what type of men we'd marry." She stopped. Didn't go on.

"And what type of man is that?" He held her gaze, lost in the emotions flashing in those green depths. Was he the type of man she could fall for?

She dropped her attention to her plate. "I don't remember anymore. It was just a childish dream."

Once they'd paid the bill, he and Leah headed outside to the SUV to another day slipping away.

Dalton settled into his seat and secured his seat belt. The exhaustion of the past two days gathered around him. His head hurt. His eyelids grew heavy as Leah drove him to her house.

Her place was as generic on the inside as it appeared from the street. He was under the impression she'd owned the house for a little while. Had she not settled in yet, or was it hard for her to put down roots?

The house's air-conditioning hummed as it struggled to keep up with the heat of the day.

Leah gave him a tour of the place. "Kitchen's through there. It's sort of stocked." She shrugged, and he wondered what that meant. "I've hesitated moving Kitty into Marge's house because she doesn't take to change well. I found her behind the police station. She was all alone and crying. Someone had dumped her there." She stopped and shook her head. "But with Mom's dementia worsening, I think it's time to move Kitty and myself in with her permanently. Kitty will adjust."

Dalton wondered how much of herself Leah saw in that kitten. He couldn't imagine what she'd gone through back then, losing everyone she loved. Feeling alone.

"I'll see if I can find her." She continued down the narrow hall and opened a door. He slammed into her when she stopped suddenly. "Oh no." Dalton barely caught the whispered words. Leah's hand covered her mouth; her eyes stared at something on the bed.

"What is it?" He gently moved her out of the way and saw

what she'd seen. Dalton recognized the piece of jewelry because it was similar to the one Colette had given them. It was a locket turned over to display initials engraved on the back.

"He's been here. Dalton, he's been here." The words came out in a sob. He put his arm around her shoulders and stared at the dark reminder on the bed.

Anger rose at the realization that the killer had been inside her house. Had probably touched her things while planning how he would kill her.

And he might still be here.

Dalton let her go, unholstered his weapon, and searched the bedroom and adjoining bath. He grabbed his phone and called for backup.

Together they cleared the rest of the house.

"Kitty." She looked up at him with huge, worried eyes. "She's probably in the laundry room. That's where she goes when she's scared."

The cat had wedged herself behind the washer. Leah managed to coax her from her hiding place. She held the cat close and stroked her fur. "It's okay, girl." She put the cat into a carrier and grabbed her food.

"Let's take Kitty to the SUV and wait outside for backup. Your house is now a crime scene. We don't want to disturb any evidence."

Darkness settled around the countryside. Another day was ending, and they were still no closer to having the answers they needed.

Dalton started the SUV and turned the air-conditioning up to keep Kitty comfortable while they waited. The nightfall made him feel vulnerable. "Let's wait inside the SUV until they arrive." He held the door open for her and she climbed in. As soon as he got behind the wheel, he locked the doors and laid his weapon across his leg.

"I can't believe this is happening again," Leah said so softly he almost didn't hear her. She leaned her head against the headrest. "I've waited for ten years for him to come after me. I've always known he would, and yet now that it's actually happening, I'm scared, Dalton. I'm scared."

"You're not alone. I'm going to be right here with you."

She turned her head to him. "That locket. I think it's the same one John gave me before."

He remembered she'd told him she kept it under her mattress. The locket had been missing for a long time. "Why do you think it's the same one?"

She rubbed her scar absently. "The initials on the back. John had turned it over so I'd be sure to see the initials he had engraved there. L and J." Another part of the game for the killer.

Within minutes, Sam and Henry arrived with lights flashing. With Ethan stationed at Marge's, the team was stretched thin.

Both Leah and Dalton got out.

"The crime scene unit's behind us," Sam told them.

Dalton nodded. "Good. The house is clear. He left a locket." He glanced at Leah. She was barely hanging on. "It's still on the bed."

Once CSI arrived, he and Leah left. She'd been through enough. There was no need to watch the tedious process.

She stared out the windshield without saying a word. Dalton could almost feel her fear escalating. The killer had made it clear he planned to kill her.

"I'm not going to let him hurt you again, Leah." Dalton reached for her hand and entwined his fingers with hers.

She slowly nodded.

Ethan had heard the news over the radio when they arrived at Marge's house. "You want me to assist, Chief?"

Dalton shook his head. "If you don't mind, I'd like you to stay here. The killer is stepping up his attacks. We could use the extra manpower here."

"Sure thing." Ethan settled back into his cruiser while Dalton and Leah went inside.

She set the cat carrier on the floor and opened the door. Kitty cowered inside the carrier, too frightened to leave. "Sorry, sweetie. Take your time."

The only sound in the house came from the living room.

Leah stuck her head in the room. "Marge is sleeping in front of the TV." She turned toward him. Mere inches separated them. "I think I'll sit with her for a while. You should try to get some rest, Dalton. I'll show you to the guest room."

He stopped her before she headed up the stairs. "I can use the sofa. We're assuming the killer is planning his next move to hurt you on the anniversary, but nothing about his behavior is rational. We can't count on that. For my own peace of mind, I'm going to check the rest of the house. Come with me."

Once they'd cleared the final room, Leah opened the door to where Marge slept. "There's the sofa in the corner. It may not be very comfortable, though."

She was worried about him. He kind of liked having someone care about him.

"I'll be fine. If anything comes up, wake me."

Dalton kicked off his boots and stretched out while Leah slipped into the chair next to Marge's. He watched her for a second longer before he closed his eyes. The only sound was the murmur of the TV. Ethan was outside. The house was secured.

Leah was a strong, courageous woman. She could handle herself.

He placed his arm under his head, and his Glock rested within a few inches of his hand.

"Find out what happened to our Harrison, Dalton. Please," the family had begged him when he'd gone to deliver the news of Harrison's death.

"I will. I promise," he'd murmured, yet he hadn't. Ten years had passed and there was still no clear answer to what happened.

The grief of losing her son had left its mark on Harrison's mother. Every single time Dalton returned to Rexford, she asked about the case. His answer was always the same—he was working on it. For the first time since Harrison died, he actually believed he might be able to fulfill the promise he'd made to the family.

The inevitable showdown coming had been a decade in the making. When it was over, would any of them be left standing?

"Why did we have to come here? This place is awful." Eva glanced around at the abandoned Amish farm with distaste. She'd waited until her family had fallen asleep and then slipped out through the cellar door like she had before and met him on the road that ran at the back of their property.

"This isn't where I wanted to take you, but it will have to do," he said with a glint in his eye.

Eva wanted to ask him where that might be, but she was afraid she already knew.

She had been so excited to see him again. Now, it was as if she were drowning in doubts over the man she once trusted completely. "My mamm will be worried if I do not return."

He grabbed her hand and chuckled. "Would you stop worrying? I'll have you back before your mother knows you're gone. I have a surprise for you inside the barn. Don't you want to see it?"

"Can't you bring it out here?" She glanced around the dark, ominous countryside. The next closest farm was the Zooks' place, and that was several miles away. Eva had lived all her life here in this remote portion of Montana, and she loved everything about it. The darkness had never bothered her before. Until now.

"Don't be a baby. Come on. We don't have much time." He smiled and tugged her close. "We'll only be a minute." He pulled her along beside him.

Suddenly, the things she thought she knew didn't ring true about the man standing beside her now. She tried to yank her hand free, but his grip tightened.

"Come on." He opened the door and drew her inside. "See, there's nothing to be afraid of. It's just a barn." There was an edge to his voice that she hadn't heard before.

"I don't want to be here," she murmured and was starting back toward the door when he brought her close.

"You aren't afraid of me, are you?" The gleam in his eyes held a brightness. Almost as if he enjoyed her fear.

Her heart hammered in her chest. Before, he'd always seemed so daring. Now there was something frightening about the way he looked at her. It made her want to run away. She thought about what the police officers had said about him. They'd told her that he was dangerous. That he'd killed Beth and others.

"What did you want to show me?" she asked when he continued to stare at her.

He laughed, and the sound sent goose bumps up her arms despite the heat.

"Always so eager. Just like Beth . . . and her." Something dangerous entered his eyes.

"H-her?"

"Leah."

Fear pressed in. Though Eva had not known Leah Miller well when her family was killed, the story of the Millers' deaths had been circulating for years.

"How do you know her?" But deep down she knew.

He didn't answer but dragged her to the center of the barn with his grip tightening on her arm.

"It's not where I wanted to do this, but it will have to do. Beth didn't fight back very much. She came to the Miller barn willingly and didn't even know what I was talking about when I told her about the others."

Her blood ran cold. She couldn't look away. He was confessing to killing her *gut* friend. And others. If she stayed, he would kill her too. Eva jerked her arm free and ran for the closed door.

He grabbed for her shoulder. She lost her balance and hit the ground hard. The wind expelled from her body. He stood over her, watching as if he were looking at some strange bug.

"You shouldn't have tried to run." He grabbed her and hauled her to her feet.

"Help!" Eva screamed, knowing no one would hear her. Her cry was cut off when he slammed his fist into her midsection and covered her mouth.

He wrapped his arm around her waist and dragged her back to the spot in the middle of the barn.

She wasn't about to let him do to her what he did to Beth without putting up a fight.

Eva kicked him hard enough to free herself. She ran for the door once more. Once she reached it, she fumbled with the handle and got it open. Without hesitating, she ran toward the old, dilapidated house, her prayer kapp strings flying around her face. Her skirt tangling her legs.

His footsteps tromped after her. Eva was almost to the porch when something slammed against the side of her head. Her vision blurred. Her stomach heaved. She struggled to keep her feet beneath her but couldn't. Her hands reached for the porch post. Felt the weathered wood beneath her fingers. She tried to scream, but another blow struck hard. And her world tumbled to darkness.

ten

Something woke Dalton from a hard sleep. He sat up quickly, the darkness outside the curtains proving he'd been asleep for hours. He grabbed his phone. The time showed past midnight of a new day. He was now alone in the living room. Where was Leah? Fear catapulted him from his seat.

With his weapon close, he stepped out into the hall. Quiet conversation came from the kitchen. Marge's and Leah's voices drifted his way. He lowered the weapon and gulped in several breaths. His phone reflected several missed calls from Sam. There had been no DNA left at Leah's house. Not a surprise but a definite kick in the gut. The killer seemed to be familiar with how the police gathered evidence.

Dalton was heading for the kitchen when his cell phone buzzed. Henry. Dalton stepped away before answering it. "What's wrong?" The bad feeling that had been his constant partner hit him full force.

"Two of Eva Hostetler's brothers came to the station. Eva is missing."

"How did she get out of the house without our officers seeing her?" Dalton asked in astonishment.

"We think she may have snuck out through the cellar door. The officers were watching what they believed to be the bedrooms at the front of the house. They didn't have eyes on the back."

"Unbelievable." A door opened behind him. Dalton turned as Leah came over to him. "What is it?" she mouthed.

"Hang on a second, Henry." He held the phone at his side and told her the news. "Let's go into the living room." Once the door closed, Dalton put the phone on speaker. "What did the brothers tell you?" he asked Henry.

"Her mother checked on her only to find Eva's bed was empty and she was gone. The two brothers searched the property. Found footprints leading to the road behind the house. The two tribal officers are canvassing the property now. Sam is on his way to the Hostetler place now to assist."

"Send the brothers home, Henry. I'd like the family to stay together. I'll have Ethan meet Sam over there. Have the officers at the house keep them inside. I'll be in touch soon." Dalton ended the call and gave the order to Ethan. They couldn't leave Marge alone with a killer out there somewhere. "I'm calling for assistance. We need someone watching the house and Marge at all times."

"I'd better let her know." She returned to her mother while Dalton placed the call for help.

The sheriff's department as well as the tribal police force had given them the extra manpower needed to hunt for the killer. Until John was captured, routine patrols had been suspended. Only emergency calls were being investigated. Everything else was filtered to the sheriff's department in the next county over.

He joined Leah and Marge in the kitchen. "They're on their way," he told them.

"I can't believe this is happening." Marge grabbed for Leah's hand. "That poor family."

Dalton's thoughts raced over the facts he knew. If Eva's family had searched their property, either the killer had taken her somewhere or she had agreed to meet him.

A text message came through. "Backup is outside. Make sure you lock up behind us, Marge."

The older woman went with them to the door.

"Try not to worry," Leah told her and kissed her cheek. After they stepped outside, the locks slid into place.

"This is bad stuff," the tribal police chief said when they stopped next to his cruiser. "You think she's still alive?"

Dalton didn't want to share his dark thoughts yet. "I sure hope so. I'll call you when we have more information. I appreciate the assist." He flew from the neighborhood.

"If he has her, he'd want to take her to the barn," Leah said.

Dalton checked in with the deputy who was watching the Millers' barn. "Has there been anything unusual happening there?"

"Nothing, chief. There's been no one near the barn. I checked it just recently."

"Well, keep your eyes open. If anything looks out of place, radio for backup immediately."

"Copy that."

Dalton glanced Leah's way and saw her struggling to keep it together. "So if he didn't take her to your barn, then where?"

"He'd want someplace like the barn to mimic the experience in his mind."

"Like an abandoned farm?" Dalton asked.

She nodded. "Exactly like an abandoned farm." Her eyes widened. "There's one down the road from my place. It's been vacant for several years. He'd take her there."

Dalton turned onto the road leading through Amish country. Most of the houses were dark. "I can't believe she'd go anywhere with him after we talked to her."

"These young Amish women are trusting. Unaccustomed to violence of this kind being part of their world." Her brows drew together. "I get that, but why target them in the first place if it's me he wants?"

Dalton had thought a lot about that. "It's all part of the game. He may be reliving his relationship with you through them. He enjoys killing, and he's becoming more unhinged with each victim. All of this—killing Beth, whatever is happening with Eva—is leading up to the grand finale in his mind."

"Killing me," she whispered.

"That won't happen, you hear me? I won't let him hurt you."

She closed her eyes and slowly nodded.

Dalton hadn't used the lights and siren since entering the Amish community. If the killer was still there, he didn't want to alert him to their coming. He prayed they'd find Eva alive.

He parked the SUV along the edge of the road near the barn.

Leah got out of the vehicle and aimed her flashlight beam on the ground. "Tire tracks. They're recent. Someone's been here."

According to Leah, the place had been abandoned for several years. There was no reason for anyone to be here, unless it was kids coming out to drink. But his gut wouldn't let him believe it.

Dalton's misgivings doubled. He clicked on his light and headed for the barn.

"Footprints." He indicated the set and shined the light around. "Here's another set." They were close to the tire tracks. "She came here with him."

They carefully avoided the footprints on the way to the barn. Another message was splayed on the door. *I did this for you.*

Leah stared unblinking at the writing. "She's dead."

Dalton didn't have any doubt the blood belonged to Eva. "Are you okay to go inside?" He couldn't imagine what she was going through. Being stalked by a killer who had taken out her entire family.

Her hands balled into fists, then slowly relaxed. "I'll be okay."

Dalton wasn't nearly as certain. He pulled his weapon and stepped inside. It only took three steps before his flashlight hit Eva's body, lying in the exact location where Beth's had been found in the Miller barn. Revulsion churned through his body. John had tried to re-create the murder to the last detail.

A gasp from Leah had him whirling her way. She covered her mouth with her hand. Tears gathered in her eyes.

"Take a step back, Leah. You're too close to this. I never should have let you get involved in this case." He radioed dispatch. "I need Sam and Ethan over at the abandoned house that's down the road from the Miller place immediately. Call the medical examiner and CSI. We found Eva. She's dead." He could barely force the last part out. He watched as Leah struggled to pull herself together.

"I'm okay," she said. "I want to be part of the investigation, Dalton. I have to. This is my fight. I've earned the right to be part of it."

He eyed her for a long time, then nodded his head.

Dalton turned away from her, put on gloves, and knelt beside Eva. He felt for a pulse. "She's cold. She's been dead for a while." He looked up at Leah. "Looks like she was struck in the head multiple times. That's not normally part of the killer's MO."

Leah knelt down beside him. "My guess is Eva fought back. Her fingernails are all broken." She gasped. "Look. There's a note in her hand."

"I see it." He bent closer. "'Songbirds must die.' He knew Eva came to see us."

Leah stared at the sightless eyes of the young Amish woman. "She imagined herself in love with him. Probably didn't want to believe it."

John was good at luring young girls into his trap. Making them feel important. Convincing them he loved them. He'd done as much with Leah. Beth and Eva too. Probably those girls in Wyoming.

"She wanted to tell me," Leah whispered. "That's why she came to the station. Maybe she didn't want to believe he killed Beth, but deep down she knew."

Dalton shook his head. "This can't happen again. I want our people to speak with every Amish family who has a daughter close to Eva's age. I won't lose another young Amish woman."

He noticed something peeking out of Eva's apron and leaned closer. "What is that?" He removed the paper. Another note from the killer?

He opened it and read the four words written there. *His name is Jonathan.*

"The writing's different," Leah said. "Eva must have written it and stuck it in her pocket when he asked to meet her. She knew something was wrong. My guess is she wanted to make sure we had his name. Jonathan, John for short."

He put the note into an evidence bag and slipped it into his pocket. "He's stepping up his kills. He knows the area. Knows how to avoid the surveillance cameras, and enough about our procedures to be one step ahead of us. We have to assume his connection to this area goes beyond his desire to get to you."

She didn't blink. "So he wasn't just passing through the area like he told me. He lived here for a while at one time, either before he met me or afterward. We could check high school photos from the past. If he lived here, chances are he attended school."

Outside, sirens screamed through the night. Multiple police officers were headed their way. By now, the tribal police as well as the sheriff's people would know about the victim.

"Chief, you copy?" It was the deputy stationed at the Zook place.

"Go ahead," Dalton said. He rose and helped Leah to her feet.

"Josiah Zook has asked for Leah to stop by and speak with his daughter Katie. He said the girl may have seen something."

Dalton shot Leah a look. "Any idea what he's talking about?"

"Negative, sir. Whatever it is, he says the girl will only speak with Leah."

"As soon as our people arrive, we'll head that way."

"I can't believe this is happening," Leah said once the transmission ended. "Why would she choose to go with him when she clearly suspected him of killing Beth?" She glanced at Eva's lifeless body. "I should have done something more to protect her. Maybe I didn't stress enough how truly dangerous John is."

Dalton went over to where she stood and clasped her shoulders. "You did everything you could. Don't go there, Leah."

"How can I not? If I'd insisted Ellis check into John instead of going after Harrison, Beth and Eva wouldn't be dead now." Her voice cracked under the weight of guilt.

Dalton tugged her close. "That's on Ellis—not you. For whatever reason, this guy chose to target you. It just as easily could have been another family."

She sighed deeply. "I hate this." She pulled away.

"I know. But he's stepping up his attacks and getting more

reckless, which means the chance of him making a mistake is strong. We'll get him, Leah. For Harrison. For you and your family. For Beth and Eva and all the others who encountered this guy and lost their lives."

She searched his face. "You speak about Harrison almost as if you knew him."

As much as he would have liked to hide the truth, he couldn't, and she saw it.

"You did know him. How? Dalton, tell me," she insisted.

Dalton chose his answer carefully. "I know his family. They're good people. So was Harrison."

Her incredulous eyes held his. "Is that why you took this job? To prove Harrison wasn't the one who killed my family?"

He looked away. "I told the committee the truth. I came here because I'd grown tired of the big city life, but it wasn't the only reason why I accepted the position. I wanted to find out why Ellis Petri targeted Harrison, because his family has a right to know."

She put space between them. "Why haven't you told me this before?"

Her eyes narrowed as she continued to watch him with a wintry look on her face. She didn't trust him. That hurt, but he couldn't blame her. There was something else she didn't know. Something he wasn't ready to share with her yet.

"She was likely killed between ten and midnight." The medical examiner confirmed what Leah already believed. "It appears she was struck in the head several times by a wooden object." He pointed to splinters of wood in the wound.

"Something went wrong." Leah ran her theory by Dalton

and the doctor. "Eva resisted. He had to silence her before she alerted the deputy at the Zooks' place." She looked around for the object used. "It's not here."

The medical examiner removed his gloves. "I'm guessing when you find the object, there won't be any fingerprints. The killer is known to wear gloves."

Sam entered the barn, spotted them, and came over. "We found something at the house. There's blood."

Eva had made it as far as the house. Maybe she thought she could lock the door behind her. "From the note, she obviously had doubts about him. Why did she still choose to go with him?"

Dalton shook his head. "I wish I knew. Sam, take one of the crime scene techs with you to the house and collect the evidence." He glanced around at the activity taking place inside the barn. "Our people have this. Let's go speak to the Zooks."

They returned to the SUV, where Dalton radioed the deputy to let him know they'd be there soon.

As they approached the Zook house, the deputy got out and told them the family had been awake for a while.

Leah glanced at the home lit with lanterns. The family was to bury their daughter soon. Now, they would be told about another murder.

Leah thought about the struggle that had taken place not far from here. How frightened Eva must have been. No one knew the nightmare Eva had gone through except her killer.

It was almost four in the morning. The Amish would be beginning their chores soon. How long before the rest of the community found out that someone else had died? Even though Eva's family was sequestered in their home, she and Dalton would need to speak with them soon.

Josiah opened the door before they reached the porch. He stepped back to let them inside. "He's killed again." A statement rather than a question.

"I'm afraid so." Leah confirmed the awful truth.

"My daughter is in the kitchen. If you do not mind, we will speak in there. The living room is prepared for Beth's funeral."

Though it was still early, Miriam hovered over the stove, preparing the family's breakfast. Katie sat at the table, her hands clasped together in her lap. She glanced up as they entered. The fear in her eyes reminded Leah of herself. As if her entire world had been shattered.

Miriam whirled from the stove, nervous hands fluttering in front of her apron. "What has happened?"

"I'm afraid it's Eva Hostetler," Dalton told her. "She was killed earlier."

Katie whimpered and covered her face with her hands.

She slipped onto the bench beside Katie. "Did you see something, Katie?"

The little girl's shoulders quaked.

"Katie, you must tell her," Josiah said in their language.

The child lifted her head, her face ravaged by tears. "I-I saw him."

Surprised, Leah glanced at Dalton. "Who did you see?"

"The man who Beth was seeing. I was feeding the chickens and I saw him walking in the woods behind the Miller place. I watched him until he disappeared."

If he kept going that way, he'd eventually reach the abandoned house where Eva was found.

"When was this?" Leah asked the child.

"Yesterday," Katie said tearfully.

"Did you see his face?"

Katie scrubbed her hand across her eyes. "Jah. It was the same man I saw Beth talking to before . . ."

Leah put her arm around the child's shoulders. "Thank you, Katie. You did good. This will help."

"But he had a beard," the child whispered. "He looked like that man you showed me before, only he had a beard."

"What if he comes back?" Miriam exclaimed. "What if he realizes our Katie saw him? She could be in danger!"

"The deputy will be stationed outside your home," Dalton assured the family. "Please make sure he is with each of you when you go outside. We can't be too careful."

With a sniff, Miriam turned back to the food she was preparing.

Leah squeezed Katie's arm and stood. "Thank you for being so brave."

After thanking Josiah, Leah and Dalton left the house. Dalton stopped briefly to speak with the deputy and tell him about Katie's experience. "Don't let them out of your sight no matter what. We don't believe he saw the girl, but at this point, we can't take any chances."

When they returned to the SUV, Dalton climbed in beside her and drove away from the property. "I'll call our sketch artist and have him update the sketch to reflect a beard. Then we need to send the new photo out to every news outlet around. He's obviously using a fake beard to change up his appearance."

So much death. Her family. Beth. Now Eva. All brought on because John had become obsessed with her.

Dalton covered her hand with his as if he'd read her thoughts. "He used your innocence to lure you in. I can't help but feel his motives go much deeper than his obsession with you. There's something else we're missing. Something important."

His attention went back to the road. She thought about what Dalton said concerning his connection to Harrison's family. Leah couldn't help but believe he hadn't told her everything.

Dalton turned onto the Hostetlers' drive. In front of the house, a buggy had been tied off. Eva's brothers. The officers stepped outside along with two young Amish men. Leah recognized Peter, Eva's older brother.

She and Dalton exited the SUV together and climbed the steps.

A look of surprise passed over Peter's face when he recognized Leah. "I had forgotten you were a police officer now."

Peter was five years her junior. He resembled Eva, whereas Tanner, the younger of the two, was fair-headed and the spitting image of their dad. She'd heard Peter had gotten married last November.

He glanced between them and immediately grew suspicious. "Did you find her?"

"Can we come inside?"

Peter's dark eyes held hers for a long moment before he went back inside. Dalton left the two officers stationed outside.

In the small living room, Gertrude and her husband waited for news of their daughter. Tanner sat down beside his parents. Gertrude's troubled eyes latched on to Leah's.

Eva's father, Noah, rose. "Is she dead?" He directed the question to Leah.

Leah confirmed with the tiniest of nods. "I'm sorry, she is."

Gertrude screamed and collapsed against her son while her husband dropped down to his seat, a stunned look on his face.

Leah did her best to explain as delicately as she could what had happened.

"This is the same person who killed Beth?" Noah asked in a monotone.

"We believe so," Dalton confirmed. "When was the last time you saw Eva?"

Noah seemed to struggle with his answer. "At bedtime. She went to her room. I waited until her door was closed before I went to bed." His chin wobbled as he tried not to fall apart. "We checked her room this morning. She was gone." Noah shook his head. "Why would she leave?"

Leah wished she could answer that question. After everything they'd told Eva, she still met up with John, and it cost her life.

Leah remembered what Gertrude had said to Eva during their last visit. "Gertrude, you mentioned you saw Eva with someone."

Noah whipped his head toward his wife. "What is this? Eva was seeing someone? Who?"

Gertrude wiped her eyes. "I guess there is no point in keeping secrets now." Her shoulders sagged. "I saw her near the barn with an Englischer man before Beth died. When I questioned Eva, she told me he had stopped to ask directions."

"But you didn't believe her." Leah saw it on her face.

"Nay. I saw the way she looked at him. The way she smiled."

Leah brought up the sketch on her phone. "Was it this man?"

Gertrude studied the sketch. "*Jah*, this is him. He is the one."

Peter looked at the sketch as well. "I noticed a man in a green truck driving on the gravel road behind the property a few days ago. It was odd because that road is rarely used except by buggies." He gave a description of the truck.

Dalton looked at Leah. "Call Sugar. Get the description out to all the law enforcement agencies around the county."

She made the call.

"We'll continue to have a police presence outside your home,"

Dalton told the family. "Not that I believe you're in any danger," he assured Noah before he could voice the question. "It's just for my peace of mind."

Noah inclined his head.

"If you need anything at all, please let the officers know. As soon as we have more information, I'll stop by. I'm so sorry for your loss. So very sorry," Dalton said in a voice thick with emotion.

Leah and Dalton quietly left the family and headed out to the SUV.

After Dalton got in the vehicle, he gripped the wheel tightly. "I have a bad feeling about this, Leah."

She looked into his eyes. "Me too, Dalton. Me too."

eleven

Dalton pulled onto the overlook he'd noticed just outside of town. The twinkling lights from the streetlights and shops penetrated the darkness. The mountains were black shapes in the distance, but they were always there. Just as God was. Even in the darkest moments when it was hard to feel his presence.

Leah shifted in her seat. "Why are we stopping?"

He killed the engine and sighed. "It's been a gut-wrenching day. I thought we could take a minute."

Her expression softened. "You're right, it's been a horrible day." The word ended in a sob. He put his arm around her shoulders.

He held her without speaking and wished for a different time. When death wasn't shadowing them at every turn. A time when the past wouldn't stand between them.

"What aren't you telling me about Harrison?" she asked so softly he almost didn't hear.

She deserved to know the truth, no matter how hard.

Leah pulled away. "You two were close. I understand that, but there's something else, isn't there? Please, just tell me."

Dalton rubbed his palm across the front of his shirt before answering. "Harrison is my brother."

She searched his face. "But you aren't Amish."

"No, my family lived next to Harrison's. We'd played together since we were toddlers. When I was around ten, my mother died and my father, well, I guess he decided he didn't want to be strapped with a kid. He took off."

"Oh, Dalton." She touched his shoulder.

Talking about his old man was hard. It brought back the pain he'd gone through at the time. Losing his mother had been devastating. But to have his father take off like that . . . "Harrison's mother and father took me in and raised me like their own." He swallowed a couple of times. "I owe them and Harrison everything. Who knows where I would be if they hadn't taken me in?"

"I'm so sorry," she whispered. Something shifted in her eyes while a soft breath escaped.

He leaned in and searched her face. Dalton cupped her cheek and brushed his lips against hers. A tender moment shared within the darkness closing in.

"Chief, you copy?" Sugar's transmission broke them apart. Dalton couldn't look away from Leah. He wished more than ever they had met at a different time. "Chief, the tribal police have located a dark green truck fitting the description." Sugar gave him the address.

Dalton expelled a breath. Their gazes still tangled as he responded. "I copy you, Sugar. Leah's with me. We're heading there now," he said in a rough tone.

He wasn't sure what to say to Leah. Should he apologize?

She placed her finger over his lips. "Don't you dare. That was a nice kiss, and I don't regret it for a second."

Dalton chuckled. He didn't either. His attention went to her lips regretfully. He hit the lights and sped down the road.

"That location is nowhere near the Amish community." Her voice appeared unsteady. Was she remembering their kiss? He sure was.

He cleared his throat. "Could be he's staying close by. We have to canvass the entire area. Show the sketch door to door. Maybe someone will recognize him." Dalton spotted the flashing police lights and pulled up behind them. The officer he'd met before had begun searching the vehicle.

"Chief Cooper. Leah." Officer Rebecca Trahan straightened and addressed them.

"Appreciate the call. Any identification in the truck?"

Officer Trahan shook her head. "Nothing so far. It's kind of eerie, though. The glove box is empty. No plates on the vehicle. I've called in the crime scene unit, but I have a feeling we'll discover it's stolen."

"I'm guessing the plates were removed recently." Dalton observed the missing back plate. "Otherwise, someone would have stopped him by now."

"For sure," Officer Trahan responded.

Sam arrived on the scene and pulled in behind the SUV.

"This is a new twist," Sam said while watching the activity around the truck. "Why would he leave the truck here?"

Had the killer deliberately removed the plates and left the truck for them to find?

"Looks like we're going to be able to pull some viable fingerprints on the driver's door," Officer Trahan told them.

"That's a little too convenient if you ask me," Leah said. "Those are probably not his."

Dalton glanced around the area.

"It's a quiet neighborhood. Very little crime—" Leah suddenly stopped. "Wait, our second shift dispatcher Justine Raber's family lives around here, don't they, Sam?"

"They sure do. A couple of blocks over, I believe."

"She could be in danger." The urgency in Leah's tone vaulted Dalton into action.

"Radio for assistance, Sam. We need to go door to door and see if anyone has seen the man in the sketch."

They headed for the SUV. Dalton followed Leah's directions. After several turns, they reached an older neighborhood, where Justine lived.

"This is it." Leah pointed to the house at the end of the cul-de-sac. She barely waited until he'd stopped before jumping out. "I sure hope she's okay."

Dalton stepped up on the porch and knocked. "Why would he target Justine? So far, the other victims here were Amish."

Leah reminded him that Justine's family had once been Amish, then added, "Justine wants to join the force one day. I'm helping her prepare for the academy, and we've gotten pretty close."

When his knock went unanswered, Dalton rang the bell multiple times. Each ring was met with silence.

A disturbing thought occurred to him. Had Justine been targeted because of her former Amish roots or because of her relationship with Leah?

Before he could voice his concern to Leah, Justine opened the door with an incredulous look. "Chief. Leah. What are you doing here? Is something wrong?"

How did he explain their suspicions? "Have you noticed anything unusual happening around the neighborhood last night or this morning?"

"Unusual? No. Why?"

Dalton explained about the abandoned truck. "We believe it may belong to the killer."

"You think he's coming after me?" Her hand flew to her chest.

"We don't know for certain," he assured her. "It could just be a strange coincidence. To be safe, keep the doors locked and we'll have a patrol sit in front of your house."

"Is that necessary?" She averted her gaze. A strange question considering the danger she might be facing.

"Yes, as a precaution."

"All right," Justine said at last.

"Are your parents home?"

"No, they went to the morning breakfast for the homeless at the church. Mom and Dad help prepare the meal and serve, so they get there early. I decided to stay home." Justine still wouldn't look at Leah.

"The chief and I will stay until we can get a police car to sit at your house," Leah said. "I'll call your mom and let her know."

"No." Justine rejected the idea too quickly. "I mean, that's not necessary. I'll be fine alone."

Leah's gaze swept to Dalton. "We'll wait outside. Lock up behind us."

"Really, this isn't necessary . . ." Justine stopped and waved her hands in front of her. "But I appreciate it. Thank you."

"She's lying," Leah said once they were in the SUV. "Justine never misses a chance to serve at church."

"You think there was a reason beyond what she claimed?"

She blew out a breath. "Maybe I'm just being paranoid after everything that's happened."

But he shared her doubts. "No, I agree with you. She's hiding something. I'll get someone to sit at the house." After making the call, he went over in his mind the details they knew so far. For whatever reason, the killer had chosen to leave the truck behind. Without it he would be on foot until he found a replacement. "Where would he go to get out of sight?" He looked Leah's way.

Once their backup arrived, Dalton drove to the outskirts of town, where the valley separating St. Ignatius from the mountains spread out in front of them, filled with unknowns.

"There's no place to hide until he reaches the high country."

"The weather wouldn't be a problem this time of year. He could survive. Which means there are miles of possible hiding places." Dalton did his best to curb his disappointment.

"Unfortunately, yes. And the mountains mark the beginning of the Mission wilderness and private tribal land. We'll have to reach out to the tribal police."

"I'll speak to the chief and ask them to start a search at daylight." He checked the time. "Which won't be long. Why don't we gather the case files and take them to Marge's? We can relieve Chief Perez." With a final look at the vast unknown in front of them, Dalton turned the SUV around and headed back to town.

Once he'd gathered the information he needed at the station, he told Sugar where they'd be should something come up.

"Uh-huh," Sugar murmured. She appeared distracted and not her usual vivacious self.

"What's wrong with her?" Dalton asked once they were outside.

"She's worried about Justine. I asked her if she'd spoken to her niece recently. Sugar said she called, but Justine hadn't wanted to talk. And Justine's mom says she's been acting strange lately."

Dalton stopped walking and faced her over the top of the SUV's hood. "In what way?"

"Keeping secrets. Missing church more than just this morning. And her mother said she overheard Justine talking to someone on the phone. When she came into the room, Justine abruptly ended the call. None of that's like her."

They both climbed into the SUV. "She might just be acting out." But he'd seen how cagey the young dispatcher had been when they showed up at her door. Almost as if she were hiding something . . . or *someone*. "Do you think Justine is seeing someone in secret?" He couldn't bring himself to say what he thought. The killer encouraged women to keep their relationship secret so no one could identify him.

"Maybe. But it doesn't exactly fit John's MO. I was only sixteen at the time. Beth and Eva were around the same age. And all were Amish. Justine is older and no longer Amish."

Dalton turned onto Marge's quiet street. "She was at one time, and she's lived a sheltered life. I've done some checking on the other two cases from Wyoming. Those women were young as well. The coroner believes probably in their late teens. Most likely runaways. If they came from Amish communities and left the faith, there might not be anyone looking for them. They'd make easy targets."

He pulled alongside Chief Perez's cruiser, and they climbed out.

"Sounds like you've had an interesting morning," the chief said once they stopped beside his window.

"To say the least. Thanks to your officer for finding the truck." Dalton told the man about the idea the killer might have disappeared into the mountains.

"I'll have some of my men go up there. If he's still there, we'll find him."

"I appreciate it." Dalton stared up at the house. "Everything okay here?"

Perez nodded. "Yes. It's been quiet most of the night."

"That's good to hear. Thank you. We'll take it from here."

The chief fired the engine. "You got it. As soon as I have anything, I'll give you a call. If you need us to watch the house again, let me know. I'm happy to help. I want this guy caught the same as you."

Dalton waited until the vehicle disappeared before he turned to Leah. "How are you holding up?"

The light breeze blew her hair across her face. "I just want this to be over."

He felt the same way. "I want that too. For you. I want it for you."

She held his gaze for a moment, then turned and unlocked the door.

The house appeared quiet. He assumed Marge was sleeping.

"I'll make some coffee. You want some eggs?"

He smiled and tried to remember the last meal he'd eaten. Probably the burger with Leah. "That sounds wonderful."

In the kitchen, she put on a pot of coffee. Once it was brewing, she took out a frying pan and stuck her head in the fridge. "There's bacon." She looked over her shoulder.

"I won't pass on bacon ever. Let me help. I'll fry it up. You handle the eggs."

She grinned. "Deal." She retrieved another frying pan. Dalton washed his hands and went to work while Leah cracked eggs.

"I sure hope we're wrong about Justine. She's an only child

and her parents have shielded her, but the thought of her being involved with this man and knowing what he has in mind for her . . ." She shook her head. "It's terrifying."

After everything Leah had been through, she'd grown into a strong woman, one more than capable of taking care of herself. His feelings for her were growing stronger, and he realized there were so many things he wanted to know about her. "It must have been incredibly difficult moving beyond what happened. Learning to trust people again. Opening your heart up to love." The last part slipped out.

She froze with the egg suspended over the bowl.

"Sorry, that's none of my business." What was wrong with him?

"No, it's okay."

He waited and watched her expressive face.

"I've never been in love—at least not the romantic kind of love. I love my parents. Ellis and Marge." She shook her head. "But after what happened with John . . ." She set the egg down and faced him. "I feel like my life is suspended in time."

He understood all too well. Even though he'd married, his life had been permanently put on hold the day he heard the news of Harrison's death.

"I have to work."

She was stalling. Someone had created doubts in her head. "Call in sick. Come on, you know you want to."

She giggled despite her reservations. He imagined her blushing. "I can't. My job is important. You know that. I won't be able to see you today."

"How about tonight after your shift ends?"

She remained quiet for a long moment. "I will have to let you know. Please, don't be mad at me."

He slowly smiled. She was still worried about what he thought. "Only if you promise to see me after your shift."

"Oh, I want to," she said longingly. "I will try. I have to go. Someone's coming."

The call ended abruptly. He shoved his phone into his pocket. Silly girl. Always so needy. Just like the others.

He parked the car he'd stolen some distance from the farm in the trees so it wouldn't be discovered should someone happen by. A police cruiser was parked out front of the Hostetler home. He stayed in the woods until he was past the property. He'd slip in the barn from the opposite side and away from the cruiser. He'd have to be careful, but he had to find the phone he'd given to Eva. She'd taken pictures of him. They couldn't be allowed to surface. He moved through the woods until he spotted the back of the barn. Being as cautious as possible, he ran across the road and flattened himself against the building.

Eva had told him she kept the phone hidden inside the barn. She'd placed it behind a support beam out of sight. Running his hand along the back of the structure, he found the loose board Eva told him she'd used to slip out of the barn without her mother spotting her. A pity he'd had to kill her so soon. He'd enjoyed Eva's company more than anyone apart from Leah.

He moved the board aside. It let out a squeaking protest as he squeezed inside. The smell of the place descended on his nostrils. How could anyone live like this?

At first, Eva had thought it was a game to not tell him where she'd hidden the phone. He'd finally elicited the information from her. He slowly eased over to the spot she mentioned. She'd told him she'd hidden cigarettes there as well. She and Beth had played around with smoking while on their time of running around. He felt around the spot. A pack of cigarettes and a lighter. Movie tickets. No phone. He pocketed the lighter. Where was the phone?

It was just like Eva to play games. Anger had him pacing the barn while the animals housed there protested his presence. He searched every square inch of the place. She'd moved the phone.

A noise outside caught his attention. He quickly hurried past the loose board. From a distance, he watched the property through the trees. A flashlight moved across the yard to the barn. One of the cops must have heard him and gone to investigate. Well, it didn't matter. The phone wasn't in the barn. There would be no reason to go back.

He stormed back to the car and drove away. Eva was conniving. She'd done something stupid. He just hoped it wouldn't come back to haunt him.

Because he'd stolen the car, he drove on the less traveled roads. Pulling around behind an abandoned house outside of town, he killed the engine. He needed money, which meant he'd have to go see her soon. She owed him.

The house smelled of dank decay. It had been standing vacant for years. He lit the lantern he'd boosted.

More times than he could remember, he'd been forced to live in the shadows. Exist in places such as this when he deserved so much more. He'd gone through things no human should have to survive.

The mattress where he slept had been shoved against the corner. He grabbed the bag of food he'd purchased with the last bit of money and gobbled it down. Once he'd finished the burger, he tossed the bag among a growing pile of trash and brought out his phone.

He'd taken a picture of Leah standing in front of her little house with *him*. He'd wanted to see her reaction to finding the locket, and it was everything he'd anticipated.

He brought up the message app.

Thinking of you.

He texted Justine the sappy sentiment. Women like her loved that drivel. So easy to sway them with a few words. A smile. Some kisses.

Her response came quickly.

I miss you. As soon as I can I'll call you.

She believed he loved her, but he had no interest in her or Eva or Beth or the others. The one he wanted had betrayed him.

Soon. We will be together soon.

He waited for her answer before he dropped the phone onto the mattress. She had no idea what he had planned. But soon she would. He thought about where he would do it. They'd be watching the barn, expecting the move. Someplace daring. A smile spread across his face. A place that would shock them all.

"That was the lab. They're running the fingerprints from the truck now." Dalton reclaimed his seat at the table.

"Even if they find a match, it won't be John's. He wanted us to find it for some reason," Leah said with certainty. At every other crime scene, including hers, there'd been no fingerprints left behind. Leah's house had been no different. And the chances of finding out who had engraved the locket after so long was the equivalent of finding a needle in a haystack.

Dalton picked up his cup and swallowed the last of the coffee. "The question is why?"

Leah pushed her plate away and leaned back in her chair. "Marge will be waking up soon. We should probably put these away." She indicated the files they'd been going over. Crime scene photos scattered around. Gruesome details that no civilian should witness, especially not someone as fragile as Marge.

"You're right." He rose and gathered up the photos and documents.

"Why do you think he killed Ellis?" she asked. Nothing about his crime scene matched the other victims, including the cause of death.

Dalton put the files away. "I think Ellis figured out the identity of the killer."

Leah ran her finger around the rim of the cup. "If that's true, then John or whatever his real name is has been back in St. Ignatius for at least a year. Why did he wait so long to start killing again?"

He sat down next to her once more. "It's all about the timing. He planned all of this to coincide with the ten-year anniversary of your family's deaths."

"Yes, but why now? Why not the first anniversary or the fifth? Why now?" What was so special about ten years?

He covered her hand with his. "There may be something significant about the number ten. Only he knows the reason. But we're close, Leah. I truly think we're close to having the answers."

As she looked into Dalton's eyes, she believed him. Dalton would fight to find the answers she needed to finally put John's atrocities to rest.

She pulled in a shaky breath and thought about their kiss.

A little more of her heart was opening up to him with each second they spent together, but it scared her. She'd lost so much to the killer.

He framed her face with his hands. "This will end soon. You'll be free of him once and for all. Free to live. Free to love." The last part was whispered softly.

The promise she saw in him filled her with hope. "I want to believe that so much."

"Then do." His faith in the outcome was so clear. For the first time since that night long ago, she believed it might be possible to finally lay the past to rest.

She took his hands in hers. "Thank you, Dalton."

"For what?" he asked quietly.

"For understanding that I needed to stay involved in the investigation." She leaned over and kissed his cheek, then let him go.

Leah gathered their dishes and carried them to the sink. She rinsed the plates and placed them in the dishwasher. While she worked, she thought about her and Dalton's connections to the case. She turned from the sink. "Did you ever speak with Ellis about the case?"

He came over to where she stood. "Many times. After I left the marines, I came here for a while before I started college."

She searched his face. "It didn't go well?"

"You could say that. He didn't want to speak to me at all. Ellis wasn't forthcoming with information, to say the least. He insisted Harrison had done the murders, though he couldn't give me a believable reason other than Harrison knew you." Dalton shook his head. "Ellis believed Harrison was in love with you and was jealous of John."

She shook her head. "That doesn't make sense. I told him Harrison and I were only friends."

"It was a flimsy excuse that Ellis knew I didn't believe."

"I'm sorry, Dalton."

"Ellis was covering for someone. In the end, it cost him his life."

Disgust rose up inside. "What he did went against everything he had dedicated his life to." She reached out and took his hand. "I'm so sorry this happened to you and your family. So sorry."

"He's my brother. I owe him. It could just as easily have been me that Ellis framed."

She frowned. "What do you mean?"

"That summer I'd been working with some of the neighbors in the field. Isaac—Harrison's dad—didn't want to pull me away, so he sent Harrison to St. Ignatius to help the family. It was just dumb luck that he was here instead of me."

"Oh, Dalton." She didn't know what to say. All those times she'd expressed her guilt over what happened to her family, he'd understood completely because he carried his own guilt.

"My family deserves to know the truth about what happened. I owe my brother."

twelve

He hadn't told his story to another soul besides his former lieutenant, Mark Sorenson. Until now. But he and Leah had a lot in common. They'd both suffered much at the hands of a killer. "I should have told you everything sooner."

She shook her head. "No, I understand completely. It's hard sharing the worst part of your life with anyone."

No matter what the future held for Leah and him, they would forever be united in tragedy.

"Wait, you said you'd spoken with Ellis many times?"

Dalton nodded. "I did. I wanted to make it clear I wasn't going away."

Leah poured them both more coffee. "What did he say?"

"Not much. Ellis didn't want to talk to me, but I kept pestering him. I had the right to know what happened to my brother. Eventually, he gave me some more information. He said after Harrison killed your family and it became clear he was about to be arrested, Harrison tried to escape, but Ellis tracked him to an abandoned house outside of town. Harrison realized there was no way out, so he set the house on fire. Ellis tried to go in after him, but by then the fire had spread quickly through the house."

"He told me the same thing."

Yet through the years, Dalton couldn't accept Ellis Petri's explanation, and he wasn't the only one. Both his adoptive parents believed Ellis had lied. "After Harrison's death I wanted to stay with Isaac and Rachel. They'd lost their son. How could I leave them?" He recalled Isaac's reaction when he told him he'd decided not to enlist in the marines. "Isaac sat me down and told me both he and Rachel always knew the Amish way was not my future. They wanted me to continue with my plans." Dalton thought about that time. He'd been riddled with guilt. Harrison wouldn't have the chance to live his life. Have a family.

"I came back here often. I must have stopped by the station to speak with Ellis a half dozen times—to the point where he told me he didn't want to see me again."

"What did you do?"

He smiled. "Started investigating on my own."

"How?"

"I went to your old barn and combed every inch of the place. Then I visited my cousins."

"Did you learn anything useful?"

"Nothing that would change Ellis's mind," he said with bitterness. "At the time, the oldest son shared a room with Harrison. He confirmed Harrison couldn't have slipped from the room without him seeing, and they'd told Ellis this. It didn't matter. He ignored the family entirely."

Leah appeared baffled. "None of this makes sense. Ellis was always a by-the-book cop. I don't know why he would ignore evidence."

"Ignore what evidence?" Marge's angry tone had them both whipping around. "What are you accusing my husband of doing?"

Leah went over to the older woman. "Nothing."

Marge crossed her arms over her chest. "You were talking bad about my Ellis. He doesn't deserve that from you, Leah. He's a good man. Ellis took you in when you had no one. And he gave me the child I so desperately wanted to replace the one I lost."

Leah recoiled. "What are you talking about? What child?"

Marge's glazed eyes darted past Leah to Dalton. "Who are you? Why are you here?" She grew more agitated.

"I'm Dalton Cooper, ma'am. We've met before."

Marge focused on him for a long moment; her expression eventually cleared. "Oh yes, I remember. You're the new chief. You replaced my Ellis."

Dalton smiled gently. "That's right."

"He gave me the child I so desperately wanted to replace the one I lost." Marge's strange comment stuck in his head. Just part of the disease?

A strained silence filled the air.

"Are you hungry?" Leah said to her mother. "We made break-fast." She looped her arm through Marge's.

The older woman glanced around the kitchen and then at Leah. "You did? Thank you, Leah."

"You're welcome." Leah gently guided her to the table. "Come and sit. I'll fix you a plate."

Dalton pulled out a chair for Marge. With a smile, she lowered herself down to it. "Why thank you, young man."

While Dalton poured coffee, Leah placed bacon and eggs on a plate and set it before her mom.

"Here you go." She kissed Marge's cheek.

"Thank you, baby girl." Tears brimmed in Marge's eyes.

"I'm sorry you overheard what Dalton and I were saying

earlier. We're trying to figure out what happened to those two Amish girls. Somehow, they're connected to what happened to my family." Leah sat beside Marge. "Do you feel up to answering some questions?"

Marge's brow furrowed in confusion. "Leah, you know Ellis never spoke much about his cases—not even yours—with me. He wanted to spare me."

Marge picked up her fork and began to eat while Leah exchanged a brief look with Dalton.

"What did you mean earlier when you said he gave you a child to replace the one you lost?"

Marge's eyes widened. Immediately, her back straightened and her chin lifted. "What? Why would I say such a thing? You know Ellis and I weren't able to have children."

"Maybe I misunderstood." Leah let the matter drop. She patted the older woman's shoulder.

Outside, the first pinks and oranges of the new day peeked through the kitchen window. Another morning and they were no closer to understanding what the killer's true motives were than the day she looked into the sightless eyes of Beth Zook.

Sugar met them at the door before they had a chance to step inside the station.

"Something came for you, Leah. I'm not sure when it arrived—it must have fallen behind some paperwork. I'm sorry, I just found it." She handed Leah a small cardboard box.

There was no other name on it except for Leah's scribbled across the top.

"That's Eva's handwriting." She recognized it from the note Eva had left them.

Dalton leaned closer to examine the script. "You're right, it is."

Sugar stopped next to her desk. "She obviously didn't mail it. She must have dropped it here before . . ." Before she was murdered. "Anyway, I grabbed my purse to leave once Sylvia arrived and knocked over the picture right here. It must have slipped behind it."

"Wait, where's Justine? She mentioned wanting to come in and get in a few extra hours doing some paperwork."

Sugar tsked. "She told me the same thing, but then she called and said she wasn't feeling well. I'm about to give that girl a piece of my mind. She's up to something."

Leah had a feeling she knew what that entailed. "Let me speak to her first. I'll see if I can find out what's going on." She stared at the box in her hand.

"I opened it," Sugar said. "There's a cell phone inside." She glanced between Dalton and Leah. "Don't worry. I wore gloves and I didn't touch the phone."

"Bring it to the office. I have a kit and will see if I can lift some fingerprints before we turn it on." Both Leah and Sugar followed him to his office, where he dusted the phone and pulled several usable prints from the phone and the box. "Sugar, get Henry to take these to the lab. It's worth a shot. I'm guessing the killer gave it to her. Chances are he wouldn't have worn gloves around Eva."

Sugar stepped out into the hall and yelled, "Henry, get yourself in here."

Dalton cringed over every shouted word. Once Henry poked his head in, he explained what was needed. "Tell the lab to put a rush on the prints."

"You got it, Chief."

Dalton hit the button to power the phone up with his gloved hand. He examined the phone while they waited. "It appears to be a cheap phone like you might buy at any store."

The phone's welcome screen appeared. Leah and Sugar moved to stand over his shoulder. A message icon appeared.

Dalton tapped it. "Just one person." His attention shot to Leah. "It's from a Jonathan."

"That's the name Eva gave us."

"There are dozens of messages between Eva and Jonathan."

Dalton read the messages aloud. "'Meet me at our place.'" He frowned at the screen. "There are many more like it."

Leah's family barn came to mind. He'd want to relive her family's deaths. Beth's. Having Eva there and seeing her reaction probably intensified the experience.

"This last one is curious. It sounds as if Eva was beginning to have doubts about Jonathan. The date is after we spoke to her that final time. She told him what we said." Dalton sat forward in his chair. "She must have had an inkling that something was wrong. That's why she delivered the phone here. Why she left the note giving us Jonathan's name. Eva must have thought he might try to kill her."

"That poor girl," Sugar muttered.

"Why did she go to meet him if she'd become suspicious?" After all their warnings, Leah couldn't believe Eva had agreed to meet Jonathan.

"He's good at convincing women to trust him." Dalton clicked on the photo app. "There are pictures of Eva here."

Leah studied the photo of the young Amish girl smiling into the camera. Several more like it. Dalton swiped left and stopped. "Wow. This must be him. It looks a lot like the sketch." He showed it to Leah and Sugar.

A chill ran down Leah's spine.

"That's John." The ten years had aged him, and yet she recognized his smile. He'd used it on her many times to persuade her to do what he wanted. "I can't believe it."

"Do either of you recognize the location in the background?" Dalton asked.

"I do," Sugar confirmed right away. "That's the old bridge outside of town."

Leah studied the background a second longer. "She's right. It's about five miles out. He had to have picked her up and taken her there."

"Probably instead of going to work. Henry spoke to the store owners. They said they had hated to let her go, but Eva was repeatedly late or a no-show for her job."

"She was sneaking off with Jonathan instead so as to not draw her family's suspicions."

Dalton set the phone down. "I'll see if there's a way to get the history of the phone number assigned to these text messages from Jonathan, but I'm guessing he's using a burner as well."

"We need to talk to Justine right away before she does something foolish. She's in danger." Leah had a sick feeling that the killer would try to take her out to eliminate another witness.

"You want me to call her?" Sugar snatched her phone from her pocket.

Leah understood the dispatcher's concern about her niece, but they couldn't afford to have Justine alert John.

"Let me handle this."

Sugar reluctantly agreed. As Leah and Dalton prepared to leave, Justine herself walked in. Judging by the younger woman's forlorn expression, Leah believed Justine might open up more if she spoke to her alone.

"Girl, I thought you were sick," Sugar burst out.

"Sugar—" Leah clamped a hand on the older woman's shoulder to keep her from a full-on interrogation. "I've got this. Why don't you go home. I'll call you later." Leah faced Dalton. "I think it would be better if I speak to Justine alone. If you don't mind, I'd like to show Justine the photo of Jonathan on Eva's phone."

Dalton handed her the phone. "Use my office."

Leah led Justine to the room and closed the door. She waited for her to take a seat. The young woman covered her face with her hands. Justine was obviously troubled.

"Hey, what is it?" Leah asked gently as she claimed the seat beside her.

"I'm so sorry," Justine muttered between sobs.

"What are you sorry for?"

The young woman swiped her hand over her face. "I lied to you earlier. My boyfriend was there with me when you and the chief arrived."

"It's okay," Leah said carefully. She didn't want to scare Justine into silence. "What's his name?"

"Jonathan," she admitted reluctantly. "But he's not the person you're looking for. He isn't," she insisted when she saw Leah's startled reaction. "He's kind and sweet and he wouldn't hurt anyone."

"Can you show me the number he uses to call you?"

Justine hesitated before bringing out her phone. She brought up Jonathan's contact number. The same one that Eva had for him.

Leah sighed. Justine needed to know the truth. "Justine, that number you have for Jonathan is the same number we found on a phone Eva Hostetler possessed. There was a photo on it of the man Eva was seeing." Leah brought it up and showed it to Justine.

All the color left Justine's face. "That's him. That's my Jonathan."

They knew about him and Justine. For the first time since he'd returned to St. Ignatius, he was worried.

Using his phone was no longer safe. The police had the number. He'd taken all the precautions by using a disposable phone, and yet Justine had betrayed him.

Foolish Justine. He'd planned to reel her in deeper before he ended her life. Now, the choice had been taken from him. There would be no more games to play with her. He'd have to kill her soon, before she had the chance to expose him further.

He passed by the police station. When he saw her car parked in front, his anger became like a living presence in the car.

He turned on the road behind Justine's house and parked. There was a cop guarding the front of the place. He'd have to go in through the rear entrance. It would be empty now. Both her parents worked. He hopped the fence and advanced to the back porch. Using gloves, he retrieved the key from beneath the plant and slipped inside. The silence of the house pleased him. He'd grown fond of silence after that place.

Justine had told him about her happy childhood growing up Amish. So unlike the one he'd experienced. There were no loving parents to guide him into adulthood.

Upstairs in Justine's room, he searched through drawers until he found where she kept her money and pocketed it. Then he brought out the letter and left it on her pillow. She would find it and know it came from him.

In the kitchen, he gathered food, a handful of drinks—whatever he could grab to survive on.

He slipped out the back door and returned to his car.

As he headed back through town, he noticed the new chief of police heading into the station. The chief didn't look up as he passed by.

The man wouldn't have his job if it weren't for him. He'd make him pay the way he had Ellis Petri.

The urge to kill again grew stronger. Soon, he'd track Justine down and end her life. Make her pay for betraying him like he had the others. Assuage his desire to kill. Until the next time.

Once he was out of town, he removed the wig he'd used as a disguise.

Behind him, a police vehicle approached, and his pulse went wild. He'd made a point of keeping his speed below the limit to avoid drawing attention to himself, and yet the cruiser slowly closed the space between them.

He spotted a road ahead on the left and turned. The police officer did the same.

He clasped the gun. Having it in his hand—feeling the metal barrel—helped to calm his nerves.

The cop wasn't letting up. He flashed his lights and hit the siren.

Running wasn't an option. The cop probably knew the car was stolen by now.

Which left one choice. He eased onto the shoulder of the road and tucked the gun under his right leg.

The cop exited the vehicle with his weapon draw. "Driver, get out of the car with your hands in the air."

John wasn't about to do as the cop asked. He watched the man tap his mic and call for backup. John had to get away while he still could. He whipped back onto the road and jerked the car around, barreling toward the cop who stood in the middle of the road. John recognized the officer from the roadblock near the lake. The cop shot once and then dove for cover at the back of his cruiser. As John passed by, he fired off several rounds, striking the officer in the shoulder. The cop dropped to the ground. John floored the vehicle and flew down the road.

He reached the intersection and whipped the car to the left.

Gunning the car's tired old engine, he flew down the road. He almost missed the turnoff to the abandoned home and had to swerve to make the turn before flooring the car once more.

For the first time, the pressure of being hunted weighed on him. Shooting a cop hadn't been on his agenda today, yet it wasn't the first time he'd taken one out. And it probably wouldn't be the last.

thirteen

"Chief, I can't reach Henry on the radio." Sylvia poked her head into Dalton's office without knocking. She had a worried look on her face. "He was heading into the station but that's been some time ago."

Dalton vaulted to his feet and grabbed his weapon. He headed for the door. "What's his last location?"

"Off 93."

"Call Ethan. Tell him to head that way now," Dalton tossed over his shoulder.

"I'm coming with you." Leah scrambled after him.

Dalton stopped in his tracks. This could be a ploy by the killer to get her out in the open. "Leah. It's not safe. He wants you."

"This is Henry. I'm going. I'll be fine as long as I'm with you."

Still, his misgivings warned that taking Leah with him was a big mistake.

"Dalton, Henry could be in trouble."

Against his better judgment, he agreed. He and Leah raced out to the SUV, and he hit the lights, flying down the road toward Henry's location.

Both their radios squawked to life at the same time. "Help me. I'm shot."

"That's Henry," Leah exclaimed.

Dalton responded, "We're on our way, Henry. Where's the perp?"

"I don't know." Dalton barely recognized Henry's words, which were slurred. "I stopped the driver of a stolen car on our watch list and he shot me. I've lost a lot of blood."

"Ambulance is en route," Leah reassured him. "Hang on . . . it won't be much longer."

"Where were you shot?" Dalton wanted to keep Henry talking until they reached him. He spotted the county road and whipped onto it. Behind him another siren screamed toward them. Ethan.

"My shoulder."

Dalton spotted Henry's cruiser. "I see you." He screeched to a halt behind Henry and grabbed the first aid kit from the back.

Henry was slumped sideways in his seat and unconscious.

Dalton shook him. "Wake up, Henry. I need you to stay with me. Leah and I are here. Paramedics are on the way."

Henry wasn't wearing a bulletproof vest. If the bullet had been a few inches to the right . . .

Dalton unbuttoned Henry's shirt and moved it out of the way. The bullet had not exited his shoulder.

"Here." Leah handed him gauze to pack the wound.

Ethan reached them. "Ambulance is right behind me."

The young officer opened his eyes and looked straight at Dalton. "I recognized him." Henry gathered a couple of breaths. "It's the same person who was driving the truck we impounded. I stopped him near the lake when we found the car. The truck that was registered to a woman. He said it was his sister's truck.

The face was the same, but now that I think about it, I'm pretty sure he was wearing some type of wig before to disguise his appearance. Chief, this is the killer."

Dalton's gaze shot to Leah briefly. "We'll need to find the name on the registration."

Henry had stopped the killer and almost died. Dalton had little doubt this was the work of John.

"He's driving a dark blue, two-door compact car."

The ambulance arrived. The three stepped away to let the ambulance crew work.

"He'll ditch the car soon," Leah warned.

"Get an APB out on it right away," Dalton told Ethan. "We need to catch him before he unloads it."

Ethan turned away and enforced the command.

"He's spiraling." Leah shielded her eyes and panned the countryside. "That should work in our favor."

"But he's not ready to give up on the game yet." Dalton had no doubt the killer had planned his next victim, and he believed it was Justine. He watched the paramedics prepare to take Henry to the hospital, then went with Leah to have a word with them before they left. "How is he?" Dalton asked the senior paramedic.

"Very lucky the bullet didn't hit any major arteries," Adam Reece told him. "He'll be sore for a while, but he should be back on his feet in no time."

"I'm sure Henry's glad to hear that." Dalton leaned over to speak with his officer. "Take care of yourself. Get some rest."

Henry nodded and was wheeled away into the ambulance.

This part of the countryside was remote. Isolated. "Chances are he wouldn't head back to town with the car stolen now that he knows we'll be looking for it and him. It's too big of a risk."

"There are a few abandoned farmhouses in the opposite direction," Leah suggested. "He could be crashing at one of them."

And they could be walking into a trap set by a very cunning murderer. Dalton's instincts screamed to take her back to the station.

Leah placed her hand on his arm. "I'm coming with you."

Dalton looked into her green eyes and tried to hide his fears as he slowly nodded.

The tow truck arrived to take Henry's patrol car back to the station.

He and Leah returned to the SUV and turned around. Ethan pulled out behind them.

Dalton hit the mic. "Let's split up. There are several roads coming up, and we don't know which one he may have taken." They'd relayed the description of the vehicle out to every law enforcement agency around. Dalton just hoped they found him before he ditched the car. "We'll take this first one. I'm calling in the tribal police to assist. If you spot anything, hold back and wait for backup. I repeat, wait for backup."

"I copy you, Chief."

This case had once again become personal for all of them. One of their own had been hurt.

He slowed his speed according to the rough road. "What's down this way?"

"A few deserted houses. More down the many roads that cut through the county." Leah blew out a sigh. "In other words, he could be anywhere."

Dalton spotted an old farmhouse coming up on the right. "Like this one?"

She leaned forward in her seat. "Exactly. I don't see the car."

A small, garage-sized building peeked out from behind the house. "He could have hidden it."

Dalton stopped out front. He faced her. Couldn't hide his misgiving. "Stay here and lock the door."

Leah shook her head. "I'm not letting you go in there alone."

He ran a hand over his eyes. "Fine, but—"

"I know. Stay close." She smiled gently before climbing out.

Dalton carefully closed the door to keep from making too much noise. A search of the garage proved it was empty. "Let's check the house," he whispered. "I'm going in first, and that's not up for debate."

Her smile reminded him of things he'd written out of his life after Allison.

The door stood slightly ajar. A sign someone had been there recently. Leah saw it too. Dalton eased the door open with his weapon and stepped inside.

The room was small and dank. Wallpaper peeled off in sheets. The smell alone was noxious. A mattress had been slung in one corner. Fast-food wrappers were scattered all around. Something lay on the mattress.

Dalton and Leah approached slowly. A small gasp escaped from Leah when she spotted a handful of instant photos that had been left deliberately for her to find.

The killer had taken them when she had no idea. In front of her house with Dalton on the day they'd found the necklace. At Beth's house the day of the murder.

"He's been watching me," she murmured. The fear in her eyes scared him.

"We need backup right away. And I want to get CSI out here. Let's leave this to them." He'd feel safer with her inside the SUV.

Dalton stepped from the house with Leah against his side.

He'd barely taken a step when something hard slammed against his head. He dropped to his knees. The world around him blurred. Another blow sent him sprawling against the ground. As darkness closed in, all he could think about was Leah.

"Dalton." Leah whirled toward the attacker, her weapon drawn. John anticipated her move and slugged her hard. Her eyes watered. He took advantage and snatched the weapon from her hand and tossed it out of reach. Then he took out her Taser and shoved it into his pocket.

"Hello, Leah." His voice washed over her. He grabbed her and hauled her against him. "I've been anticipating our day together. Have you?" Something cold and familiar touched her neck. Revulsion rose in her throat. The knife.

He pulled her around to the side and into the woods. She noticed something hidden in the trees. A car. Small. Blue. Like the one Henry had identified.

"Your officer almost had me," he whispered. John didn't appear to be concerned about Dalton. "Can you imagine a rookie like him capturing me?" He laughed as if the thought were hilarious. "I should have killed him. Like I did the former chief."

Her legs failed her, but John caught her and propped her up. "Such a pompous person. Thinking he could control me."

"Thinking he could control me"? Had John spoken to Ellis?

Her mind struggled to push through the fear so she could remember everything he said.

"Should I kill him now or would you prefer to wait until our special day?" he said, as if sensing her concern for Dalton.

Leah shook her head frantically. She couldn't bear the thought of John hurting Dalton.

"No?" His laugh sent chills through her. It sounded un-hinged. He nuzzled her cheek. "Well, if not him, then someone else must die. Can you guess who?"

She fought to free herself, but his grip tightened.

"You and I both know it's not our time yet. I'll be seeing you real soon, Leah." Her heart thundered in her chest as he kissed her cheek. "I think I'll go ahead and kill him after all."

No. Please no. John retrieved the Taser. Before she had time to think, he held it against her side then let her go. The voltage shot through her body, and Leah dropped to her knees. She tried to scream, but it came out as a whimper. Another jolt crumpled her against the ground. Her last thought was for Dalton. *Please don't let him die.*

fourteen

Whoosh! The strange noise pulled Dalton out of the darkness. He struggled to open his eyes. From somewhere close by, car tires squealed as they sped down the road. He rose to his knees. Pain shot through his head as he stumbled to his feet. All he could think about was Leah.

When his vision cleared, he saw the SUV engulfed in flames. Leah! Was she in the vehicle?

Dalton ran toward it, battling the heat and flames to get close enough to confirm the vehicle was empty. He fought to keep from losing it. Had the killer taken her? "Leah!" he called out before he hit the radio and quickly explained what had happened. Dalton gave their location. "Leah is missing." Those words were the hardest to say.

"Backup is on its way, Chief," Sylvia said. "We'll find her."

Engine noise disappeared down the road. He was without a way to give chase. Dalton ran a hand over his eyes and searched around the wooded place. "I need your help, Lord. I can't lose her." At the edge of the trees, something grabbed his attention. It was Leah. He kept his legs beneath him and ran.

"Leah." Dalton dropped down beside her and shook her. Leah moaned. She was alive.

Her eyes shot open. When she saw him, she sat up quickly and hugged him close. "I was so worried. He told me he would kill you. Are you okay?"

John had been close enough to taunt her, but he hadn't wanted her dead yet.

"I'm fine. It's just a little bump," he said, even though he felt far from it. "You're hurt."

"He Tased me. We need help, Dalton. He's getting away." She stumbled to her feet and started walking. When she saw the fire, she stopped short.

A siren raced down the road and reached the house. Ethan bailed from the cruiser and ran toward them.

"Tribal police cruisers are trying to cut him off before he escapes," Ethan told them.

"They won't reach him in time. We have to go after him. Where does the road lead?" Dalton asked Ethan.

"It loops back to the main road a little closer into town."

The three jumped into the cruiser. Ethan jerked the car out onto the road and sped down the direction the car had taken.

They reached a fork in the road. "Now what?" Dalton asked as he looked both directions.

"Is that smoke?" Ethan pointed to where a gray plume billowed up to the clear sky.

"It is." Dalton had a bad feeling that any evidence in the car had been destroyed by fire. Ethan hit the siren and raced toward the blaze. As they neared, Dalton spotted a car almost completely engulfed in fire.

Ethan slowed to a stop near the car. "From what I can see, it fits the description."

A couple of houses were off in the distance.

"If he heads toward those, the owners could be in danger." Dalton hit the radio on his shoulder. "We've found the car." He gave the dispatcher the location and requested the fire department on site. "Leah, maybe you should—"

She gave him a "you've got to be kidding" look. "I've been through far worse. And you're hurt worse than I am."

The reference to the attack that had started everything became a grim reminder of the enemy they chased.

The three spread out, searching for evidence of the killer's intentions.

"Footprints." Leah pointed to the set that veered off to the left toward a wooded area beyond the pasture they were in now. "He came this way."

Dalton radioed in their location to dispatch. "Where are the tribal police?"

"They're close, Chief," Sylvia assured him. "Stay safe."

"Ethan, wait here for them. We'll continue searching for the perp."

As he and Leah entered the woods, a prickling of unease lifted the hairs on Dalton's neck. The thick trees turned the bright sunshine beyond them to dusk.

As they eased through the thick foliage with their weapons drawn, Dalton was aware of every little sound around them. "Where does this lead to?"

"There's a neighborhood in this direction. We're close to Marge's house." Her worried eyes met his.

"Sam's with her now. I'm sure she's fine." But he understood that the coincidence was a little too much for Leah to be satisfied.

They exited the trees into a quiet neighborhood.

"He probably hopped a few fences and then disappeared into the rest of the foot traffic around town," Leah told him and scanned the backs of several houses.

So far, the killer was like a ghost. He'd reappeared after ten years, and yet he'd left not a trace of himself behind at any of the crime scenes.

The pain in his head continued to throb, and he struggled to stay focused.

"I have no idea which way he might have gone from here," Leah said, but she pointed up ahead. "We're only a couple of blocks away from Marge's home." She glanced around at the summer foot traffic in town. "Do you think he'd come after her to get to me? If he killed Ellis—"

What happened to Ellis didn't make sense. Still, they couldn't afford to dismiss anything.

She hugged her arms around her waist. "This is the last thing Marge should be facing right now. There are days when she doesn't even remember Ellis is dead. It breaks my heart to see her like this."

Marge's back gate stood open slightly. He grabbed her arm. "Hang on." He pointed to the gate.

Leah wrenched her arm free and rushed through the gate and up to the porch. She tried the door. It opened easily in her hand. She glanced back at Dalton with a terrified look before unholstering her weapon.

Dalton did the same. They proceeded carefully inside.

The back of the house opened into a laundry room. Followed by the kitchen.

Dalton stopped to listen. Voices came from somewhere within. A TV perhaps?

Leah pointed to Ellis's office and he nodded. Together they

eased toward the room. She reached for the doorknob and slowly opened the door.

Marge sat in the recliner Leah had told him belonged to Ellis. She must have heard them enter because she jerked toward the door and their weapons.

Her hand flew to her throat. "Leah? Oh my word. What on earth is going on?"

Leah quickly holstered her weapon and went to Marge. "I'm sorry. Are you okay?"

"Of course," Marge managed, though she seemed agitated. "Why are you here and why do you have your weapons drawn?"

Leah explained what happened. "You haven't seen anyone unusual around the house, have you?"

"You're scaring me."

Leah did her best to calm her nervous mom.

"Stay here with her. I'll check the rest of the house and speak with Sam." Dalton left Ellis's office and carefully searched each room of the house. The place was empty. He headed out the front door to where Sam remained in his patrol car.

The officer spotted his approach and quickly got out. "What happened to you, Chief?" Sam indicated the two bloody gashes on Dalton's head.

After Dalton told him about the attack, he glanced up and down the empty street. "You haven't seen anyone suspicious around the neighborhood?"

The officer's eyes widened, and he shook his head.

"I'm going to call the sheriff to send over a couple of deputies. I want extra patrol here at the house." Dalton released a breath. "I'd like to leave Leah here with Marge and you to come with me." He made the call before he returned to the women.

Leah must have been waiting for him. She stepped out into

the hall and approached him. "Marge said she's been watching TV for a while. She hasn't seen anyone around the place."

"And the back door?"

"Marge feeds the stray cats in the area. She probably forgot to relock both it and the gate."

"Leah, she can't be leaving the house unsecured. It's too dangerous." He ran a hand through his hair. "Sheriff Ingalls is sending over a couple of deputies to watch the house. Marge needs you. It's going to be dark soon. Why don't you stay here with Marge tonight. I'll get a ride with Sam. If we come up with anything new, I'll give you a call right away."

Leah glanced back at Marge. "You're right. She does need me."

He smiled at her. "Try not to worry." He just wished he could take his own advice.

Something shifted in her eyes. Leah stepped closer and touched his shoulder. "I will be okay," she whispered.

But would she? He'd read her record. Seen for himself what a strong person she was, and yet this killer had left his mark on her and him.

He covered her hand with his. "I know you will."

This moment, amid the storm raging around them, felt like a safe harbor, and he didn't want to leave it.

A knock on the front door had them both jumping apart.

Leah laughed nervously. Dalton reluctantly stepped back and looked through the peephole on the door. "The deputies." He turned back to her, regret weighing him down. "I should go. Lock up behind me."

"I will. Be careful, Dalton. He's coming after you too."

He took one last look at her lovely face before opening the door and stepping out onto the porch. Dalton explained to the deputies what had happened and sent the photo of Jonathan to them. With the two deputies safeguarding the house, Dalton climbed into the patrol car beside Sam.

"How's Leah holding up?" Sam asked.

Her face came to mind. He'd admired her for her courage. Wasn't sure when that admiration had turned to something more. "She's strong but . . ."

Sam understood. "Yeah, she doesn't like to talk about what happened back then. I've known Leah a long time. That's her MO. She keeps her feelings to herself."

"You were on the force at the time of Leah's family's murders. Let me ask you something. What did you think about the way Ellis handled the investigation?"

Sam eyed him curiously. "Are you asking if I thought he made a mistake targeting that Troyer kid?"

Dalton nodded, his full attention on his senior officer.

"Yeah, I did. That kid was scared to death when Ellis dragged him in for questioning. He and I literally pulled that boy from the field. The poor kid didn't know what to do. He was only here temporarily to help out his cousins."

Dalton couldn't imagine how frightened Harrison must have been, being accused of such a heinous thing. "Why did Ellis target Harrison Troyer when Leah told him about this John person back then, not to mention the man she believed was following her?"

Sam rubbed his chin. "Good question. The chief never really gave them much attention. He was convinced Troyer did the murders." He looked over at Dalton. "Enough to arrest him."

"He arrested the kid?" As far as Dalton knew, Harrison had never been arrested. "How did Harrison end up at that abandoned farmhouse then?"

"I'm not really sure. On the day Troyer killed himself, I had come in early that morning, and Ellis told me he had to let the boy go. He said he didn't have enough to hold him on."

Dalton bit his tongue. Harrison's faith was strong. He would never have taken his own life. Had Ellis deliberately killed him to shield the real killer?

"Then why did he arrest him in the first place?" A hard edge entered Dalton's tone.

"To this day, I honestly don't understand why he did that."

Neither did Dalton. Why go to the trouble of placing him under arrest only to let him go? It almost seemed as if Ellis was setting Harrison up to take the fall so he could bury the problem once and for all.

After a fitful night of tossing and turning, Leah had risen early and made breakfast for Marge. Having the extra time with her mother was a blessing, but she couldn't get John and the upcoming anniversary out of her mind.

Morning shadows filled the room. Marge had fallen asleep. Leah muted the TV, so the only sound was the air conditioner working overtime to keep the blistering heat at bay.

Too restless to sit, Leah drifted from room to room, glancing out the windows. The two deputies were at their stations. She'd done enough surveillance to know it was long periods of boring monotony, only rarely broken by a few moments of heart-palpitating excitement. Leah made iced tea and first took a glass out to the deputy around back. "It's hot out. I thought you might like something cool."

"Thank you, ma'am," he said, accepting the glass with gratitude.

Leah recognized him from Beth's crime scene. "Please, it's Leah." She'd spent a lot of time here in the backyard that first year. At times, she still liked to come here and think. "Everything okay back here?"

The deputy took a sip. "Yes, nothing but a couple of squirrels."

"Good to know." She smiled and pointed to the glass. "If you want some more, just knock."

"I will. I appreciate it."

Leah went back inside and prepared a second glass for the deputy out front. When she returned to Ellis's office, Marge still hadn't stirred. Leah slipped into the second recliner. Her phone announced an incoming message from Dalton.

"How are things there?" Dalton asked when she called him, his husky voice a reminder of the tender moments they'd shared before and the hope taking root in her heart.

Leah quietly left the room so as not to disturb her mother. "Fine. Marge is sleeping, and I feel as if I should be doing something. Are there any new developments?"

"Not much. It's clear the killer is familiar with the layout of the town and surrounding countryside. He's probably planned out every possible scenario and has an escape route in mind." She could hear Dalton's frustration.

"Was there anything salvageable from the burned car?"

"No, nothing." He stopped. "I'm worried, Leah. It's almost the anniversary."

She shivered involuntarily. It felt like watching sand slip through an hourglass.

"Can you remember anything from when you knew John? Did he mention his family? Something to help us find his true identity?"

She'd gone over every single word from their conversations

dozens of times. "John didn't really talk about himself. He told me he'd been hiking across the country and had come to St. Ignatius to climb the mountains."

"Did he mention where he'd come from before? Or where he was staying?"

"No, he didn't, and I never thought to ask. I assumed he might be camping up in the mountains, but I don't know that for sure."

"You believe he drove a black car."

Leah could tell where he was going with this. If John had a car, how could he be hiking across the country? "Yes. He obviously stole the car like he did this time. And the pickup that followed me, I don't think it's the same one we impounded but I do believe John was driving it back then." She couldn't imagine how difficult all this was for Dalton. If only Ellis had listened to her, Harrison might still be alive. "I did give Ellis the description of the car John drove as well as the pickup. He told me nothing ever came from the search. Now I wonder if he even followed through with them."

Dalton remained quiet for a long moment. "I had the chance to speak to Sam yesterday. Did you know Ellis arrested Harrison and then let him go on the day he supposedly killed himself?"

She couldn't believe it. "You're kidding! I had no idea, but then I really didn't ask Ellis much about the case, and he didn't volunteer. By that time, I'd been released from the hospital and he and Marge had taken me in. It was hard . . ." Everything she knew had been taken from her along with her Amish way of life. It had forever tainted her memories and was the reason why she'd chosen to leave the faith. Everyone around town knew about the murders, including her new classmates at school. She'd endured the whispers, the accusations that she had something to do with her family's deaths.

"I can imagine," he murmured. "I remember how difficult it was to move on after the news of Harrison's death reached us."

He'd suffered too. Losing the boy who had become his brother had to be agonizing. She and Dalton had been thrown into a situation that was unimaginable, the bond connecting them to a killer unthinkable.

"Do you feel up to attending Beth's funeral this afternoon?" Dalton asked, jarring her from her thoughts. "There's a chance the killer might show up to try and relive the kill."

With everything that had happened, she'd almost forgotten Beth Zook would be buried today.

"Yes, of course. But what about Marge?"

"I'm sending Ethan over. I told him to stay inside with Marge and leave the two officers to handle the outside."

"Good." She wondered about the owner of the truck. Henry had said he'd run the registration. "Did you find the woman who owns the truck yet?"

Dalton sighed deeply. "Not yet. The address on the registration was a dead end. We're still looking for her, but I can't imagine how she fits into all of this."

Leah couldn't either. "We'll figure it out," she told him. "I'll see you soon."

She made lunch for herself and Marge, but neither had much of an appetite. While Leah went upstairs to change, Marge returned to Ellis's office to watch TV.

Leah quickly changed into the only black dress she owned. She'd worn it for Ellis's funeral and had left it behind in her old bedroom because she'd hoped there wouldn't be a need to wear it again. She wound her raven hair into a knot at the nape of her neck. When she was ready, she went back downstairs. Ethan and Dalton had arrived and were quietly talking by the door.

"I'll just stick my head in and check on Marge before we go." Leah went to the office, where Marge appeared to be struggling in a fitful sleep.

"No, Ellis," Marge murmured. "That's not right."

Leah shook her gently. Marge's eyes snapped open. She stared up at Leah with a terrified expression. "Oh, Leah. You scared the daylights out of me!" She sat up slowly.

"I'm sorry. I was just checking on you before we left. You were having a bad dream. Are you feeling all right?" Leah sat down beside her mother.

Marge raised a shaky hand to her forehead. "Yes, I'm fine." She focused on Leah's appearance. "You look nice. Are you going somewhere?"

Leah gathered the other woman's hands in hers and told her about the funeral.

"Oh, that's right. I'd forgotten. I feel so sorry for the family. I remember—" She stopped and focused on Leah. Both Marge and Ellis had attended her family's funeral. "It's good that you are going."

"Ethan's here to sit with you, and those two deputies are still outside. You're safe."

Marge smiled. "Well, of course I am. Ellis wouldn't let anything happen to me." Her smile slipped slightly as she struggled to recall reality and couldn't.

Leah leaned over and kissed her cheek. "I'll be back soon. In the meantime, don't spoil Ethan and the deputies too much." She rose and started for the door. Once she reached it, she turned.

Marge stared at the muted TV as if unaware of the lack

of sound. Leah covered a sob and slipped from the room. She scrubbed her hand over her eyes to wipe away the tears. Marge needed her to be strong.

Ethan was in the kitchen talking with Dalton. Both turned when she entered. Dalton's dark eyes slipped over her.

Ethan cleared his throat. "I'll take Marge a cup of coffee. She and I were playing checkers before. Maybe she'll want another game." Ethan excused himself.

"You look nice," Dalton said when it was just the two of them.

Warmth spread up Leah's neck. "You look pretty handsome yourself." And he did. The dark suit accentuated his tall frame and reminded her how quickly she was losing her heart to him.

As they drove to the Zook farm, Leah couldn't stop thinking about Marge's reaction to her dream. She'd appeared to be arguing with Ellis about something. The times she'd seen Ellis and Marge disagree were few. She suspected they kept their arguments from her.

Leah remembered something Ellis had said to her once. He'd told her Marge was fragile. She'd had a hard life and he'd do whatever he could to spare her further heartache. Leah hadn't understood what he meant. She'd asked Ellis to explain, but he'd refused. Now she wondered if Ellis had kept something hidden about Marge.

"Everything okay?" Dalton's voice brought her from the past. She turned to stare into his eyes. The tenderness there washed over her.

"Yes. I'm just worried about Marge, I guess. It seems her periods of confusion are growing. It's bringing back a lot of bad things. And with her losing Ellis, well, it's almost as if she doesn't have a reason to hang on."

He gave her a curious look. "She has you."

Leah smiled. "Yes, she does. And I don't want to lose the only family I have left."

⸻

The funeral was simple and painfully familiar. Beth's pine casket had been set up near the windows in the Zooks' living room. Everyone in the Amish community and many locals from town had turned out to show their respect to the family.

The preacher moved to the front of the room near the casket, where he read the words to several hymns and quoted John 11:25: "Jesus said unto her, I am the resurrection, and the life: he that believeth in me, though he were dead, yet shall he live."

After the sermon, the preacher prayed.

Leah bowed her head. She couldn't get her family's funeral out of her head. Members of the community along with the Zook family had arranged everything. She still remembered leaning against Ellis and Marge, Colette holding her hand as she stood before the four coffins. Her body had gone through the motions, her mind numb.

"He's not here," Dalton whispered. "He probably guessed we'd be expecting him to show. Let's head back to the station."

They returned to their vehicle and left the funeral early. The trip back to the station was a silent one. The solemn ceremony had left Leah feeling emotionally drained. She wondered if Dalton felt the same way.

Her exhaustion seemed to go straight down to her soul. Each second seemed to tick off in her head. A constant reminder that what had begun ten years ago was quickly coming to a head. And she wasn't sure she was ready for the showdown that was to come.

fifteen

The door was locked. He knocked loud enough to catch the officer on duty's attention.

The man glanced up and eyed him curiously before he headed over and unlocked the door and stuck his head out. "Can I help you?"

He shoved the door open. The cop stumbled backward and grabbed for his gun, but not before John slammed the butt of his against the cop's temple. He dropped to the floor, out cold.

The dispatcher screamed and grabbed the phone. John crossed the room and knocked her out too. She dropped to the floor with a loud thud.

"Aunt Sugar?" Justine stepped from a room. The second she saw him she started running.

He charged down the hallway after her. "Oh no you don't." Reaching out, he snatched a handful of her hair, and she lost her balance and fell. Justine slid across the floor, but he lunged for her before she could get back on her feet. She flipped over on her back and kicked him hard.

Anger rose inside him at her reaction. She'd not only betrayed him but she was now trying to escape. How dare she.

John grabbed her leg and pinned it to the floor before sitting on both legs to keep her from kicking him again.

She clawed at his face. He snatched her flailing hands in one of his and smacked her hard. Her head bounced off the floor.

"You told them about me," he snarled, inches from her face. "You disappoint me, Justine." He pulled the knife from his pocket. Her eyes grew wide, and John smiled. This was the part he loved. Watching them realize their fate. It was exhilarating.

"No, please," she whimpered. Of course, she was weak like Beth. The others. Eva had tried to fight back, but she was no match for him. There was only one who was his equal, and he looked forward to the day when she would spar with him again.

"Please what? Don't kill you?" He laughed incredulously. "You told them about me, Justine. Now you'll see what I do to traitors."

She screamed at the top of her lungs. If someone heard her yelling, they'd come to investigate. Best do it fast. Sadly, there would be no time to savor her pain.

He clamped his hand over her mouth and fought past her hands with the knife slicing into her fingers. Her palms. And then he slashed the shiny blade across her throat, and she stopped fighting. John jumped to his feet, towering over her as she stared up at him with terror-filled eyes.

"That's what happens to traitors," he sneered as a tear slid down her face.

They turned onto the street in front of the station. Dalton parked in front.

"So what happens next?" Leah asked.

Something about the door caught his attention. It was open. He'd specially asked Sam to keep it locked.

Leah saw it too. She jumped from the vehicle and ran toward the door. Dalton unholstered his weapon and was right behind her.

Dalton stopped her before she went inside. "Let me go in first." He had to force the door the rest of the way open. As soon as he was inside, he realized why. Sam was unconscious and blocking the entrance.

Dalton knelt beside Sam. He'd been struck in the head, but he was alive. "Call an ambulance," he told Leah.

Where was Sugar? Justine?

A low-sounding moan answered his question. He eased toward the sound. Sugar lay on the floor, holding her head.

Dalton dropped down beside the dispatcher. "Don't try to move. You're hurt."

Sugar ignored him and tried to sit up. "Where's Justine?"

"Stay here, Sugar, and don't move." He looked to Leah, who informed him that an ambulance was on the way. He motioned for her to follow him, and they headed down the hall with their weapons drawn.

Near the conference room something moved.

Dalton couldn't get there fast enough. Blood splatter spread out around the young woman. Justine's frightened eyes latched onto his. She tried to speak but couldn't. Her throat had been cut.

He holstered his weapon and knelt. "I need something to stop the bleeding."

Leah sprang into action.

Dalton placed his hand over the wound and did his best to stem the blood flow. "Help is on the way. Try to stay calm."

"Here." Leah handed him a towel to cover the wound.

Through the chaos going around in his head, Dalton registered sirens approaching. Within minutes, the paramedics arrived and began working on Justine. Sugar and Sam hovered nearby, having waved off medical attention.

By the paramedics' skillful hands, Justine was quickly readied for transport.

"I'm going with her," Sugar insisted in a tone that dared anyone to protest.

"Go with them, Sam," Dalton told his officer.

Sam shook his head. "I should never have opened that door. This is my fault."

Dalton clasped Sam's arm. "This isn't on you," he assured the man. "Get yourself looked at and then stay with Justine. Leah and I will secure the crime scene until CSI arrives."

A single set of bloody footprints headed back toward the rear entrance. He indicated the tracks to Leah.

"The perp inadvertently stepped in Justine's blood," she said. "He left in a hurry."

Dalton nodded. "When we showed up, he had to vanish. He got sloppy and it probably saved Justine's life. We need to follow the footprints." Dalton locked the front door. "Let's see if we can catch him before he gets away." They carefully avoided contaminating the footprints as they left out the back. The footprints led to some trash bins. The killer had discarded his shoes inside.

"He could be anywhere," Leah said, her voice laced with frustration.

"I'm guessing he'll find another car to steal soon enough. Let's check the shops and then go back and wait for CSI to arrive. We'll turn the investigation here over to them."

No one at the shops remembered seeing anything unusual. Dalton and Leah gave each shop a thorough search, but there was no sign the killer had been at any of them.

They returned to the station as the CSI technicians arrived.

Leah appeared shell-shocked as they drove in silence to the hospital. Once they arrived, Dalton parked and faced her. "How are you holding up?"

She rubbed her hands across her arms. "I don't even know anymore."

More than anything, he wished he could end this for her, but Dalton had a feeling the killer had his own plans, and the game wouldn't end until he was ready for it to be done.

"Let's see how Justine is doing." He climbed out and went over to her side, opening the door. Together, they crossed the parking lot to the entrance and rode the elevator up to Justine's floor.

Sam stood guard outside Justine's room. His injuries had been treated.

"How are you feeling?" Dalton asked his officer.

"Other than a headache I'm fine. Justine is sleeping. The doctor who worked on her says she'll be okay."

Sugar heard them talking and stepped from the room, her head bandaged. "I sure am glad to see you both."

Leah gave Sugar a hug as they entered Justine's room, while Sam remained at his post by the door.

Justine's throat was bandaged. Spots of red had seeped through the white, a sharp contrast. Dalton clenched his fists. No matter what it took, he vowed to capture this cold-blooded psychopath and make him pay for the lives he'd destroyed.

"Doctor said there shouldn't be any permanent damage to her vocal cords. But he warned her against trying to speak for a while. This creep didn't take his time with her like he did the others, thankfully." Sugar's mouth twisted bitterly. "She's been out since they brought her to the room. They gave her a sedative to make her more comfortable, and it could be hours before she's awake."

"What happened, Sugar?" In all the chaos surrounding the attack, Dalton hadn't gotten her information. "Did you get a good look at the man?"

Sugar visibly shuddered. "I sure did. But he'd disguised his appearance. He wore sunglasses and a ball cap. And he was clean-shaven."

Dalton raked a hand across the back of his neck. The beard was part of the killer's disguise. John had been one step ahead of them at every turn. All his fault. He should have insisted on putting Justine in police protection instead of thinking she'd be safe at the station with Sam close.

"Justine's parents are on their way in now." Sugar's voice sounded brittle, as if she were about to cry. "I told them I would watch out for her. I'm a former cop myself."

Leah touched her arm. "I'm so sorry, Sugar."

Justine's parents rushed in. Her mother's hand flew to her mouth once she had a good look at her daughter. "Oh, my baby." Tears filled her eyes and rolled down her cheeks.

Sugar put her arm around her sister. "Justine is going to be all right. She'll have a scar, but the doctor said he'll send a plastic surgeon by later on to talk about options. She's alive. That's all that matters."

"Who did this, Chief?" Justine's father demanded. "Who hurt my little girl?"

"We believe it's the same man who killed the two Amish girls." Though it was of little comfort, Dalton assured him there would be an officer stationed outside of Justine's room at all times.

"Thank you. Please, find the person who did this. None of us will sleep until we know he's in custody."

His jaw flexed. "We will," he said gruffly. "Apprehending this killer and getting him off the streets is our top priority." He wasn't just making empty promises. Dalton wouldn't stop until they put an end to this man's reign of terror once and for all. "If I have your permission, I'd like to dump Justine's phone records and see if we can find anything that might help us with his name."

Justine's father readily agreed. "Whatever we can do to help."

Dalton shook the man's hand. "Thank you. We'll stop by later to check on Justine. She'll be in our prayers." With a final glance at the unconscious young woman, he stepped out into the hall, where Sam waited. "No one goes in without being identified. That includes medical personnel as well."

"You got it."

He and Leah headed down in the elevator. "He gave Justine the same fake name as Eva," Dalton said. "Probably Beth as well. So far, we haven't been able to get any prints belonging to him, or at least none that have led to anything."

They reached the ground floor and headed out into the fading day.

"But he's definitely afraid of something," Leah said. "Otherwise, why risk entering a police station in broad daylight to take out a witness?"

"Exactly." Dalton hit the key fob to unlock Leah's cruiser they'd used since his SUV had been destroyed. "We have permission to obtain Justine's phone records. Let's go back to the station and start on them." With the killer becoming more unhinged with each attack, and with Leah in his crosshairs, no one who stood in his way would be safe.

When they got to the station, CSI had finished their canvass and the building was locked up. Dalton unlocked the door and stepped inside with Leah.

"I'll start the paperwork to get Justine's phone records released to us," Leah said.

He reached for Leah's hand before she left. She slowly smiled, and some of his worry dissipated.

As much as he wanted to be out there on the streets involved in the search for the killer, if something happened to her because he wasn't being diligent . . . He sat down at his desk and stared at his laptop. Dalton couldn't get the two murders in Wyoming out of his head. He looked over to where Leah worked and marveled how she still managed to look so poised despite the madness swirling around them.

Dalton brought up the information on the two women and tried to focus. Both were young—probably sixteen or seventeen, according to the medical examiner. They were dressed simply. No identification found on them. Due to the state of decomposition, a forensic facial artist had created molds of what he believed the two women looked like. So far, no one had come to identify them. After so many years, he wondered if they would forever remain Jane Doe 10 and 11.

"I have Justine's records." Leah stopped in the doorway. Dalton's dark head was bent over his desk as he read something. She bit her bottom lip. So strong and courageous. He was fighting hard to bring the killer to justice for her. She had to stay strong. For him. "What do you have there?"

He held up one of the photos of the mold depicting Jane Doe 10. "Trying to figure out the connection between the two women in Wyoming and our killer." Dalton dropped the photo and leaned back in his seat with a heavy sigh. "Did you find anything in the phone records?"

"Not really. I've gone over them twice. It appears Justine just started seeing Jonathan two weeks ago." She handed him the records.

"And according to Eva's phone conversations, he's been here at least two months. He could have come back to kill Ellis and then left again, returning as the tenth anniversary got closer." Dalton scanned the page she'd given him. "Where's he staying? And how is he able to survive? He'd need money. Even if both his vehicles were stolen, he'd still have to find a way to eat. Buy gas."

Leah had thought the same. "There's been no reported break-ins or robberies. Someone could be giving him money, or he's stealing it."

She suddenly remembered the missing money at Marge's and felt sick. She told Dalton about the envelope. "I assumed Marge just misplaced it or some kids broke in and stole it, but what if it was John? Maybe when he left the envelope with the bullet enclosed, he stole some of Marge's money too."

Dalton slowly rose and crossed the room. "You think Marge let him in?"

"It's possible. She's trusting and . . ." Her condition was worsening.

"What about farm and ranch work?" she said when the idea popped in her head. "Most pay their day workers in cash." It would be a perfect way to obtain money for someone looking to keep their identity secret. "Some of the Amish hire extra help during the busy times." Which meant there would be no way to call the farm owners.

"There are an awful lot of farms around St. Ignatius, and we're stretched thin as it is." They couldn't afford to waste manpower on what could prove to be a dead end.

Like Dalton, she couldn't let go of the two dead women in Wyoming. "I've been thinking about the Wyoming connection and our Jane Does. What if our killer was in jail or hospitalized in that area? The women were probably runaways. Easy kills."

Dalton nodded. "I'll check in with law enforcement in the area and see if there are any prisons or hospitals around where the murders happened." He rubbed a hand down his tired face.

"You look like you could use some coffee," she said.

He smiled. "Sure. I need a little more acid in my stomach."

She chuckled. "I'll get it."

She returned with the two coffees. Through a window she could see the late-afternoon breeze rustling through the trees near the station. In the distance, long shadows reached their tentacles across the valley below the Mission Mountains.

"They're beautiful, aren't they? When I lived in Denver, I was surrounded by mountains and yet I rarely took the time to appreciate them."

Leah looked at him curiously. "Do you miss living in the big city?" Though the case pressed in around them, just for a moment, she wanted to have a simple discussion that had nothing to do with John.

Dalton laughed. "Not at all. My roots will always be here in this country."

She knew exactly what he meant. "I felt the same way when

I went away to college even though Missoula wasn't exactly huge. I couldn't wait to get home."

"I guess we're both small town people. Allison was just the opposite. She loved everything about Denver."

A comfortable silence fell between them.

"When was the last time you visited your family?" she asked softly.

"About six months ago for the holidays. Isaac and I went hunting together. We haven't done that in years—not since Harrison's death. It felt strange, but I'm glad we went."

"Do they know you're here?"

Dalton shook his head. "Not yet. I'm sure by now my family here will have heard. As soon as the case is over, I'll go see them. Hopefully be able to give them the answers they need at last." He faced her. "And you. You and I both need answers if we're ever going to be able to move on. I think God brought us together for a reason." The look in his eyes hinted at so much more than just the case.

"You really believe that?" Leah's faith had been faltering for a long time. She'd been angry with God for taking her family. Now, with two innocent women dead and Justine's life threatened, she questioned how God could allow so much pain. Her father's and mother's walk with God had been a shining example to Leah growing up. They believed everything that happened was God's will and for his purpose. But how could a benevolent God wish for so many people to die?

"I do," he said sincerely. "But it wasn't always the case. I grew up not believing in anything. After Isaac and Rachel took me in, I saw how God was there in every part of their lives, and I wanted that for myself. I don't think I would have been able to survive Harrison's death—and my wife's—if it hadn't been for clinging to God and his promises."

While Dalton had run to the shelter of God's presence in his time of trouble, Leah had done the opposite.

"I wish I could reach that place." She was so tired of blaming God. It had taken almost a year after the murders to be able to sleep in her bed and not curl up inside the closet with the light on. Just as long to stop expecting John to show up at Marge and Ellis's house and kill everyone.

Dalton touched her cheek, and Leah closed her eyes, her heart beating a crazy rhythm against her chest.

"You have to find a way to let go of the anger, Leah. Because it will eat you alive if you don't."

She swallowed several times, but the lump in her throat would not go away. Tears were close. No matter how hard she tried, she couldn't stop them.

He tucked her into his arms and rested his cheek against her head. Dalton made her feel safe. Leah hadn't felt this way in a long time. Probably not since she was a child when she'd wake up afraid and her daed would hold her and tell her everything would be oke. A dam broke inside, and Leah started crying. Dalton held her tighter without saying a word.

When the tears finally subsided, she let him go and scrubbed her palms across her cheeks. "I'm sorry." Her voice was as unsteady as she felt. "I'm not normally this emotional."

"Don't be." Dalton tipped her chin back and looked deep into her eyes. "You've lost so much."

"And I brought it all on my family." If she'd been a *gut* Amish girl, she wouldn't have let her head be turned by John.

Dalton's expression gentled. "No. You're a victim. Like Beth.

Eva. Those two women in Wyoming. Justine. It isn't your guilt to carry."

She so wanted to believe him. Something shifted in his eyes. Leah pulled in a breath as Dalton leaned down and touched his lips against hers. The breath evaporated from her body and she melted against him. Leah could count on one hand the number of times she'd been kissed. None of them compared to Dalton's gentle touch.

He ended the kiss and stepped back.

She could see the apology in his eyes, and she reached for his hand. "No, there's nothing to be sorry for. Just—thank you."

He searched her face. "Why are you thanking me?"

"Because you made me remember I'm human. I'd forgotten for a long time. So, thank you."

A slow smile spread across his face. "We should probably get back to work," he said with what sounded like a hint of regret in his voice.

As hard as she tried to focus on the case, Leah's thoughts were dominated by the man at her side. They were both damaged. Both victims of the same killer. Both trying to find a way to move beyond the past. Was it possible? Or would what John had done that fateful night be forever part of their DNA?

sixteen

"There's a state hospital not far from Cheyenne," Laramie County Sheriff Allen Tucker confirmed. And close to where their Jane Does were murdered.

"Can you tell me the name of the administrator?" Dalton grabbed a pen. It was a long shot, but perhaps the person in charge would remember someone who fit John's description.

"Hang on a second." Papers rustled and then, "Charles Hopkins." Tucker gave Dalton the number. "I sure hope he can be of assistance. Keep me posted. I'd love to help these two women's families find closure."

Dalton left a message for the administrator and set the phone down. Outside, dusk quickly approached. The case he should be working was the furthest thing from his mind. Leah had been occupying growing space there. Was what was happening between them real or simply because of their shared history? Guilt riddled his heart. Allison had been gone for five years, and yet every time he'd thought about moving on, he couldn't. She'd loved him completely. Tried to convince him to let go of his quest to find Harrison's killer. Many times, he wished he'd listened. The years he'd wasted chasing ghosts gnawed at him. Instead of doggedly pursuing leads that didn't pan out, he should have been at her side. Should have realized how sick she was becoming.

Someone tapped on his door. Leah stuck her head in.

Tension filled him as he looked at her. The kiss still fresh in his mind, he felt as if he'd betrayed Allison. "Yes, what is it?" His tone came out harsher than he intended.

"Is anything wrong?" she asked, the hurt in her voice clear. She came into the room.

Dalton ran a hand through his hair and felt like a heel. "No, nothing."

"I didn't mean to interrupt, but I'm on my way over to see Marge. She's been asking for me." When he didn't respond, she started from the room.

"Leah, wait." Dalton went after her and stopped her. "I'm sorry. I didn't mean to come off like a jerk. Guess I'm just dealing with my demons. I'm coming with you."

She slowly smiled. "It's okay." Her forgiveness made him feel worse. "Sylvia ordered chicken from the café across the street. I thought we could take it with us to Marge's."

"That's a good idea." Dalton gathered the files, and they stepped out into the growing darkness.

Leah's gaze swept the shadows near the station. "Believe it or not, until Beth's death, the county was quiet."

Dalton unlocked the vehicle and slid inside. "Quiet sounds good right about now."

On Marge's street, a new shift of law enforcement had arrived to relieve those watching the house.

Ethan met them at the door as they approached.

Leah held up the bag of food. "We brought you dinner. How's Marge doing?"

"She beat me at checkers five games to three."

Leah laughed. "Don't feel bad. That's her game. She beats me every time."

Marge saw the number of people in her kitchen and clasped her hands, a look of delight on her face. "It's been a while since there's been so many guests in my home. It reminds me of when I was just a girl and all the family would come to the house to celebrate the holiday."

Leah eyed her cautiously. "I didn't know you came from a large family."

Marge frowned, an uncertain look on her face.

Leah went over and hugged her close. "We brought dinner. Dalton and I will be here with you through the night."

"Oh, honey, I'm happy to have you here, but he won't hurt me."

Leah looked at Dalton in surprise. "Who won't hurt you?"

Her mom's expression clouded again as if she were trying to pull out the answer. "Well, no one. Not with you two here."

Was this just dementia? Or was Marge hiding something?

———

Leah couldn't get Marge's strange remark out of her head. *"He won't hurt me."*

Ethan scraped back his chair as he prepared to leave. The sound grated along Leah's nerves. She was on edge and expecting John to make another attempt to get to her. Had he found his next victim? The thought of another life being taken because John wanted to play games was heartbreaking. They'd alerted all the Amish families with teenage girls, but John was good at convincing innocent girls to trust him.

"I think I'll stop by the hospital and see our people, then go to the station and do a little work," Ethan told them. "I can catch some sleep there if I get tired. Finding this guy is the most important thing."

Dalton rose as well. "I'll walk you out." He turned to Leah. "Be right back."

Their voices faded down the hall. Leah gathered dishes and took them over to rinse.

Marge put the remains of the meal in the refrigerator. "The chicken was as good as always. Eliza and Ben are good people."

The Amish couple who ran the diner had been at the same location since Leah was a child. She'd gone to the Amish school with their two boys. "They are indeed." Leah finished the last of the dishes and closed the dishwasher. She went over to Marge and put her arm around her shoulders. "Want to play some checkers?"

Marge chuckled. "If you're sure you're up to losing."

Leah shook her head. Marge was vicious when it came to her checkers matches. "I heard you showed no mercy to Ethan."

"He's a seasoned police officer. He should be showing me mercy."

The checkerboard was set up and ready in Ellis's office.

But as hard as Leah tried to concentrate on the match, she was distracted.

Dalton stuck his head in the room. "Can I speak with you for a second?" She could tell from the eagerness in his eyes he'd found out something.

"Excuse me for a minute, Mom."

Marge looked up from the checkerboard. "What? Oh, sure, baby girl."

Leah stepped from the room and closed the door.

"I received a text from the administrator of a state hospital in Wyoming. He had a patient there by the name of Jonathan Stephens who was admitted around ten years earlier showing symptoms of schizophrenia."

Shock waves rippled through Leah's frame. "You're kidding."

"Nope. Stephens was prescribed medication and released. His symptoms appeared to worsen as he got older, and he was committed again after one particularly severe psychotic episode led to a mental breakdown. The doctor claims he never showed signs of violence to himself or toward anyone else, though."

"Still, the time frame fits. He could have been committed after the murders here. This is huge."

"Exactly." His excited tone confirmed there was more. "I spoke to Stephens's father, who told me he lives in Montana."

Her eyes widened. "He's here in Montana?"

"Near Helena with his wife and daughter. But get this— Jonathan Stephens's wife is named Marissa."

Leah stared at him and tried not to get her hopes up. "Wait, wasn't the registration on the truck a Marissa something?"

"Pennington. As soon as I got off the phone, I did a search. Marissa Pennington married Jonathan Stephens. I guess she never updated the registration on the truck."

"This is huge. This ties Jonathan Stephens to the truck."

"There's something else," he said. "Marissa reported her husband missing a couple of hours ago."

Leah's head swam with the new information. "Could this be our guy?"

"It's possible, but we can't get ahead of ourselves. His wife said Stephens received a call from a friend here in St. Ignatius and told her he had to go and help him out. He said he'd be back in a few days. When those days passed, she became worried and tried to call him without any answer. That's why she reported him missing."

"I can't believe it," Leah said. "It finally feels like we may be getting somewhere."

"I sure hope so. I notified the chief of police in Helena, and he's getting a warrant to dump Stephens's phone records. Let's see if he actually received a call or if he made the whole thing up to give him an excuse to return to St. Ignatius. We're getting closer, Leah. I can feel it."

Leah pulled in a breath and prayed this might really be the beginning of the end. "I should get back to Marge. She loves her checkers and especially loves beating me."

He laughed. "From what Ethan said, I don't want to take her on."

Dalton's phone beeped, and he glanced down at it. His smile disappeared. "I requested Stephens's DMV photo." As he continued to stare at the image, Leah's heart sank. "This doesn't look like our guy." Leah leaned in close to examine it.

The man in the photo resembled the John she knew but . . . Her heart sank. "This isn't John."

Dalton's mouth thinned. "So much for a breakthrough." He sighed. "Still, I'm wondering if Stephens may be somehow connected to our killer. I mean, the name is too close to be a coincidence in my book. If they were at the same state hospital, it's possible they became friends. Maybe our killer has been using Stephens's ID and Stephens found out about it." His gaze locked onto Leah's. "Stephens may have been trying to help our killer."

"And he could be in danger."

Dalton agreed. "I'm going to see if I can get some more information on him."

While he did that, Leah returned to Marge.

"Everything okay?" her mother asked.

"Yes, it is." And it was. Though Jonathan Stephens might not be their killer, he could help them identify him. She was finally starting to feel hopeful again, her heart softening over the possibilities of a future without the shadow of the past dragging her down.

She and Marge were on their second game when Dalton came into the room.

"There's my boy." Marge exclaimed with an odd smile on her face that worried Leah.

Dalton froze and shot Leah a startled look.

"Marge, this is Dalton."

Her mom's mouth opened and closed. Tears hovered in her eyes. "My boy isn't here."

Leah watched Marge with a sinking feeling in the pit of her stomach. "You don't have a boy, remember?"

"Yes, I do." Marge flashed anger her way. "But he had to go away."

Shock waves rippled through Leah. "When did he go away?"

Marge focused hard. Clarity slowly returned to her eyes. She touched her hand to her head. "What?"

"You said your son had to go away. I didn't know you had a son."

Her mom grew more confused. "Honey, I don't have a son. You know that."

Leah wanted to press for answers, but Marge looked ready to drop. "You should go up to bed. It's been a long day."

Tears fell from the older woman's eyes. "You are such a good girl. I don't know what I would do without you."

"Get some rest. I'll see you in the morning."

Marge slowly rose. "Okay, honey." She shuffled from the room as if she had doubled in age.

Leah waited until she heard her labored footsteps heading up the stairs before she moved to the sofa. "Why would she think she has a child?"

She remembered the few times she and Ellis had spoken about personal things. He'd told her that he and Marge hadn't been able to have children of their own.

"Do you think she's mixing up memories?"

If this were the first time, Leah might have dismissed the claim. "Possibly, but this is the second time she's mentioned having a child."

Dalton claimed the spot beside her.

"What do you know about Ellis's and Marge's past?"

She thought about the few things they'd told her through the years. "Not much, really. Ellis told me they'd met when he first became a cop." Leah clamped her hand against her forehead. "I can't believe I didn't remember this before. Ellis mentioned once that he and Marge had lived in Wyoming at one time. In a small town."

"Wyoming. That's a pretty big coincidence. Is it possible we've been looking at this all wrong and the killings are in some way related to their past?"

She didn't want to believe it. "I don't see how."

"We could do some checking into Marge's background. See what we can find out."

Was she searching for problems that didn't exist? Marge's memory had been fading since Ellis's passing. Her doctor had told Leah that sometimes a traumatic experience could worsen dementia.

"I'll call her doctor tomorrow and tell him about it. But yes, in the meantime, I think we should check into her background. Just to be sure." What if Marge *was* telling the truth? Leah might have a brother out there somewhere. "It's hard watching her fade before my eyes. I feel like I'm letting Ellis down, but I don't know how to help her."

He placed his hand over hers. "You are helping her. She depends on you."

Leah leaned her head back against the sofa. "I don't want to think about . . ." She didn't finish but he seemed to understand. He put his arm around her, and she leaned against him. It had been a hard year coming on the heels of nine heartbreaking ones. Still today, after so long, when she closed her eyes, she could see her family before that night. Happy. Hardworking. Her brother and sister learning the ways of the Amish. All the good memories were returning that for so long had been tainted by that night. She turned her head to him. "I'm sorry about Harrison. If he and I hadn't become friends . . ."

Dalton brushed her hair back. "Don't go there, Leah. One day, I hope we can figure out why Ellis chose to make Harrison the bad guy. There must be an explanation. But this isn't on you. *None* of it is on you."

She leaned her head against his shoulder and closed her eyes. The weight of the past few days settled around her. The exhaustion seemed to bear down past flesh and bone, marrow and sinews, deep into her very soul. With John still out there, her soul wouldn't find rest until he was stopped. "I feel like we should be doing something," she murmured and felt him smile.

"Me too. For now the best thing we can do is get some shut-eye. Start fresh in the morning. Hopefully after a good night's sleep we'll see something that we may have overlooked before."

Dalton rose and pulled her up beside him. "Get some sleep. I think I'll bunk down here."

Leah stifled a yawn. "I'll see you in the morning." Before she turned away, he captured her hand. The look in his eyes made her heart go crazy.

"Good night, Leah." He let her go.

Before turning in, Leah checked in on Marge. Her mother had turned on her side, her steady breathing a sign she'd fallen asleep.

Leah gently closed the door and returned to her room. She lay down on the bed fully clothed, her mind racing. Dalton and Marge mingled in her thoughts. She turned on her side. Why would Marge think she'd had a child? Was it all connected to dementia? Maybe she'd wanted a child of her own.

Closing her eyes, Leah couldn't get her mom's strange sentiment out of her head.

She grabbed her phone and called the office of the doctor who was treating Marge and left a message. It might be time for some adjustments to Marge's medication. On an impulse, Leah asked the doctor if Marge had ever given birth to a child.

After ending the call, she stared up at the ceiling, the phone resting on her stomach. As much as her body craved sleep, her mind refused to shut off. Every single detail of what had happened since the team found Beth's body played on a loop in her head. John had waited ten years to finish the game he'd started with her, and nothing would stand in his way no matter how much Dalton and the rest of law enforcement tried to protect her.

Leah turned off the light and squeezed her eyes tight. She should take advantage of the time to rest while she had it. She'd need to be sharp for what lay ahead.

The faintest of sounds had her eyes jerking open. Leah glanced at her phone now lying on the bed. Several hours had passed. She must have fallen asleep, but something had awakened her. Leah searched the darkness. Just the house making its noises, Marge used to say when Leah would wake up scared by some sound. Yet the fear chasing down her spine wouldn't let her go back to sleep. She sat up and swung her legs over the side of the bed. She reached for her weapon. It wasn't there. Before she could scream for Dalton, a hand clamped over her mouth, stifling the scream.

"Hello, Leah," he whispered and pulled her up beside him. The voice was the same as in her nightmares. His hot breath spread across her cheek. "Did you enjoy what I did to Justine? Did it remind you of what I did to your family?" An eerie laugh followed. "Are you ready for our big moment? It's so close." He breathed out an excited breath.

She listened for any sign that Dalton might be awake. But she heard nothing. *My phone*. She couldn't reach it.

John realized what she was thinking and snatched it up. "Oh no. You weren't going to try and warn him, were you?" Excitement flowed through each word.

The familiar feel of the knife sent her back to that time, and her fear spiraled out of control.

"Don't worry," he whispered once more as the knife glided over her skin. "It's not time for you to die yet, but *soon.*"

Something soft and pungent replaced his hand. A cloth soaked in chemicals. She clawed at it, trying to free herself. Time slipped by in slow motion while the sickly smell invaded her senses. Slowly, she felt herself losing consciousness, and there was nothing she could do.

Leah fought with all her waning strength, but whatever

he'd used to knock her out was too strong. The last thing she remembered was the kiss he planted on her cheek before she collapsed against the bed. And then the darkness that overtook her.

Dalton jerked awake. Someone was moving around upstairs.

He jumped to his feet and flew through the doorway. After taking the stairs two at a time, he reached Leah's room. "Leah, are you awake?" No sound came from inside. He jerked the door open and flipped on the light. Leah lay on the bed without moving. He saw a drop of blood on her bedspread and then a small nick on her neck. Dalton glanced around the room. No one was there.

He rushed to her side and shook her. "Leah! Are you okay?"

Her eyes slowly opened. She stared at him before terror filled her face. "He was here, Dalton." She slurred the words out and tried to sit up. "John. He was here."

She touched her neck and saw the blood. "He was just here. We have to go after him."

"Let's get you to Marge's room. I'll check the house." He helped her to her feet and hurried her along to Marge's room. Dalton opened the door and ushered her inside the bedroom. The woman sat up in bed and stared at the door as they came inside.

"It's okay. I'm with Leah." He did his best to explain what happened. "Lock the door and stay here while I check the rest of the house."

Dalton systematically cleared each room. At the end of the upstairs hallway, he saw that the door to the attic was open. With his weapon ready, he climbed the stairs and clicked on the light. A light breeze blew the curtains over an open window. John had come this way.

Dalton slipped through the window and carefully walked across the roof until he reached the lowest part near Marge's neighbor's home. Nothing was visible. This was how the killer got away. He probably had a car stashed somewhere close by. Dalton alerted the deputies outside and called for backup before returning to Leah.

Dalton knocked on Marge's door, and Leah opened it. "I'll be right back," she told Marge and stepped out beside him.

Dalton's gaze landed on the cut on her throat. "If anything happened to you, I'd never forgive myself."

"I'm okay, Dalton. Just a little scared."

Sirens filled the still night.

He told her that he believed the killer had slipped out through the attic and had somehow managed not to alert the deputies. "We need to search the area in case he's still around." He waited until she'd locked up before he went outside to where Sam, Ethan, and other law enforcement had arrived. "Check the street behind the house. He entered through the attic window and jumped from the roof into the neighbor's yard."

Dalton went back inside to where Leah waited for him.

"We have people looking for him. Tell me what happened."

She told him about falling asleep. "Something woke me. I reached for my weapon, but it was gone." She shuddered. "He covered my mouth with his hand so I couldn't scream and then he put the knife to my throat. That's how I got this." She touched her throat and winced. "He kept talking about the anniversary, and I could tell he was excited about it." She swallowed several times. "And then he put a cloth over my mouth and nose, and it knocked me out."

He frowned. "Like chloroform?"

"I'm guessing so. It had a sweet smell, like the disinfectants used at hospitals or doctors' offices."

Chloroform wasn't allowed to be sold to individuals. If it was indeed the chemical used to knock Leah out, John would have taken it from somewhere. Tracking down where John had gotten it from would be difficult.

Dalton indicated the cut on her throat. "Let me take a look at that." He clasped her hand and led her to the kitchen and onto the closest chair. He brought a damp cloth over and carefully cleaned the blood from the wound before inspecting it. It was almost right on top of the original one.

"It's not so bad," he assured her. The wound was about an inch in length and had barely broken the skin's surface.

"Thanks," she said once he'd applied some antibiotic ointment. She held up trembling hands. "I can't believe he was so brazen."

"I'm just relieved you're okay." Dalton sat beside her and gathered her cold hands in his. "How's Marge?"

"Terrified," she choked out. "This is the last thing she needs."

"I know, and I'm sorry."

Dalton's cell phone rang, and he picked it up off the table. "It's Sam." He answered the call.

"We're still searching, but it looks as if he might have gotten away."

"Unbelievable." Dalton shoved a hand through his hair. "He used something to knock Leah out. We don't know how long she was unconscious. In other words, he had a head start. Keep looking. We need to find this guy."

"Sure thing, Chief. If he's still around, we'll get him."

"Thanks, Sam." Dalton glanced up as Marge entered the kitchen, anxiously searching the room for her daughter.

"Oh, Leah . . ." Tears flowed from Marge's eyes.

———

Leah scraped back her chair and rushed to the woman's side. "You're safe. He's gone."

Marge touched Leah's throat as the tears rolled down her face. "He hurt you. He hurt my baby girl."

"No, it's just a scratch. It's not like before."

Her mom's nervous hands fluttered all around. "But he wants to."

Leah gathered her close. "Maybe. We're just not going to let him."

Marge wept in her arms. After everything her mother had been through, Leah wished she could be spared having to go through this, but this was just another part of John's game. Making those around her suffer.

A knock at the back door startled Leah. Her nerves were on edge, and Dalton noticed.

"It's probably Sam." He went to answer the knock.

Both Sam and Ethan came inside. "We're still looking, but it isn't good," Ethan said. "My guess is he had a vehicle. Patrols are canvassing every street around the neighborhood. We'll head back out now and help with the search. We just wanted to update you in person."

"Thank you both. Keep me posted."

———

Dalton knew it was no longer safe for the women to stay here. He went back to the kitchen, where Leah and Marge talked quietly at the table.

"I think it's best if we move you and Marge to another location until this is over." He expected pushback from Leah, but Marge rejected the idea immediately. "I won't leave my home. No, sir. Not under any circumstance."

Leah clasped her mom's hands. "It won't be for long. Just until we catch this man."

Marge pulled her hands free and jumped to her feet. "I won't leave. Don't ask me again." She stormed from the room, leaving both Dalton and Leah watching in shock.

"I'll go after her," Leah said.

"I'm sorry about upsetting her. But you and I both know it's not safe to be here after what happened."

Leah touched his arm. "You're right, but her doctor told me being at a place that's familiar helps with the memories. Change is hard for her."

With a resigned sigh, Dalton placed his hands on her shoulders. "All right, but I want as many law enforcement officers as we can spare here with her at all times."

"Thank you," she said and left the room.

Dalton sank onto one of the chairs and put his head in his hands. "God, I need you. I don't know what to do next."

He was trying so hard to stay strong, but there was so much coming at them that it was difficult to see the next move clearly. He exhaled wearily. Leah, Marge, and this entire community were counting on him to keep them safe. But what if he couldn't? Slowly pushing to his feet, Dalton decided to make a pot of coffee because he wasn't going back to sleep anytime soon.

Afterward, he returned to the room where he'd slept, set his steaming mug aside, and pulled out his laptop. He wanted to know more about Jonathan Stephens. According to what little was available on the internet, Stephens had been married for nine years. He owned an insurance business and was by all accounts a pillar of the community.

Dalton typed a message to Sugar. He hoped Justine could settle the matter for him.

A few seconds later, his phone rang.

"I hope I didn't wake you." Dalton realized it was almost midnight.

"Oh no, I can't sleep. All I can think about is what happened."

He felt the same way. "Did Justine have a chance to look at the photo of Jonathan Stephens?"

Sugar sighed into the phone. "She did, and she's never seen the guy. It's not the man she was seeing."

His heart sank. "That's what Leah said as well." Dalton wasn't even sure why he felt the need to ask Justine. He hadn't really expected a different answer.

"Is there anything new with the case?" Sugar asked.

Dalton hated having to tell Sugar about the attack on Leah but reluctantly filled her in.

"Is she okay? I can't imagine how terrifying that must have been."

"She's fine. Both she and Marge are pretty shaken up."

Sugar made a clicking sound with her tongue. "We need this guy off the streets before he can hurt anyone else."

"Amen to that. Call if you need anything."

Someone entered the room. Dalton turned and saw Leah. After everything she'd gone through, did she even realize how strong and beautiful she was? "How's Marge?" he asked while clearing his throat.

"Upset. Still refusing to leave her home."

"I'm sorry. I sent Ethan back to the station but Sam and the two deputies are still outside. They'll stay through the night and then I'll make other arrangements to ensure there are people with her at all times."

Leah smiled wearily. "I appreciate that."

Her smile stirred something deep inside. Something he couldn't quite put a name to.

"What are you working on now?" She pointed to the laptop.

He struggled to bring his focus back to the case. "Stephens's phone records came in." He had them pulled up on his laptop. "According to the sheriff, the wife said he received a call from a friend several days ago." He scrolled through the report. "I don't see the number for the killer's burner phone." The sheriff had made notes on the numbers that belonged to the family.

"Just calls to and from his wife and his parents. And to his office." Leah sounded discouraged. "If his friend called for help, he didn't use this phone."

"Maybe he called Stephen's work number."

"It's possible." Leah sighed wearily.

"Do you mind if we talk about Marge for a second?" he said quietly.

Leah sat beside him. "Of course not. What do you want to know?"

"I've been thinking about her claim of having a child. Do you think there's a chance she was remembering correctly?"

Leah frowned. "I don't see how. Ellis would have mentioned it if they had a son."

"What if he wasn't the father?"

She searched his face for a long moment. "You think she had a baby before she and Ellis married?"

"Maybe. I realize this has nothing to do with what's happening, but we have several hours before we can call Stephens's family, and I need something to distract me." Dalton ran a hand through his hair. "I'm thinking Marge had a child, and she either had to give it up for adoption or maybe it died. If we can find out for sure—if the child lived and was adopted—maybe we could give Marge some closure that she did the right thing for the baby."

"That's sweet. She could use something positive. I left a message for her doctor to see if he can tell me if Marge had a child. But what if we find out it's bad news? What if the baby died?"

"We'll know for certain. We don't have to share the bad news with her," he said gently. "When did Ellis and Marge marry anyway?"

She leaned back against the sofa. "They celebrated their twentieth wedding anniversary a couple of months before Ellis died."

"You had said Ellis and Marge lived in a small community in Wyoming. Do you know where?"

"Not really. They didn't like to talk much about their past. I assumed it was family problems. Maybe their parents hadn't approved of the marriage. There was never any family to visit at the holidays. After coming from an Amish background where the family get-togethers were important, it seemed odd, but they were happy. I do know they lived in Missoula after Wyoming."

"What about Marge's maiden name?"

She shook her head. "I'm sorry, I'm not much help. Marge is short for Margaret. Ellis called her that once." Leah looked around the room. "Maybe there's something here. Ellis kept all his important papers in his file cabinet."

Leah went over and tried to open it, but it was locked. "Hang on." She looked under a ceramic bear and retrieved the key. After unlocking the cabinet, she opened the first drawer while Dalton peered over her shoulder.

"These look like a bunch of old cases." She flipped through the files and replaced them. The bottom drawer contained a single folder. The label on it grabbed Dalton's attention right away. It was marked "Personal."

Leah pulled it out and looked inside. "Ellis's birth certificate." She held Dalton's gaze a second. "He was born in Crook County. Isn't that in Wyoming?"

"It is."

The next document was their marriage certificate. "Margaret Beiler." Dalton read the name aloud. He leaned forward, a sliver of excitement running through his body. "Let's see if we can find any record of a Margaret Beiler from Wyoming having a child." He grabbed his laptop once more and searched records in the area. "I'm not finding any record of a birth."

"Maybe the birth wasn't recorded," Leah told him.

If Marge hadn't wanted anyone to know she had a baby—and from her silence on the subject, it seemed that was the case— then it made sense.

"Private adoption records are usually sealed," Leah murmured to herself. "There would be no way of checking."

Dalton could see the idea was unsettling to her. "Let's table this for another time."

She turned his way, and inches separated them. More than anything he wanted to kiss her. Did she feel the same way? They stared at each other for the longest time.

"Leah," he whispered. She dropped her gaze. He tipped her chin toward him. "I think we need to talk about what's happening between us."

Color filled her cheeks. "Dalton . . ."

"I'm not going to deny I have feelings for you, but the timing—it feels off," he said with regret.

She slowly agreed. "I care for you too." A sad expression crossed her face. "More than I've ever cared for another man. But we have to finish this case for both of us. Once and for all, we have to bring justice to those who gave up so much."

He'd been so close he could smell her hair. See the scar on her throat. He enjoyed toying with her. Letting her know there was nothing her chief could do to stop him. Leah's strength crumbled around him. Her fear excited him.

The time was coming soon when he and Leah would meet again for the last time.

He drove away from the house where he was squatting. The thrill of killing called out. He would need to assuage that desire soon.

The Amish community spread out before him. He didn't use headlights because there was added police presence. He parked the car some distance from where it all began.

Getting out, he made his way through the trees until he caught glimpses of the barn through the leaves. Faint voices drifted his way. Police officers were stationed nearby.

"Foolish." They wouldn't stop him.

He sniffed the air. Could almost smell the blood again. But he had his eye on another one just as innocent. Ready to do whatever he told her to do.

He went back to the car and drove to her house. Close to the same age as the others and just as eager to experience life. She thought him interesting. She'd told him that law enforcement had warned all the Amish families with girls between sixteen and eighteen about the Englisch killer on the loose. But that hadn't stopped her from falling prey to his charm. He'd gotten past her reserve so easily. She believed everything he told her.

He parked the car down the street from her home and sent her a message. She didn't make him wait for long. Despite the darkness, her white bonnet shone like a lantern as she climbed from the window and down the tree by her room. She hit the ground with a thud. Some distance from the house, she ran toward him. Her eagerness made him laugh.

He reached for her hand and smiled at the way she turned away and giggled.

"I cannot stay long. They might check my room."

"We should take advantage of the time we have." He tugged her close. She appeared embarrassed, and he marveled at how simple it was to persuade these girls to do whatever he wanted.

"Do you want to take a walk?" she asked shyly.

He laughed, and her brow furrowed. She didn't understand, but she would soon enough. He entwined his fingers with hers. "Yes, let's take a walk."

They started down the dirt road hand in hand.

"I like your car. Will you give me a ride in it one day?"

"How about tomorrow?" He'd find a way to take her to his favorite place, and he would see that look of sweet anticipation turn to abject terror before his eyes. He couldn't wait.

"Why can we only see each other at night?"

Her question surprised him. "Because I work during the day."

"What do you do for work?"

He thought about what he might have done, had he been granted the opportunity afforded to others.

"I'm a carpenter."

Her eyes lit up. "Oh, such a nice job! My uncle is a carpenter too. Perhaps you know him." She rattled off a name.

"Sorry, I don't."

They reached the end of the road where it turned onto a county road. She stopped. "Well, I should head back. My mamm and daed are being overprotective. They are worried after what happened . . ." She didn't finish, but he knew what she meant. If she blabbed about him to anyone, it would be all over.

"I can understand. Perhaps you shouldn't tell them about us. Let it be our secret."

She stopped walking. "But why?" She clutched his hand tight. "I want to go away with you. I am tired of the Amish ways."

"Soon, but for now we must keep our love secret; otherwise, your parents would try to stop us."

She sighed and shook her head. "I won't let that happen. I won't let them take you from me."

They reached his car once more. It amused him how passionate the young were and how easily manipulated. "Then keep this our secret for now."

seventeen

ugar stuck her head into Dalton's office. "Someone's here to see you both." She stepped inside and closed the door. "A woman—she's Amish—just walked in with her daughter. She said she had to speak with Leah Miller or the new chief about the murders."

Leah's heart jumped to her throat. "Where are they?"

"In the conference room. You want me to send them this way?"

"No, we'll go to them."

Sugar opened the door and stepped out. Leah and Dalton exchanged a troubled look before they followed Sugar to the conference room.

Two women sat at the long table. The deep-set traveling bonnets covering their prayer kapps prevented Leah from seeing their faces. Clasped hands on the table gave them a prayerful look.

"They'll be more comfortable speaking with you," Dalton told her.

"All right." Leah stepped inside the room with Dalton. Both women turned quickly. She recognized the older of the two.

Esther Lapp. The young woman seated beside her was the spitting image of Esther right down to the same golden blond hair.

Esther's troubled eyes shot between Leah and Dalton before she rose. "Leah, I believe the man who killed Beth and Eva has been talking to my Willa." She turned back to the young girl, who remained seated, her attention on her hands. "We were warned about this terrible man. *You* were warned. He could have killed you. Tell her what has been happening."

Willa's shoulders quaked. She turned tearful eyes to Leah. "H-he isn't that bad man. He isn't. I tried to tell Mamm so, but she wouldn't listen."

Leah pulled out the chair beside Willa. "Why don't you tell me about him? What's his name?"

"He told me his name is Scott and he'd come here to visit family." Her pleading eyes held Leah's. "He has light brown hair, and he is a carpenter. Scott isn't the one who killed Beth and Eva."

The description wasn't close to John's. Was Esther mistaken? "Willa, can you tell me how you two met?" Leah kept her tone friendly, as if she and Willa were simply having a conversation.

A dreamy smile spread across her face. "I had problems with the buggy wheel. It came loose. He helped me fix it." She turned to Esther. "He is kind, Mamm. He would never hurt me."

Esther's mouth tightened. "He has encouraged you to sneak around behind our backs. To disobey us. He is not a *gut* man." She reached into her apron pocket. "And he gave her this, so she could call him. I found it tucked under her mattress." She brought out a small cell phone. It fit with John's MO.

"How long have you been seeing this man, Willa?" Dalton asked.

Willa twisted her hands in her lap. "For a few weeks."

The timeline definitely overlapped when Beth and Eva were seeing John, as well as Justine. He'd been seeing them all at the same time.

"Do you mind if we keep the phone?" Leah addressed the question to Esther.

She shoved it at her. "*Jah*, take it. It is not part of our ways, and I do not want my daughter having it."

Dalton retrieved an evidence bag and placed it inside. "Thank you, Mrs. Lapp."

"When are you supposed to see this Scott again?" Leah asked the distraught young woman.

"T-tonight, but we have not set a time. He will contact me when he is able."

Leah touched the girl's shoulder. "Listen to me, Willa." The young woman turned troubled eyes her way. "He isn't who you think. You believe Scott would never hurt you, but both Beth and Eva were given phones by an Englischer to have a way to contact them. He had them meet him at night without anyone knowing. He killed them. He is *not* a good man."

Leah showed Willa the picture of John. "Is this the man you've been seeing?"

An expression of disbelief froze on Willa's face. She slowly nodded. "His hair is a different color, but jah, it is."

Leah could tell the young woman still didn't want to believe. She had to find a way to convince her that her life was in danger.

Leah pulled her shirt away from her scar. "The same man did this to me. He told me he loved me just like he did you."

Willa stared at the bright red scar.

"He said his name was John. Ten years ago, I was a young Amish girl like you, and I believed him like you, and I fell for what he told me." She glanced up at Dalton. The encouragement

243

she saw in him helped her go on. "He talked me into sneaking around behind my parents' backs. When he asked me to leave with him, I was afraid. I couldn't do it. He came back later that evening and he killed my entire family." She stopped. Saying the words aloud never got easier. "He's the one who killed Beth and Eva, and he will do the same to you, Willa, because he is not the person he claims to be."

The girl shrank back as if Leah had struck her. "He said he cares for me."

"He doesn't. He's very sick and dangerous. You cannot see him again."

Willa brushed her cheeks and looked up at her mother. "I am sorry, Mamm."

Esther's expression softened, and she gathered her daughter close. "It is *oke*, *kinna*." She looked over Willa's head to Leah. "What if this man tries to come after my child?"

"I'll have someone stationed outside your house," Dalton told her. "But Willa, you mustn't meet this man again. No matter what."

Willa slowly nodded. "I won't."

"How does he contact you? Does he mostly call or text?" Leah asked.

"He texts me usually."

"Good. That helps. Stay here while we arrange to have an officer see you home." Leah squeezed Willa's arm. "You did the right thing."

They stepped out into the hall and moved out of earshot. "When he reaches out to her, we'll arrange a meet," Leah said.

Dalton turned toward her. "That was brave of you to tell her your story. I'm not sure she would have believed us if you hadn't opened up."

"Thanks to you. I don't know if I would have talked about what happened if you hadn't been there with me."

While Leah sent the Amish women on their way, Dalton arranged for two of the tribal police to follow them home.

The burner phone given to Willa rested in the plastic evidence bag.

"I'll dust for prints, but I'm guessing all we'll find are Willa's and her mother's."

Leah watched the buggy disappear while heat vapors rose off the street, reminding Leah of the day this had all begun again. The first time she'd met Dalton. The day she showed up at the Zooks' home to find their pasts were about to collide dead-on with a killer.

Now, it seemed as if things were quickly coming to a head, but would she survive another showdown with John? Though she'd thought herself strong, Leah realized she'd been living in fear. Knowing somehow John would come back. Finish what he started all those years earlier. But she was different. She wasn't that scared little girl any longer. She wasn't about to let the man who had ruined so many lives escape his reckoning this time.

***

"Chief, we have a situation." Sugar's tone was the first thing to alert Dalton something was wrong.

Dalton faced his senior dispatcher. "Go ahead."

"A couple of hikers found a body up in the mountains. Tribal police are on their way there now since the mountain territory falls in their jurisdiction, but I thought you would want to know."

"What do you know so far?" Dalton's eyes met Leah's. A tempest of doubt raged in hers.

"Not much. Two people out hiking stopped to take in the view and saw a body instead. They were shaken up pretty bad. Not sure if it was a man or woman. They said all they saw were legs."

Dalton rose and retrieved his weapon. "We're on our way there now."

"Do you think he's killed someone else?" Leah whispered as she followed him outside.

"We don't know that yet. Let's not get ahead of ourselves." Dalton climbed inside Leah's cruiser. "Is it normal to have hikers die up in the mountains?"

She shifted his way. "Not usually. But it does happen every couple of years or so."

Dalton slipped on his sunglasses against the glare of the day.

Heat waves rose off the hood of the vehicle as they headed toward the mountains. Was the deceased person just a coincidence? If this case had taught him anything, it was that *everything* had meaning.

He eased the cruiser to a stop at the trailhead, where multiple police and rescue vehicles were parked. He and Leah started up the mountain trail.

"This is one of the easier paths," she said with a frown. "It's wide, and I can't imagine anyone falling unless they were intoxicated."

They walked some distance before they reached the spot where the body was found. The tribal chief spotted them and came over.

"Have you been able to identify the deceased yet?" Leah asked.

Chief Perez shook his head. "There was no ID on the body. He's a white male with dark hair. Average build. About your height." The chief indicated Dalton.

"Any cause of death yet?"

"Not yet. The ME believes complications related to the fall, but come with me."

They followed the chief over to the stretcher holding the deceased man. The men carrying the body stopped. Chief Perez lifted the covering.

Leah stared into the face of the man they had been searching for. "That's Jonathan Stephens."

Decomp had begun.

They'd been looking for a dead man.

Chief Perez lowered the cover once more, and the emergency personnel took the body away.

The medical examiner came over. "As soon as we have anything, I'll let both offices know. So far, it's looking like an accident."

"Take a closer look, Doc," Dalton told him. "We believe this man may have known our killer. If that's the case, then I seriously doubt this is an accident."

"I understand, but proving it might be difficult." The ME followed the emergency personnel down the mountain.

"This keeps getting more tangled," Chief Perez said as he walked with them to their vehicles.

"Yes, it does, and it's a long way from being over." Leah scanned the sunlit countryside.

He was out there somewhere. Waiting for Leah.

The chief shook their hands and headed after his people while Leah and Dalton got into the cruiser.

"What now?" The desperation in her tone mirrored what he felt.

"It seems like he's one step ahead of us at every turn." Dalton stared out the windshield at the activity around them.

Leah blew out a weary sigh. "He isn't invincible, Dalton. We can't give up."

He clasped her hand. Slowly smiled. "You're right. We'll get him. Together, we'll get him. Once the ME confirms the identity of our deceased, we'll call the sheriff in the family's area, and they can make the notification. I'm sure they'll have questions."

"I feel terrible for them." She rolled her shoulders. "The wife said Jonathan was meeting with a friend here. And we can assume that was the killer."

"We need to figure out how they met. If they were in the state hospital at the same time, that would make sense. Maybe the wife might know."

"How do we find out who Jonathan hung out with so long ago?" Leah asked. "Chances are that wouldn't be in any of his records. Let's show the sketch to Dr. Hopkins. Maybe he can point us to someone who remembers Stephens from back then and may have an idea who he palled around with. I know it's a long shot."

He shook his head. "No, it's something."

She leaned back against the headrest. Leah was barely hanging on, and he was worried. When the clock struck midnight tonight, it tolled that fateful day. The tenth anniversary of that night. Dalton had literally hours to find John's true identity before he found a way to fulfill his promise to finish what he started ten years earlier.

eighteen

Someone knocked on the window near where Leah sat, and she bit back a scream.

Chief Perez stood beside the cruiser holding a plastic bag.

Leah rolled the window down.

"Sorry, I didn't mean to startle you, but one of my men found this." He handed the bag to Leah. "Looks like a .38. That matches the gun used in Ellis's murder, doesn't it?"

Leah swallowed at the sight of the familiar weapon. "It's Ellis's Ruger."

"Are you certain?" Dalton asked, taking the bag from her.

"I'm positive."

"Chief Perez, I'd like to take this to the lab for testing," Dalton said.

The chief nodded his head. "Let me know what you find." He tapped the side of the cruiser and then headed back up the mountain path.

Leah shivered as the bright sunlight of the day vanished behind a cloud and a chilly breeze swept through the vehicle. As if even the weather were witness to the horror coming.

The mountains before her disappeared and she was back

there in the barn again. Crying uncontrollably and terrified as John killed each person in her family. As he taunted her and then let her live for this moment. She swallowed and ducked her head, willing the images of her family to die away.

"Leah." Dalton's voice was so gentle. He put his arm around her shoulders and pulled her close to him.

She struggled to keep from falling apart. She couldn't show weakness. She had to finish the game.

"Let's take a break to clear our heads." Dalton let her go and started the engine. He drove to the pullout overlooking the mountains where they'd stopped once before.

In the daylight, the Mission Mountains created deep shadows across the valley below, like giant ships moving over the land.

"It's beautiful here," Leah whispered. "I come here sometimes when things become too difficult."

He was no longer watching the mountains. "I wish I could take it all away," he said so softly she almost didn't hear.

She turned her head toward him. "I know." And she did. Leah wouldn't have made it through John's recent attacks without him. Every time she looked at him, she wanted things that had always been out of her reach. Leah desperately wanted to be free of John's stain.

"I will never forget the day we found out about Harrison," he said quietly. "My parents looked so broken. My dad was always such a strong man—never showing weakness. When he found out about Harrison, he cried. I don't think I'd ever seen my father cry before."

Her heart broke for him and his family. After everything Dalton's family had been through, they deserved to have Harrison's name cleared.

Something shifted in his eyes. "We've both been held captive by what happened that night." He tipped her chin and stared into her eyes.

More than anything she wanted to stay here with him. Shut John and all the terrible things he'd done out of their lives for just a little while.

Unexpectedly, Willa's phone beeped an incoming message, dispelling the tender moment.

Leah grabbed the phone. "It's him." She swiped the message open. "He wants to meet Willa tonight at eleven."

"He doesn't have any idea we've spoken to Willa. She said she always confirmed with him. Go ahead and do that."

Leah had read all of Willa's responses. The young Amish girl kept her answers short, usually only a couple of words. She typed a simple yes and waited. There was no response.

In the back of her mind, she kept remembering the photos he'd taken of her at different times. "Do you think he was watching the station when Willa and Esther came in?" If he was, this could be a setup.

"I sure hope not." Dalton glanced at his watch. "We have seven hours to prepare. He can't escape this time."

In the past, she hadn't dared go through Ellis's files, but now she wondered if somewhere in his home office there might be a clue as to why Ellis went after an innocent man. No matter how hard it might be or what it might do to Ellis's reputation, she would do whatever she could to find the truth.

———

He hadn't expected them to find the body so soon. It was a setback, but it didn't matter. Nothing was going to stand in the way of what was to come. His grand moment with Leah.

251

He could feel the anticipation growing like a separate personality inside his body.

Jonathan had been a good friend through the years. Part of him regretted having to kill him. The guy had kept his secrets in the past, but he couldn't afford to have that loose end hanging around. It wouldn't take the police long to trace the truck to Jonathan's family. He'd called Jonathan and asked him to meet him up in the mountains. Jonathan never suspected a thing until he'd shoved him off the mountain. Jonathan wouldn't be telling any secrets.

He brought out his phone. A message had come as expected, with the same tone and inflection as his Willa, and yet he had doubts. What lay ahead was too important to make even a single false move.

He texted a response only she would know. The answer didn't come quickly but when it did, it confirmed Willa had betrayed him.

He threw the phone. It hit a tree and bounced against the ground. He wouldn't be needing it any longer. Almost time.

The day was quickly fading, and he had a plan. He drove the stolen car to the place where he'd been crashing. There was a group of vagrants staying there. No one really noticed him, except for one person who appeared to want to chat him up. The man had been a minor annoyance, but he'd allowed it because he had a purpose for him.

"Hey, you got any weed?" the man who had introduced himself as Scott asked.

He covered his distaste carefully. "I don't, but I know where you can get some."

Scott's eyes lit up. "You do? Well, all right. You got a car. Let's go get it."

He shook his head. "Not so fast. You can't go there now. Someone will see. You have to wait until later."

Hope vanished from Scott's expression. "Oh, man, you're full of it. You don't know nothing."

"I do, and there's a lot of it. I can lend you the car but . . ." He lowered his voice. "You can't tell anyone else about it."

Scott didn't hesitate. "I won't. I just need something."

He grabbed Scott's arm and pulled him outside. "There's plenty there, as I said. But you have to wait until ten. They'll be sleeping."

Scott vigorously nodded. "Sure. Who are they?"

"The Amish family that grows it."

The junkie's eyes widened. "Oh, man, now I know you're lying. Those Amish don't do pot." Scott had enough brain cells still functioning to have doubts.

"They do." He looked around as if making sure no one was listening. "At least these folks do. They aren't really Amish. They're pretending to be so no one snoops around."

"Oh." A knowing smile crept across Scott's face. "Well, that's different. Where are they?"

"Not so fast." He wasn't about to let this idiot ruin things for him. "When it's time, I'll give you the address."

Scott's empty expression turned ugly. "Hey, are you stringing me along?"

He smiled and patted Scott's shoulder. "Would I do that to you, my friend?"

Scott eyed him for the longest time before smiling. "Nah, you wouldn't."

"That's right." So easy.

"What's the plan?" Scott had taken the bait.

"Tonight, once I give you the address, you can take my car."

"Wait, why aren't you going?" Scott's conspiracy-theory-addled mind wouldn't let him trust completely. He'd need more coaxing.

"Because I have to make sure they're sleeping. Once I'm certain, I'll meet you at the barn. That's where they keep the stuff. You'll need this." He handed Scott a knife much like the one he'd used to kill Beth and Eva.

"Why do I need a knife for weed?"

"You'll have to dig it out of the hay bales. They hide it in there."

Scott's full attention bore into him before he nodded. "Makes sense. No one would think to look there."

It was too easy. "Exactly." He kept his amusement to himself and started back to the house.

"Hey, why are you always wearing gloves? It's like a hundred degrees out."

His hands clenched. The last thing he needed was a pothead ruining his plan. He slowly faced Scott. "I have a skin condition, okay?"

"Show me." Scott's curiosity overtook his fear.

"No. It's contagious. I'd hate for you to get it."

"You mean like leprosy or something?"

"Exactly. You wouldn't want to catch it, now would you?" He whirled around and headed back inside the flophouse with a smile on his face. This was fun. When this was all over, he'd plan his next game. Someplace different with new players. He couldn't wait.

nineteen

eah's cell phone rang. Ethan's number popped up. He'd relieved Sam at Marge's. "What's wrong?" Her heartbeat sped into overtime. Ever since she and Dalton had left the overlook and returned to the station, she couldn't get rid of the bad feeling pressing in.

"I'm worried about her, Leah," Ethan whispered. "She's not making any sense. Marge is talking about Ellis as if he's still here, and she keeps mentioning her son. I think she's in trouble."

"I'm on my way." She ended the call.

"What's wrong?" Dalton asked.

"Marge is having some type of episode. I have to go."

He grabbed the cruiser's keys. "I'm coming with you." They passed by Sylvia at her station. "You can reach me on the radio if something comes up," he said without stopping.

Dalton reversed out of the parking spot and headed toward Marge's home at a rapid speed.

"I'm really worried about her," she said. "She's getting worse."

"I'm sure having the past rehashed is taking its toll. Have you received a response from her doctor?"

"Yes. The doctor wants Marge to come back in. He thinks

adjusting her meds will help. But she's pushing back on making the appointment." Leah sighed deeply. "With everything that's happening, I can't find it in me to force her to go."

He covered her hand with his. "It will work out. Maybe the doctor can make a house call."

"I hope so. It's the only way to get her help." Her frown deepened. "I don't understand this thing about her having a child." With Marge having had a hysterectomy, the doctor had been unable to determine if she'd had a baby in the past. She told Dalton what the doctor said.

Dalton made the turn onto her street before answering. "Maybe she wanted a child when she was young and couldn't have one. It could be manifesting itself in her current confused state."

"I guess it's possible. The stress of reliving Ellis's death is hard for her. She's always worried about me."

Dalton pulled up behind the deputy's vehicle. "No matter what, I've got your back. Whatever you need."

Despite her concern for Marge, Leah's heart swelled with something akin to happiness. She got out and they went inside. "Ethan?"

"In here." She followed his voice into the kitchen and found the officer leaning wearily against the sink.

"Where's Marge?"

"I finally convinced her to lie down." Ethan shook his head. "I'm sorry to call you, but I wasn't sure what else to do." He acknowledged Dalton with a nod.

"You did the right thing," Leah said in a thick voice, struggling to hold back tears. The woman who had been her rock was crumbling. "I'm going to check on her." She headed up the stairs to Marge's room, cracked the door, and peeked inside.

"I'm awake. I told him not to call you."

Leah sat down beside her. "Ethan was worried. How are you feeling?"

"I'm fine. I don't like everyone fussing over me," Marge said with a weary sigh. Her eyes were puffy from crying.

Leah let the matter drop. "You want me to bring you some tea?"

Marge clutched her hand. "No, baby girl. Just sit with me for a while."

Leah smiled and put her arm around her mother's shoulders. "You got it."

"Do you think I'm crazy?" Tears hovered in Marge's eyes.

"Of course not. I don't think you're crazy at all."

Marge patted Leah's arm. "I don't know how I would have survived this year without you, Leah. I miss him so much."

"Me too."

"Did I tell you that Ellis and I met around this time of the year?"

Leah couldn't remember her mom ever talking about how she and Ellis met. "You did? Where were you living?"

Marge had a dreamy look on her face as if she were remembering that time. "In Wyoming."

Right away, Leah's attention piqued. "Really? Where in Wyoming?"

Marge's brows furrowed. "I-I don't remember."

As much as she wanted to press for answers, she knew her mother was exhausted and needed rest above everything else.

"He was such a handsome man in his uniform. I fell in love with him from the start."

Leah didn't say a word, just patiently waited for her mom to continue.

"He asked me to marry him. I was thrilled." She hesitated as if she weren't sure about the memory. "But I loved him, and we had so many happy years together." Tears slipped from her eyes. "Now he's gone, and I don't know what I'll do without him. How am I supposed to keep going without my husband?" She turned troubled eyes to Leah.

"You have me—we have each other. It will be okay."

"You want me to see my doctor?" Marge appeared to read Leah's thoughts.

"I do. We need to have your medication checked. If it would make it easier for you, I can ask him to come here."

"But what if I'm getting worse? What if . . . ?" She didn't finish.

"Whatever it is, we'll get through it together."

Marge searched her face. "You promise you won't leave me?"

"Never. I love you."

Marge slowly smiled. "You are such a good girl. The day Ellis brought you home, I knew you were different from—" She stopped and frowned.

"Different from what?" Leah asked.

"Than any other child around." Marge heaved a sigh and closed her eyes. "Stay with me until I fall asleep?"

"Of course." Leah settled back against the headboard and peered around the room that was filled with memories. She'd come here when the nightmares became too bad to deal with alone. Marge would tuck her in close and she felt safe. Her mom and Ellis had pulled her from the darkness. Though she still wore the scars from that time, she couldn't imagine her life without this woman.

When Marge's breathing steadied, Leah gently slipped her arm free and rose.

Was it possible in Marge's tangled thoughts she'd created a child to help deal with Ellis's death?

Leah tiptoed to the door and glanced back at the woman sleeping peacefully in her bed, and her heart clenched. She was losing her mom to an illness that wasn't only claiming her physical health but was slowly eating away at the memories Marge held precious.

"We should go." Dalton hated having to pull her away from her mother, but it was almost eleven.

Since coming downstairs, Leah had been quiet. She appeared sad. He couldn't imagine what she was going through with her mom.

She slowly roused herself as they prepared to leave.

"Don't worry about Marge," Ethan told her. "I'll check in on her periodically. Rest will do her a world of good—you'll see."

Leah squeezed his arm, and then she and Dalton headed outside.

"We'll have to hurry to get into place before the meetup."

Dalton had moved Willa and her family and pulled back the officer stationed at the house. He didn't want John to get spooked. They skirted the town and headed toward the scattered Amish farms. At half past ten, he pulled the vehicle into a wooded area bordering Willa's family home. Once in place, Dalton radioed the patrols watching the house to confirm there had been no activity around the farm.

"I sure hope he hasn't found out about Willa coming to the station. If he has, he won't show."

Leah grabbed his arm and leaned forward in her seat. "Someone's coming."

Dalton radioed the officers. "Be ready. There's a vehicle approaching." The car slowly eased along the road with its headlights on. "If that's him, he doesn't know about Willa."

"Come on. Turn in," Leah murmured to herself. Almost as if on cue, the car slowed once it reached the drive. Headlights swept across the woods where they hid as the vehicle turned.

"That's him." Dalton hit the radio. "He's stopping in front of the barn. Wait until he goes inside and then we take him."

The man in the car got out and looked around as if expecting someone to materialize. "He's nervous." Leah watched the guy slowly open the door and step inside.

Dalton hit the mic. "Let's go." With weapons drawn, he and Leah left the cruiser and eased toward the barn. Half a dozen officers gathered near the door. Dalton jerked the door open, and the team rushed the barn. Men stood guard all around the structure in case their perp tried to flee.

Near the stacks of hay bales a man dug frantically, seemingly unaware of their presence.

As they edged closer, Dalton's flashlight beam reflected his light brown hair. Just like the man Willa described.

"Hands in the air," Dalton ordered.

The man whirled toward them.

"He has a knife. Drop the weapon!" Dalton shouted.

The man stared at the multiple guns pointed at him. "I'm not doing anything wrong."

"I'm not going to tell you again. Drop the weapon."

"All right. I'm dropping it." The knife hit the ground.

Dalton rushed forward and kicked it out of reach. "Hands behind your back."

The man seemed too dazed to react. "What's this about, man?"

Dalton yanked his hands behind his back and cuffed him. "For starters, you're being arrested for trespassing."

"For starters? What do you mean?"

"We're taking you into custody for questioning in the murders of two Amish women. And one Jonathan Stephens."

"Murder?" the man shrieked in disbelief. "I don't know anything about any murder."

Dalton handed the man off to Henry. "Take him to the station and set him up in the interrogation room."

"He doesn't know anything," Leah said once the man was out of earshot. She carefully bagged the knife. "He's a patsy. John used him. This probably isn't the murder weapon."

"You're right, but maybe he remembers something that will help us find out where John is hiding."

Leah turned toward the hole burrowed into the hay. "What do you think he was looking for?"

Dalton went over to the hole and looked inside. "I have no idea. Hopefully, he'll tell us. Until we know what's going on, Willa and her family don't come back here. They'll be guarded at all times." He glanced at the time on his phone. "Almost midnight. What kind of game is John playing?"

Leah pulled in a shaky breath. He saw her fear and kept her close as they returned to their cruiser.

John had carefully orchestrated the events of the evening. May have even been close enough to watch.

Henry met them as soon as they entered the station. "He's in the interrogation room."

Dalton nodded and faced Leah. "I want you there. This man has seen John and spoken to him. He knows something."

Leah's breath came in fits and starts. He kept a close watch on her as they entered the room. The man they'd arrested had been cuffed to the table.

"Why am I here, man?" he demanded. "All I was doing was looking for the weed."

"Weed?" Dalton couldn't believe he'd heard him correctly. "You went to an Amish farm looking for weed?" Out of the corner of his eye he could see Leah shared his reaction. "Don't jerk us around. What's your name?"

"Scotty—Scott Garner. And I'm not jerking you around. I was told there was a stash of weed hidden in the barn. That's all I was doing there. I wasn't trying to hurt no one. I swear!"

"Why would you think you'd find pot at an Amish farm?" Unless someone had told him so deliberately. Someone like John.

The whole thing was a setup. The only question? What did John hope to gain by it?

"*He* told me. He said they weren't really Amish, only pretending to be as a cover to hide their weed operation. There was supposed to be tons stored in bales of hay in the barn."

"Who are you talking about?" Leah asked.

Scotty's brow shot up a mile. "I don't know his name. He never told me."

"Scott, you're in a lot of trouble here," Dalton said sternly. "Think carefully. What does this man look like?"

Scott shook his head and blew out a loud breath. "I don't know—just a guy. I guess he looks a little like me, only taller. He has the same hair color, only his is longer and stringy."

"Where did you meet this man?" Dalton's tone was skeptical. The whole story sounded made up.

"At the house." Scott glanced past Dalton to Leah, trying to plead his case with her. "You have to believe me. I only went there for the weed."

"What house?" Leah pulled out a chair and sat across from Scott. "Tell us everything. If you didn't have anything to do with the murders, then you have nothing to worry about."

"The old adobe house outside of town. Lots of people flop there. He crashes there sometimes. He even gave me his car to use."

"To use for what?" Dalton asked.

"I told you. To get the weed. I don't know nothing about anyone dying."

Dalton pulled up the photo they'd taken from Eva's phone. "Is this the man?" He showed the picture to Scott.

"Yeah, that's him, only his hair is a different color. Like mine. Although I always thought it looked weird—like maybe he wore a wig or something."

Dalton swung to Leah. "Let's step outside for a second." In the hall, he ran a hand across his eyes. "What do you think?"

"I think he's high, but he's telling the truth."

"Chief?" Henry hurried their way. "I ran Garner's name. He has a few possession charges, but other than that he's clean."

"Anything on the car?"

"It was stolen two days ago in Polson," the officer replied.

Dalton's sigh came from his deep frustration. "John is playing with us. He knew Willa spoke to us, so he sent Garner."

"What do you want to do?" Leah asked.

"Let's go to the flophouse. Maybe the killer is still there."

A handful of lights were on inside the house. He finished buttoning the uniform. He'd carefully lured out the two cops watching the place and one by one knocked them out. Getting both inside the trunk had taken some effort, but he was determined. It was all part of the plan. He'd made sure to gag the two so they couldn't make a sound. There would be another cop inside. To overpower the man, he'd need to fool him into believing he was one of them.

He headed for the house and knocked once. The patrolman inside obviously hadn't heard the commotion. He flung the door open. "Everything okay out here?" He looked around to the patrol car. "Where's your partner?"

"He was checking around back but it's been a while."

The alarm on the cop's face was obvious. "Have you checked on him recently?"

"No, man, I thought I'd get you to help me look for him."

The cop stared back at him. "I don't recognize you. Is this your first time here?"

He gave his best cheerful laugh. "Yes. Why?"

The cop frowned at his hastily buttoned uniform.

"I'm calling this in." The cop started to shut the door in his face, but he stuck his foot in. The cop whirled toward him, and he jabbed his knife in the cop's side. Blood soaked the uniform immediately. The officer grabbed for his knife. He held it against the cop's side.

The truth dawned quickly on the officer's face.

"Nice and slow. Hand me your weapon."

"I'm not giving you my service piece."

"I'll get it myself." He grabbed the weapon and tossed it into the bushes. "Now, go." He shoved him hard. The officer stumbled inside. He almost lost his footing but somehow kept his feet under him.

"Get in there." He pointed the knife into the living room and kicked the door shut with his foot. "Sit down."

"Look, brother, you don't want to do anything you'll regret."

"You think I care about killing cops? You wouldn't be the first or the third for that matter."

The cop shrank away. "All right, well, I can still help you. Tell me your name."

"Shut up. I'm not here to make small talk with you."

"She's not coming anytime soon."

The smile on his face had the officer swallowing repeatedly. "But she will. And you know why. Do you want to die now or wait until the show is over?" He couldn't contain his glee. The cop appeared to realize there would be no negotiating for his life.

"I don't plan on dying tonight or any other." The officer held his hand to his side. It was covered in blood.

He shoved the knife against the cop's throat. "That's not your choice. Give me your cuffs."

"You want them, you're gonna have to take them."

He backhanded the officer, and his head shot sideways. Before the cop could shake off the effects of the blow, John grabbed the cuffs from his belt. He shoved the weakened officer to the floor and jerked his hands behind his back, securing the handcuffs in place. "Stay there until I figure out what I'm going to do with you."

The officer watched him pace the room.

"Where's your phone?"

"In my pocket." The words were slurred. The cop was losing consciousness. "If you want it, you'll have to come and get it."

Enraged, he charged. When he was almost right on top of the cop, the man kicked him hard. He stumbled across the room. The cop scrambled to his feet.

He slowly smiled. "You want to fight?"

Like a wild bull, the cop came for him. He slammed into him full force. The knife flew from his hand and across the floor. He scrambled for the weapon while the cop struck him again, lost his footing, and hit the bookcase, sending books flying everywhere.

Still, the wounded officer didn't give up. The cop made another move to take him down. He grabbed a bronze bookend from the floor, and the cop's eyes widened. He slammed the bookend against the officer's temple. He dropped to his knees. A second later, he fell to the floor unconscious.

twenty

Multiple police cars streamed down the highway leading to the house Scott Garner had told them about. Leah knew the place well. She'd been called out on many disturbances there. She exited the car and moved to the front of the cruiser where Dalton waited. The rest of the group pulled in behind them.

"According to the county records, the house has been vacant for years," Dalton told the officers gathered. "Our people have had numerous calls here in the past. It's a known drug house. Be careful and watch out for each other. Sam, you're with Leah and me. The rest of you take the back. Let's go."

They headed toward the house. Not a sound came from inside.

Leah pulled in a breath as Dalton tried the door. It opened freely. She exchanged a troubled look with him before he entered first.

Quiet snatches of conversation drifted their way. The back door opened seconds after they entered. Officers poured in.

"This way." Dalton pointed to an adjacent room. Inside, half a dozen people were seated. The place reeked of weed.

"Put your hands in the air," Dalton ordered.

Several people tried to run. Others gave in peacefully. The raid was over in a matter of minutes.

Leah shined her flashlight around the faces of the men gathered. None were John. "He's not here." Her stomach clenched at yet another setback in a long line of them.

"He knew Scott would give us the location." Dalton looked around the dismal interior and shook his head.

"What do you want us to do with these guys?" Sam asked.

"Run their names. If they're clean, let them go." He motioned Leah outside. "You know what today represents. Nothing that's happened to date has been a coincidence. What's his next move?" Dalton watched the men being led from the house. "What will be his grand finale?"

Leah shivered at those words. "I don't know, but I'm scared, Dalton." She hated admitting the weakness.

He brushed her hair from her face. "It's okay to be scared. It will keep you on your toes. You're not in this alone, Leah. And I'm not letting you out of my sight for a second."

She slowly smiled.

"You'll always be safe with me." Dalton clasped her hand in his. "Soon, this will all be over. And I hope . . ." He didn't finish. What wasn't said filled her with a hope she hadn't had in a long time. Was it possible for two people who had suffered so much to move beyond the darkness?

Sam headed toward them, and Leah stepped back.

"There are a couple of folks who have outstanding warrants. The rest are clean. We'll take these two to the station." He crooked a thumb behind him.

Dalton nodded. "Thanks, Sam."

"You think he expected us and cleared out?" Sam asked.

"That would be my guess. Unfortunately, he could be any-where." Leah glanced back at the run-down house. There was a purpose behind everything the killer did. Which meant he chose this house for a reason. Probably because no one here would ask him any questions. He'd found Scott and used his addiction against him. Leah thought about where it all began. "The barn. This all started in my family's barn."

"We have people watching it." Dalton held her gaze. "You think he'd still go there? Even with someone watching it?"

"I don't know, but it holds a special memory for him."

"Sam, ride with us." Dalton motioned several of the other officers to follow. Once they reached the cruiser, he radioed the patrolmen watching Willa's family at the safe house. "Every-thing okay there?"

"Yes, sir. We checked with the family before they went to bed."

"Okay. I want you to make sure Willa is still there."

"Copy that."

Dalton floored the accelerator and raced through the night. He turned onto the road leading to Amish country. Once he reached Leah's old homestead, Dalton slowed to turn.

"Chief, you there?" It was one of the officers watching Willa's home.

"I'm here."

"The girl's safe."

Leah blew out a sigh. "Thank you, God."

"Appreciate it," Dalton said with a smile. He stopped the vehicle close to the barn and released a deep breath. "Everyone, keep your eyes open."

The deputy sitting on the barn got out and came over. "There's been no sign of him, Chief."

"Still, let's check inside." They approached the door slowly with weapons drawn.

As they entered the barn, their flashlights skirted around the space.

"Nothing." Leah wasn't sure how she felt. Relieved? Disappointed? Maybe a little of both. But more than anything, she wanted this to end.

"Wait, there is something here." Dalton pointed his flashlight at the middle of the barn. They approached the object.

"It's a wig. The same color hair as Scott's." She recalled the young man mentioning he believed the killer wore a wig. "He must have slipped in through the back and left it here."

"Geez," Sam murmured under his breath. "This guy gives me the creeps."

"Search the place thoroughly," Dalton ordered. "Inside and out."

Even though Dalton was nearby, Leah still felt on edge. Every little sound had her jerking toward it. Expecting John to materialize beside her to finish the job.

At one time, Leah knew every square inch of the barn by heart. She and her sister and brother would come here after chores. Climb on hay bales stored on the top floor. They'd play hide-and-seek here for hours.

"I'll take a look upstairs," Sam told them and climbed up the ladder-like steps.

Leah looked through all the little nooks and crannies they'd used to hide things. There was nothing else here. She returned to Dalton to tell him the canvass was finished and to ask if they should try the house. He stood near the door staring at his phone.

"What's wrong?" *Please don't let it be another death.*

"I missed a call from Dr. Hopkins at the Wyoming State Hospital while we were searching the house. He sent a text. Hopkins found someone who worked at the hospital during the time Jonathan Stephens was there." Dalton scanned the message. "He said there was someone around Jonathan's age whom he befriended. The doctor showed him the sketch and he recognized it. He said the man's name is Aaron. He didn't remember the last name. Apparently, Jonathan was a sweet kid, but this Aaron, well, he had a chip on his shoulder and a penchant for violence."

"That's our guy," Leah said.

"According to the employee, Aaron was good at fooling people, even the doctors at the hospital. In his opinion, Aaron should never have been released."

The words sent a chill down her spine. Aaron was John.

She grabbed her phone and tried Ethan, terrified for Marge. Fear twisted her up inside. "Ethan isn't answering."

"Let's go," Dalton told her. "Sam, stay here with the others. If anything new comes up, call me immediately."

As they drove, Leah continued to try Ethan's number without answer.

Dalton pulled in behind the deputies' empty cruiser. Ethan's patrol vehicle was parked in the drive.

"Where are the deputies?" Leah leaned forward and studied the cruiser. It was empty.

Dalton grabbed the radio and called for backup. "It could be nothing. Maybe they went inside for something."

Adrenaline poured into her body.

She and Dalton exited their vehicle and slowly advanced to the house. Leah scanned the surrounding properties for anything out of the ordinary. Somewhere in the distance a dog barked. Most of the lights were off except for Mr. Henderson's. The older man had told Marge once that he had trouble sleeping since his wife's death.

She swallowed several times as they reached the porch. Dalton slowly nodded, and she tried the doorknob. It twisted freely in her hand.

With Dalton at her side, she slowly inched it open. The quietness of the place hit her first. Where was Ethan? The deputies? Marge?

Her hand grew sweaty on the Glock. The tiniest of sounds came from within Ellis's office. Dalton heard it too. They crept to the room.

Dalton reached it first. The door remained shut. He twisted the handle open. The room appeared empty. The TV played an old home movie from when Marge and Ellis were younger.

A prickle of unease coursed through Leah's body. "I'm going upstairs to find Marge."

Dalton grabbed her arm before she'd taken a single step. "Something's off. We stay together."

Dalton's cell phone beeped. He grabbed it from his pocket and read the message. "Aaron's last name is Beiler."

"Like Marge's." Leah covered her mouth with her hand.

"Beiler was committed to the psychiatric facility ten years ago by his father."

"His father?" Leah asked, but she knew. She knew.

"Ellis Petri. Ellis had Aaron committed because he said he was afraid he'd hurt himself and others."

Leah's legs threatened to buckle beneath her. "That had to be right after he killed my family. Ellis must have known Aaron was the killer." She felt like she'd been punched in the gut. Ellis had known the truth and had chosen to commit Aaron rather than have the truth come out. "He must've been protecting Marge. She must not know that her son was the one who killed my family."

Marge had been right. She had a *son*. "She said he had to go away. I wonder when she last saw Aaron?"

"I don't know," Dalton murmured.

"I'd never seen Aaron before that summer. St. Ignatius is small. If he were living here, our paths would have crossed at some point. He said he'd been traveling around. Hiking the country. Maybe that part was true. But how did he get out of the hospital?"

"It looks like he was released at some point. We know Aaron is good at fooling people. Maybe he fooled the doctors into thinking he was better. Aaron obviously didn't come back to St. Ignatius right away. Someone would have seen him, unless he stayed hidden. Until he lured Ellis out and killed him." He shook his head. "Whatever happened, I'm pretty certain Marge has no idea what her son has done."

The man who had murdered so many innocent people, including her beloved family, was Marge's own son. "We know Ellis wasn't the father. Then who was?"

Dalton shook his head. "I don't know, but I'm putting out an APB on Aaron. At least we now have a name." He called it in.

"That still doesn't answer where Ethan and the deputies are."

"No, it doesn't." He started for the next room. The words had barely cleared his lips when the nightmare from her past burst through the doorway and lunged for Dalton. Leah screamed. Before either she or Dalton could react, Aaron punctured Dalton's stomach and leg with the knife. Dalton hit the floor.

"Drop the weapon, Aaron!" Leah yelled with her weapon

raised. Aaron's demented smile would be forever imprinted in her memory. He raised the knife and prepared to stab Dalton again. Leah fired. The shot struck Aaron's side. He stumbled several times then charged for Leah. She fired again, but Aaron struck her arm, and the shot pierced the wall. Aaron grabbed hold of the weapon. They both struggled for control. Aaron slammed his fist against her face. The world blurred. Her eyes watered. He pried the gun from her fingers and tossed it out of her reach. She slammed her fist against his injured side. Aaron screamed in pain and hit her again. Leah fell to the floor hard. Aaron jumped on top of her and pinned her hands together in one of his. Then he held the knife against her throat.

"I told you I would come back for you. I wasn't going to let anyone—not even *him*—stand in our way again."

In his twisted mind, he'd convinced himself they had a relationship. Leah's frantic gaze shot to Dalton. He was bleeding out. Would she lose him before help arrived?

She struggled to kick him but couldn't get any leverage. The knife dug into her neck as punishment.

"Let me go, Aaron. I can help you."

Aaron pressed the knife into her neck. "Help? I don't need your help. We finish this tonight."

She had to keep him talking until help arrived. "This is between you and me, Aaron. You want me."

The knife brought blood.

Her eyes jerked to Dalton. *Please, don't let him die.*

"There's no way you're walking out of here, Aaron. Not after what you've done. This ends tonight." Leah was surprised when a calm swept over her. Fear ebbed away. Now she would finish it once and for all.

"It ends when I say it ends. When I'm ready for it to be done."

"There are multiple police officers on the way here now. If you want to live, let me help you. Drop the weapon."

He hesitated. "You're lying. There's no one coming."

"I'm not lying. They'll be here soon."

But he was too far gone for reason. Aaron raised the knife in front of them. "We'll end this together, Leah. You'll be mine for all eternity."

A gunshot cracked the air. Aaron dropped the knife and fell on top of her. Leah glanced toward the door, where Marge stood holding Ellis's old shotgun, tears streaming down her face.

Leah scrambled out from underneath Aaron and kicked the knife away. The shot had struck his upper chest. He was unconscious. She felt for a pulse. He was alive.

Leah radioed for help. "I have an officer down. I repeat, I have an officer down! Send multiple ambulances." She ended the transmission and hurried over to Dalton and tugged him into her lap. His frantic eyes met hers.

"You're okay," she whispered. "You're okay. Just hold on. Help is coming." Her eyes swept the room and saw Marge still holding the shotgun. "Are you okay?"

The older woman dropped the shotgun and collapsed to the floor. "I shot my son. My boy. My sweet boy."

"You saved my life. He was going to kill me."

Marge peered at her through tearful eyes. "I couldn't let that happen. You're my baby girl." She scrambled across the floor to her son, cradling him in her lap. "I'm so sorry, son, but I had to do it."

Sirens screamed through the night.

Dalton's eyes closed, and he slumped to the side. Leah held him close. "Please, don't take him. Please, don't let him die." Tears streamed down her cheeks.

In a heartbeat, law enforcement flooded the house. Moments later, an ambulance arrived.

Leah clutched Dalton's hand as the two paramedics worked on saving his life.

Sam knelt beside her. "What happened here?" he asked, his voice shaky.

Leah could barely get the words out.

"We need to get him to the hospital right away," paramedic Reece told them. Dalton was lifted to the gurney. Leah stood beside him. His eyes opened slightly and focused on her. He tried to talk but couldn't.

"You're going to be okay, Dalton, you hear me? You're going to be okay." Leah fought back tears. She held his hand until they reached the ambulance. "Don't you die on me." As much as she wanted to go to the hospital with him, there was still so much more to the story that needed to be told.

He managed a smile and mouthed, "I won't."

A second ambulance arrived to treat Aaron's wounds.

Leah went back inside with them to where Aaron had regained consciousness and lay moaning on the floor.

Henry ran into the room. "Leah, we need help. It's Ethan." His frantic eyes said it all.

"Stay with Aaron," Leah told Sam. She followed Henry to the hall closet. Slumped inside was a bound and unconscious Ethan, covered in blood.

"Get the paramedics in here."

Henry grabbed one of the medics treating Aaron.

Leah uncuffed Ethan's hands. The officer slowly regained consciousness.

"He stabbed me, Leah. He was pretending to be a deputy."

"We have him in custody. Let the paramedics take care of you."

Ethan gave her a weak smile before they loaded him for transport to the hospital.

"He's lost a lot of blood," one of the paramedics told her. "We need to get him to the hospital right away."

She stood beside Ethan as they took him out. "You're going to be okay. I'll stop by soon to see you."

Sam was still standing guard over Aaron while a distraught Marge watched near the door.

Leah touched Marge's shoulder. The woman who had been her mother looked at her through tear-filled eyes.

"You're mine, Leah," Aaron rasped at her. "You'll never belong to him or any other man. You're mine. Do you hear me? You're mine."

"Go with him to the hospital," Leah told Sam without looking at Aaron. The man who had been a monster in her memories was no more.

Aaron continued to scream and thrash around as he was wheeled away.

Leah put her arm around her mother. "We're going to transport him to the hospital. As soon as he's able to talk, I'll question him. I want you to come with me." There was no way she would leave Marge alone in her current state. As much as Leah dreaded having to do it, Marge would need to be questioned about the shooting. But first, she had to make sure Dalton was okay.

Marge leaned heavily against Leah as they left the house. She seemed emotionally drained, maybe from the years of living with her secret. Leah helped Marge into the cruiser and drove toward the hospital while struggling to come to terms with everything that had just transpired.

"I'm so sorry, baby girl," Marge murmured in a broken voice. "I had no idea he was the one who did that to your family. Ellis told me it was that Amish boy, but he said that Aaron needed help and he'd taken him someplace to get it. I didn't know." She sobbed.

Leah reached for her hand. "Ellis was trying to protect you."

The stricken woman shook her head. "I wish he hadn't. I know he was looking out for me, and he knew how much I loved my boy, but look how much pain it caused."

"Can you tell me what happened? Were you once Amish?" Leah knew the answer already but she wanted to hear her mother's side of the story.

Marge managed a faint smile. "I was. For the longest time, I couldn't imagine any other way of life."

Leah had felt the same way until that night. "Ellis isn't Aaron's father, is he?"

Marge appeared embarrassed. "No, he isn't." She was quiet for a moment, as if trying to remember. "I grew up in a small Amish community in Wyoming. There were only a handful of families living there. I loved being Amish so much I never wanted to leave my home and family. Even while on my rumspringa, I knew I would return to my Plain faith. And even though I didn't find someone to marry me, I was okay. I loved being with my parents."

Leah sensed something traumatic had happened to Marge. She squeezed her mom's hand. "You can tell me anything."

Tears fell from Marge's eyes. "I was . . . raped."

Nothing prepared Leah for hearing this. "Oh, Marge, I'm so sorry."

Her mother frowned as if she were struggling to pull out the rest of the story. "I was walking home from the store, yes that's what happened. A man in a car stopped to ask directions. He grabbed me and dragged me into the woods." She wiped her face. "When it was over, he left. I lay there for the longest time, not sure what to do. Then I got up and did my best to gather my torn clothes. The bag of groceries was still there where I'd dropped them. And so, I walked home."

She couldn't imagine how frightened Marge had been. "Did you tell your parents what happened?"

"Oh no. I was too embarrassed, so I told them I'd fallen. I cleaned myself up and thought that would be it, but it wasn't."

"You found out you were pregnant."

"*Jah*. At that point, I'd given up on marriage. I believed I would live out the rest of my days at my parents' home." Marge pulled in a labored breath. "I knew I had to tell them. When I did, it went as badly as I expected." The strain of how horrific it had been for her was reflected on her face.

"They didn't believe you."

"Mamm did. Daed did not. He told me I brought shame to the family." She looked over at Leah. "I was shunned, baby girl. The bishop and the church leaders took pity on my parents, but I was banned." She shuddered at the memory. "I never felt so alone before. Mamm was Mamm. She supported me and helped me prepare for the *bobbli*, but my daed never forgave me."

"So you stayed there with your parents?" Leah asked, surprised. Did Marge even realize she'd reverted back to her Amish dialect? They reached the hospital and Leah parked out front. As anxious as she was to find out about Dalton's condition and get the chance to finally speak to Aaron, she had to know the rest of Marge's story.

Marge rubbed her forehead as if searching for the answer while Leah continued to pray the answers would come. "*Jah*, I did. Daed begrudgingly took in my boy and helped raise him. All was fine until he was around ten years old and started displaying some frightening behavior."

Ten. That number lingered in Leah's thoughts.

"Such as?" she asked when Marge didn't speak.

"He would kill animals for no reason and leave them in weird poses."

Classic serial killer behavior.

"Then when he tried to harm one of the girls in school, Daed told me we had to leave. He feared for his reputation within the community." She sighed softly. "I knew then I would not be able to be Amish or pretend to be Amish anymore. So, I left the only home I ever knew and moved to Bear Creek, a small town some distance away. I found a job in a café, enrolled Aaron in school, and he seemed to be *oke* for a while. I thought perhaps the Amish life was not for him, so I gladly sacrificed my happiness for my son." She smiled as she recalled the time. "And then I met Ellis and my world changed for the better. I was so happy. He was such a handsome man in his uniform."

"And you and he got married?"

Marge's smile disappeared and her brow wrinkled. "Not for a while. I told him about what had happened and about my Aaron. Ellis told me he loved children, and he did."

Leah had witnessed Ellis's love for children through the years. He'd dressed up like Santa for the young patients in the hospital and given out toys. Just one of the many ways he expressed his love.

"We were married, and for a while, Aaron seemed to be doing okay. And then when he was around sixteen, his bad behavior started up again and he started resenting Ellis. Aaron said it was better when it was just the two of us. He tried to hurt Ellis multiple times, and when he turned eighteen, Ellis told him he had to leave." Marge glanced at Leah.

Leah couldn't imagine how hard that must have been, sending her child away. "Do you know where he went?"

Marge shook her head. "I have no idea. He would send letters occasionally. He said he was traveling around."

Like he'd told Leah.

"When Ellis and I moved to St. Ignatius, Aaron showed up here." She started sobbing. "I'm so sorry, Leah. I had no idea. He seemed better, but I think he was just better at hiding his dark side."

"This isn't your fault." Leah clasped her hand and forced Marge to look at her. "Aaron was sick. None of this is your fault." She sighed heavily. "We'd better go inside. I'll need to have Sam question you about the shooting. When we're finished interviewing Aaron, I'll let you see him for a few minutes."

Henry and Sam met them as they came in.

"Dalton's in critical condition," Henry said. "It looks bad."

Leah struggled not to fall apart. "Thank you, Henry." *Please, don't take him.* The prayer slipped through her thoughts. She cleared her throat. "What about Ethan?"

"He's going to make it."

She smiled despite her heavy heart. "Any word on Aaron's condition?"

"He'll be in recovery for a while, but the doctor said we can ask him a few questions."

Leah turned to Sam. "Do you mind sitting with Marge? I'll need you to get her statement as well."

Sam didn't hesitate. "Not at all. Come on, Marge." He led her over to one of the chairs.

Leah squared her shoulders. She had waited ten years for this moment. With Henry at her side, Leah stepped into Aaron's room and faced the man of her nightmares.

"Hello, Aaron." The man cuffed to his bed was an older version of the one who had taken so much from her.

"Sweet Leah. You've grown into a formidable opponent," he mumbled and smiled that smile that had once filled her with excitement. "I made you strong."

It sickened her that Aaron would take credit for her strength. She did her best not to react to the bait. "You've been read your rights. Do you agree to speak with us without your attorney?"

"So professional," he taunted. When she didn't respond, he sighed. "Yes, I agree. I've waited a long time to have this moment with you."

"I'll be recording this interview." He didn't react. She hit the record button on her phone and identified each person in the room.

One thing she wanted to know. Where had Aaron been before he'd killed her family and after he'd been released from the psychiatric facility? She asked him.

"I think you know where I was before, don't you, Leah?" She knew he was alluding to the two women in Wyoming. "Looking for new adventures." His laugh sent a chill down Leah's back.

"We know about the two young women you killed in Wyoming." She kept her focus on his face.

"You think that was all?"

"So there are others out there?"

Aaron smiled. "That's really up to you to find out, isn't it, Leah."

"Where did you go after you were released from the hospital?"

He didn't answer for a while. "Oh, here and there. I stayed with my friend Jonathan for a while. And I went back to where I was created."

It took her a second to realize he was talking about the Amish community where he was born. "You went back to your grandparents' community?"

Aaron seemed pleased with her reaction. "The Amish are all about forgiveness, Leah. You know that. Besides, he was gone by then. My grandmother took me in . . ." He started laughing again.

Leah wondered if he'd done something to his grandmother. She'd have someone check on the woman as soon as she finished with Aaron. "And then you came back here and killed Ellis. You shot him. Why deviate from your previous method of killing?"

"I thought it was only fitting that he die by his own weapon. He took my mother from me."

Revulsion rose inside, and she fought it. So many families needed answers. Leah kept her expression blank. "You killed my family but let me live. Why?"

Anger flared in an instant. He clearly didn't like her reaction. "Why do you think? With them out of the way, we could be together. We could be a family like I should have had with her, only she put him first. I knew from the beginning I'd have to do away with your family for you to see we were meant to be together."

Aaron had gone to great lengths to plan the murders. They would have a strong case for premeditation.

She straightened her shoulders. "You thought if you took my family away, I would run to you, but you were wrong. I had another family who cared for me and took me in. The one that should have been yours. Ellis and Marge. They became my family. They adopted me. Loved me like their own child."

At her shot in the dark, Aaron's face quickly contorted in rage. Years of pent-up anger and resentment toward Ellis for taking his mother from him came spewing out. "He made her send me away. He took her from me."

"And that made you mad enough to kill him." Leah waited for the confession she knew Aaron wanted to give.

"She chose him over me!" he yelled, his eyes wild. "I needed her—I was her son—and she ignored me just like her father did." He panted like a caged animal.

Aaron's mental issues had started long before Ellis came into the picture. He'd been old enough to feel the impact of his grandfather's rejection.

He focused on Leah again. "I hated him for taking her away from me. I knew the best place to get their attention was at the Amish community. She would understand the significance. And then I met you." Just for a second, he flashed her that smile that reminded her of why the young girl she'd been back then had been so easily swept away. "You were so easy." He was back to baiting her again. "Just like Beth and Eva. Justine and Willa. Those in Wyoming. Others. They were all desperate for kindness."

A chill sped down her spine. He'd wanted to get back at Marge for choosing Ellis, only Marge had never known the terrible things Aaron had done.

"You were different, Leah. That's why I came back for you. I loved you, but you deserted me too. We could have been good together if you hadn't refused to leave them." The depth of madness in those eyes was terrifying. "I killed them so we could be together."

"Why wait ten years to come back for me?" It sickened Leah to hear Aaron speak of her family's deaths and others without remorse.

Aaron's eyes flashed. "Everything changed when I was ten.

I was forced to leave the only home I ever had, by him." He referred to his grandfather. "I became the person you see before you now at ten. I was born at ten. You were supposed to die on the tenth anniversary." In Aaron's twisted mind it all made sense.

There was one more thing Leah needed to know. "Were you the one in the alley outside the police station, smoking?"

His smug grin confirmed the truth.

She'd heard enough. "Aaron Beiler, you're under arrest for the murders of Gretta and Matthew Miller. Ruth and Elijah Miller. Beth Zook. Eva Hostetler. And for the attempted murders of Justine Raber. Sugar Wallace. Henry Landry. Ethan Burke. Dalton Cooper and myself." She felt confident they would prove Aaron killed the two Jane Does as well as Jonathan Stephens. And probably others.

"What about him?" Aaron taunted. "Aren't you going to charge me with his killing?"

Leah leaned forward in her chair. "You mean Ellis Petri?"

Aaron smiled with glee. "That's right. I killed him. Almost to the date of when I killed your family. Did you like the irony?"

She couldn't believe it. Aaron had deliberately chosen to kill Ellis close to the anniversary of the murders, yet he'd used a different murder weapon to throw them off.

It broke her heart to realize Ellis wasn't the man she believed him to be. She understood he was trying to protect Marge, yet he'd framed an innocent man and had forced Harrison to do the unimaginable because he didn't believe there was any other way out.

How could she ever forgive him?

"I knew I had to take him out for everything he'd done to me." Aaron continued his rant. "He had no idea I'd taken his gun. When he saw me, he was so angry. He told me I had to leave. He didn't want my mother upset. I didn't give him the chance to get out of the vehicle."

Leah saw the monster lurking underneath the exterior Aaron showed to lure his victims. It was like looking into the depths of hell.

"You'll be charged with Ellis's death too." She turned to Henry. "Keep guard over him." She started for the door.

Aaron, sensing his moment of glory was ending, screamed at her. "Don't you dare walk away from me again. Don't you dare!"

Leah never looked back. It was a hollow victory to finally close the case of what happened to her family all those years ago. Yet Dalton was foremost in her thoughts now.

Leah found Marge waiting with Sam and sent Sam to help Henry. She and Marge went to the floor where Dalton was being operated on and waited for word. Hours passed before the doctor who had done the surgery came and found her.

"He's in a coma and I'm afraid his condition is still grave. Time will tell. But Dalton is strong. He has that going for him."

Leah tried not to lose hope. "Can I see him?"

"Of course. Come with me." The doctor showed her and Marge to Dalton's room. "I'll stop by later to check in."

Leah entered the room, then clasped her hand over her mouth to hold back a sob. Dalton was so pale. She pulled up a couple of chairs for her and Marge and reached for his hand. She closed her eyes and poured her heart out to God. *Please, don't take him.* She gulped several times. *I'm sorry I lost my way, but I never stopped believing in you, and I know this can't be part of your plan. It can't be. Please, he doesn't deserve this.*

As she stared at the man who had given her so much hope, a calm descended on her. Leah knew Dalton's life and their future were in God's hands.

twenty-one

TWO WEEKS LATER . . .

Dalton's eyes felt weighted down, his body so weak.

"Don't try to move." Her voice drifted through the fog, and he forced his eyes open. He slowly turned his head toward the sound, and there she was. Leah. Smiling at him. The best medicine ever.

"I've been so worried about you," she said, her lip trembling. "You're going to be just fine."

"How long have I been out of it?" he croaked. Searched the fog to remember but couldn't.

"Two weeks. Do you remember Aaron attacking you?"

Dalton concentrated hard, and pieces of that night came back. "I do. What happened to him?"

"Marge shot him. After he attacked you, he came after me. Marge shot her own son to save me."

He shook his head. "I can't imagine how hard that must have been for her."

She placed her hand over his. "He . . . Aaron was arrested and charged with the murders. He admitted to everything. He'll never see the outside of a prison again."

He couldn't take his eyes off her face. There was something more. "What is it?"

"I found something in Ellis's office," she said slowly and lifted what appeared to be a journal from her bag. Regret glimmered in her eyes. "I'm so sorry, Dalton. Ellis wrote this with the assumption it wouldn't come to light until after he'd died. He didn't figure it would be so soon." She opened the journal. "Ellis tried to shield Marge from her son. I don't think Ellis realized that Aaron was capable of murder until he killed my family."

Dalton swallowed, his throat as dry as the desert. "He deliberately framed my brother and forced him to . . ." The thought was unimaginable.

She shook her head, her eyes shining with something that gave him hope. "No, that's just it." She handed him the book. Dalton forced his eyes to focus on the entry she pointed to. It was as if the bed and the floor fell out from beneath him and he was free-falling, unable to grasp the words.

"Ellis did frame Harrison, and that is inexcusable, but Harrison didn't kill himself. Ellis confronted Harrison and told him if he wanted to stay free, he'd go along with Ellis's plan and disappear. To stay 'dead,'" Leah said quietly.

Dalton stared at the page in disbelief and then back at her. "Are you saying Harrison didn't die in that fire? He's out there somewhere?"

Leah squeezed his hand. "I believe so. Ellis staged the scene so that he could close the case. He used a body from the morgue and knew no one would question him. He planned the whole thing. I'm so sorry, Dalton. What Ellis did is unforgivable, and it will be brought to light, but Harrison is still alive. That's something."

He couldn't think clearly. His brother was still alive. "I have to find him."

"And you will. *We* will. Together, we'll find him."

Dalton winced and grabbed his stomach.

"The doctor says you're going to be on leave for a while."

When the waves of pain passed, he said, "Then I should have plenty of time to search for my brother." He wouldn't tell his parents—wouldn't get their hopes up until he was certain.

Leah squeezed his hand again. Tears filled her eyes—rolled down her cheeks—and she brushed them away. "Thank you for helping me bring Aaron to justice. I couldn't have done it without your help."

She leaned over and kissed his cheek.

He couldn't keep the smile off his face. "You are an amazing woman, Leah Miller."

He couldn't wait to see where the future would take them. And with God's help, he prayed his family could be reunited and Harrison's name would finally be cleared.

epilogue

FOUR WEEKS LATER . . .

Dalton had spent his first few days after being released going over every detail in Ellis's journal. The anger and resentment he held inside weren't healthy, and so he'd put the journal aside and focused on trying to find his brother. Though it might take months, if not years, he owed it to Harrison and his family to keep searching.

Someone knocked on the door, and he went to answer it. Dalton couldn't believe his former commander, Mark Sorenson, stood before him.

"You're alive. I'm glad to see it."

Dalton snapped out of his shock. "Sorry. I meant to call. It's been busy."

"So I've heard. When I couldn't reach you on the phone, I called the station. The acting chief filled me in." Mark pushed past him and came inside. "Why didn't you call? Leah told me your brother might still be alive? What can I do to help?"

Dalton carefully gave his friend a hug. His injuries still hurt if he made the wrong move. "Sorry, brother. It's been a crazy few weeks."

Mark looked him over. Didn't miss the way he held his stomach. He shook his head. "So, tell me about Leah. She seems like quite a woman."

Dalton understood exactly where his friend was going. "She is indeed." And he loved her. She stopped by each day after her shift ended to tell him about the case that had changed both their lives.

But they hadn't really discussed *their* future. Perhaps because it was hard to believe the past and all its darkness had finally passed. Hard to have hope again . . . but he wanted to.

"I know how difficult it was for you after Allison passed. She wouldn't want you to grieve forever. She'd want you to be happy."

Dalton's love for Leah grew stronger with every moment they spent together. "You're right. She wouldn't." It just took hearing it from Mark to believe. No matter what the future held, he wanted to spend the rest of his life with Leah. Did she feel the same way about him? He believed she did. Still, he had to know for certain and couldn't wait another day. "Mark, I have to do something. Do you mind waiting for me here? Make yourself at home. There's cold pizza in the fridge. I want to catch up, and I might take you up on the offer to help, but first—"

Mark's face broke into a smile. "Go. Tell her how you feel. Go grab your future."

Dalton hobbled out to the pickup and ignored the pain while he drove to the station. Just struggling out of the vehicle seemed to take forever. He felt as weak as a kitten.

"Well, if it isn't our fearless chief." Sugar spotted him and gave him a big hug. Dalton held in his pain until she released him.

"How are you doing?" he managed, a little embarrassed by her show of affection. "How's Justine?"

"Healing. Ready to come back to work soon, believe it or not."

"Tell her to take her time. When she's ready, her job is waiting on her."

Sugar smiled and kissed his cheek. "I sure will. She'll be pleased to hear it."

Dalton nodded. "Is Leah here?"

The dispatcher gave him a knowing wink. "I had a feeling that's why you were here."

Dalton could feel heat creeping up his neck.

"I think it's wonderful. You both deserve happiness."

"Thanks," Dalton managed. "About Leah . . ."

"Oh, she's at the cemetery. I think she's finally ready to let her family go."

Dalton didn't want to interrupt her, but he had to know her heart.

"That's a good thing, Chief," Sugar insisted. "It means she's ready to move on and start living. You should go to her."

And he did.

On the way to the Amish cemetery, all he could think about was what if he was wrong? What if she didn't share his feelings?

He spotted her cruiser and parked behind her. He slid out slowly—everything he did lately was slow.

Leah sat beside her family's simple gravestones. She wasn't alone. Her childhood friend, Colette Stoltzfus, held her hand. Dalton smiled. She'd told him the two had been working on repairing their friendship.

She'd been relieved to learn her grandmother in Wyoming was still alive, despite Aaron's insinuation. She and Marge had gone to visit the Amish woman. Slowly, the family was mending the broken bonds. It was unfortunate that Marge's father had died of a heart condition several years earlier. Dalton wondered what his reaction would have been to seeing his daughter again.

Leah turned as he approached, the smile on her face reassuring. "Excuse me," she told Colette and came over to him. "This is a surprise." Leah gave him a gentle hug before turning back to the graves. "This is the first time I've been here since the funeral. Colette agreed to come with me. It was just too painful before. Now, it feels right. We all can finally have closure."

Those green eyes swept to him, and he all but lost his breath and his nerve for a second.

"Is anything wrong?"

He shook his head and swallowed past the lump. "I love you, Leah." Tears filled her eyes as he plunged on. "But I have to know what you want. You were forced to leave the Amish way of life, and you mentioned once how much you loved the Plain ways. Do you want to return to the Amish? No one would blame you if you did." He waited for her to say something. When she didn't, he said, "No matter what you decide, I'll be there to support you because—" He didn't finish because she framed his face and kissed him tenderly.

"My heart will always have a special place for the Amish people, and I'm so glad I have my friend back." She glanced toward Colette. "But there are too many painful memories for me there. Thanks to you, I know the truth behind my family's deaths. There will be justice for them. I'm ready to be happy." She put her arms around his waist and kissed his cheek. "I love you too." She rested her head on his chest and let out a deep sigh. "I just still can't believe what Ellis did. He was my dad, and he did this horrible thing to you and your family."

He held her tightly in his arms. "That's not your blame to take. What Ellis did was inconceivable coming from someone sworn to uphold the law, and it had led to the deaths of two innocent women. But I can't let myself dwell on what happened and live in anger any longer. You shouldn't either. I have you, and one day soon, I'll have Harrison back in my family. My life is good. God is good."

And he was. The future that was once mired down by the past had never held so much promise for two people who had endured their share of pain. After ten years of living in darkness, they'd been brought into the light.

Dalton framed her face with his hands and kissed her. Through all the dark moments in his life, he never thought it possible to find love again. But God had led him to her. His Leah.

Mary Alford is the *USA Today* bestselling and award-winning author of more than fifty novels. Her books have been finalists for the Selah Award, the Daphne du Maurier Award, and the HOLT Medallion contest. As a writer, Mary is an avid reader. She loves to cook and can't face the day without coffee. She and her husband live in the heart of Texas in the middle of seventy acres with two very spoiled cats and one adorable rescue dog. Mary is very active online and would love to connect with readers on Facebook and Twitter or any social platforms listed at www.maryalford.net.

CONNECT WITH
MARY ALFORD

Get news, sign up for her mailing list,
and more at **MaryAlford.net**!

FIND HER ON

LET'S TALK
ABOUT BOOKS

Beyond the Book

Visit our Facebook page, where you can join our online book club, Beyond the Book, to discuss your favorite stories with Revell authors and other readers like you!

facebook.com/groups/RevellBeyondtheBook

Revell Roundup

Subscribe to our specially curated weekly newsletter to keep up with your favorite authors, find out about our latest releases, and get other exclusive news!

bakerpublishinggroup.com/revell/newsletters-signup